POETIC WORKS

VOLUME 3
(2006-2024)

Robbie Moffat

Palm Tree Publishing

PALM TREE PUBLISHING
Wilmington, Delaware 19801, USA
Iver Grove, Iver SL0 0LB, UK

© Robbie Moffat 1974-2024

Simultaneous published in
United Kingdom and USA

1st edition DECEMBER 2024

Typeset: Verdana 8pt

ISBN-10: 0907282644
ISBN-13: 9780907282648

PREFACE

Although this volume includes poems from 2006 onward, it was not until a few weeks before my sixtieth birthday in 2014 that I took up in earnest my poetry writing again. This I told myself was to be my last and final stage, the old man. After eight years of introspection it was hurting me, so I decided to abandon poetry for good. I did not want to continue to torture myself, so I wrote *I Am Done (12th Oct 2022)* in the belief that I truly was done. Less than three months later, while taking time out in Spain, I was missing poetry, and I started again.

I am now seventy years old and I constantly wonder if I can keep faith with myself and find new ways to express parts of me that still remain hidden from myself. As human beings we are complex and as mysterious to ourselves as we are to others. Of course, other human beings remain of interest to me. We live in a time when it seems impossible to predict when current conflicts will end and peaceful times resume. For my part I cannot shape events but I can reflect upon them.

Why do I continue to write poetry? I don't know exactly why. I used to think it was therapy, the extension of my dreams that I don't fully understand. Really? I think that is inaccurate. Often my poems are expressions of frustration on this and that, her or him, or just about me, how different I am, how wonderful I am, how I've got life all worked out, only to discover that I'm not or don't.

So why do I do it? Maybe its fear of not recording the events of my life, to let them pass without comment? This is most folks' reason for taking selfies, or snaps of their friends. The places they've been. I do it too, but I don't think there are great numbers of folk recording their inner feelings with a selfie. Video diaries, yes, that is a performance just as much as a poem is a performance, but *tiktok* messages are mass entertainment rather than personal reflection. That's how it appears to me on a surface level. Perhaps its worth a debate. I'm sure *instagrammers* believe that they are being authentic when they post their messages, but they are subject to censorship and are they not in the business of building a following rather than being honest with themselves. Also they disappear from public view after a day.

A poet is not in the business of being liked for a day, there is no reward as such, only the desire for self-expression despite all opposition or approbation. To give more of the same, this is business, a quantifiable product that can be marketed. Hence the value of influences who can guide an audience to that product that is always reward driven for the influencer.

Poetry on the other hand is difficult to write to order. If only I was that kind of poet – a crowd pleaser, a re-enforcer of the status quo, a poet of fixed style and dependable delivery. Alas, this was never meant to be – background, education and self publication set me on my own course overland whilst a number of my contemporaries boarded a ship that provided a safer passage.

But what adventures I have had in my long landward journey! Fifty years of trekking and hiking across mountains and deserts of cultural obstacles. How I craved for some plain sailing, but like some of my contemporaries, I have arrived at the same destination, but just a little later than I thought. Have I really arrived? Not really, for the journey does not end until the last breath, the last word is written down.

So to the poems. They are herein set out in chronological order as in the previous volumes to give you the reader a clear understanding of how I have progressed as I have aged. To set the scene for this volume; in 2005 I left Scotland behind and moved to south Buckinghamshire to live in Denham two miles outside of London. The preoccupations of the young adult and the middle aged man have been left behind to be replaced with the musings of my older self.

I hope that there is something in this volume to engage you the reader in a way that will prove to be worthwhile.

Robbie Moffat
30th November 2024
Iver, Buckinghamshire

AERIC'S POEM
from Axe Raiders
[9.03am, 3rd May 2006, Camden Market, London]

Sailed from shore, shipped from storms.
I sought and slayed my kin's killer
Avenged in anger, Aeric's axe
Fell foully on Aeric's foes,
Cruelly cleft Fingal's naked neck
Claimed his land with Woden's sword.

NOT TO BE SEEN
[12.13am, 1st Oct 2008, Crick Bung, Denham, Bucks]

Not to be seen, not to be heard,
The voice of the naked, the face of the child,
Wandering the alleys and lanes of the West,
Straggling the roads stretching no end.

LEAP NOWHERE
[12.17am, 1st October 2008, Crick Bung, Denham]

Leap nowhere without faith
And never look back
On the deeds of the doer
Or the sins of the pack.

THE ROAD OF NECESSITY
[10.01am, 4th April 2009, Crick Bung, Denham]

The road of necessity is the way of despair,
The need of the poor is the want of the rich:
From heaven to earth, mountain to sea
The traffic is heavy on the path to the cliff.

SHE LIKES TO RUN
For Suzie
[11.19am, 4th April 2009, Crick Bung, Denham]

She likes to run in beautiful places
Far from the cry and hue of the city,
Where she can be ordered and perfect,
Her breath the wind wed to the wild.

QAWRA
[1pm, 12th April 2009, Qawra, Malta]

Free in the sun to swim and run,
To pound the sand, brave the surf,

Take the shade in the terrace trees,
Stare at the stars in the midnight breeze:
Find the dawn in the rising east,
Kiss your lover and feast till lunch.

SEVENTH DECADE
[10.15am, 3rd Jan 2010, Crick Bung, Denham]

Each decade turns the pages of time
Between the sheets the sun revolves:
The heat of the day, the ice of the night
I wake to eat, I wait in line,
I walk the moors, I wade my brooks,
I whittle every passing hour -
Watch the waves turn the sand,
Wish and want my fading child
To turn, retrace the wandering road
I first trod so well alone.

SUZIE
[7.54am, 7th July 2011, Estonia]

I am an island in a sea of dreams
Caught in a storm - harbour with me.
I am fresh water, shelter and calm -
A rock in an ocean of wild drowning fear.

I'M STILL BREATHING
[10.24am, 20th January 2014, Denham]

Today I woke up and thought –
I owe forty thousand,
I can't pay the rent this month,
In two months time I'm sixty.
You know what – who cares!
I'm still breathing.

SIXTY
[1.40am, 26th March 2014, Denham]

Today I return to poetry
Like I said I would twenty years ago –
I am ready to fill in the gaps,
Re-find my purpose in life,
Throw off the trappings of comfort,
Strip the veneer of convention from myself,
Re-discover my reason for breathing.
I am sixty – I have made it this far –
How much further is there still to go?

ALEX THE COUNTESS
[2.13am, 26th March 2014, Denham]

A talent with a voice and a smile –
A woman on a mission, but no nun.
The world owes her nothing, so she fights
Her corner – every round brings some hurt.

Her courage takes her the distance –
On the ropes or punching above her weight,
She covers the ring like a dancer
And is on her feet at the ringing of the bell.

AT LAST THE SUN IS HERE
[12.20pm, 29th March 2014, Denham]

At last the sun is here –
The wind has dropped, and Spring
Like the heads of drooping daffodils
Floods our garden with colour.

Once more I can sit in the yard,
Catch the early ultra-violet light
As our planet whizzes round the sun,
And our days lengthen.

Wet the winter may have been –
Yet I did not miss the snow,
Nor the cold and icy Northern blast
Endured last year.

Joy! It comes on us thus –
The birth of new and better days,
The hope of better times before me,
And an end to all decay.

EASTER MONDAY
[10.15am, 21st April 2014, Denham]

The resurrection and the life,
Blue skies clear to heaven,
Schoolboy days of boiled eggs
Rolled down parkland knolls.

I laze in slumber mode –
Through the haze of condensation,
The ticking clock counts down
The hour to morning mass.

I will not attend or pray –
Age has not destroyed my will.
If God exists, then I know
I will keep him to myself.

A BETTER MAN
[10.32 am, 21st April 2014, Denham]

If I were a better man,
And not some flimsy artist,
I would have made my mark,
Done something to be proud of –

Instead I've spent forty years
Engaging in self-absorption,
Soaking up my own persona
In a series of dramatic acts.

A better man would have done
A single feat of outstanding merit,
Instead I've been hacking on,
Making little headway through the jungle.

A better man is plain to all,
Stands above, leads the crowd,
Moves us on to better things,
Asks for nothing in return.

Instead, I think on myself -
Preservation of my own lifestyle,
Protection of my worldly goods
The hoarding of my next twenty years.

WOMEN
[10.38am, 21st April 2014, Denham]

Women are creatures of fickle nature,
Prone to blowing with the wind –
Reason does not wrestle with them,
It bullies them into submission –
Cursed with worry, they give up,
Throw themselves into the nearest arms.

OVER THE HORIZON
[11.27pm, 29th April 2014, Denham]

When you get older you start looking back
At where you have been, not where you're going.

It's easier to turn and look over your shoulder
Than to face the future shortening in length –

Whilst the past is longer and getting longer still,
What waits ahead is nearing each day –
It takes some courage to greet it warmly
For it does not offer comfort or certainty.

Whilst the past contains days of hope,
Times of joy, lost summers of plenty –
The path before us goes over the horizon
Where those we knew, never turn back.

LOOKING BACK ON LETTERS
[11.10pm, 30th July 2014, Denham]

Looking back on letters written forty years ago,
I didn't like myself as I was –
But after two days of depressed reflection
I re-read them all in posted order –
Realised that – out of context
The actions of my past were ordered.

The fear brought on by the rediscovery
That I was a wild thoughtless youth,
Had been groundless. I was nineteen,
Full of life, and energy, and lust –
A boy who couldn't get enough excitement,
Nor restrained by the obligations of love.

MADE HOMELESS BY COMMITTEE
[11.22pm, 30th July 2014, Denham]

I'm being made to vacate my bungalow
By a heartless bunch of capitalist democrats –
By committee my life has been decided;
By cold letter the order passed down.

At first, I thought to fall on reason,
Request an answer as to why?
Deaf ears and cruel cynical rebuff
Followed on my cries for redress.

Now I fight to some soon-end
That must come somewhere down the line;
In the sand is drawn my destiny,
And in my heart the battle lost.

Yet still a small flame burns –
Perhaps justice will be done?
I'll be rescued from my homeless future
by a new enlightenment.

It is small beer for seven years –
A home's a home, home is here;
Uprooted at the age of sixty
Is not a tragedy I predicted?

I will adapt, depart my idyll,
Like I did from far Argyll –
For life's a wheel ever turning,
Rolling on to other lands.

FUCHSIA SAGS IN DISARRAY
[11.17am, 7th September 2014, Denham]

Autumn draws us to our windows
To dwell on the summer now lost,
The hope for sunshine breaking through
And warming us with some love.

The cricket field empty now
Reminds us of lost hot-days –
Apples droop from bending boughs,
Fuchsia sags in disarray.

THE 45
[1.31am, 21st September 2014, Denham]

They made their mark in ordered fashion
Without allegiances to a single party –
They registered their voice for freedom,
Showed the world how it was done.

The Brits threw in the kitchen sink
And half the contents of the living room,
Yet still they could not shake belief,
Their lies, their peddled ware.

The vote to separate is over –
An aftermath of unchanged ways,
An emptiness that leaves Scots nothing,
Turns now to renewed effort.

Scotland our land, beloved by all,
We fight to free it from its past,

Not what we were, but what we'll do
Dangles before us within our grasp.

16th NOVEMBER

[11.21am, 16th November 2014, Denham]

The bastards still don't have me out,
And Christmas is on its way –
A court date will not be set
'til well after Hogmanay.

So for the now, I live rent free,
Get to think about my future –
Get the time to enjoy small things
And triumph over small adversities.

IT IS TOO PEACEFUL

[11.33am, 16th November 2014, Denham]

The leaves hang on the trees like no tomorrow,
The birds sing as if it is Spring –
What's happened to our usual weather?
Or are we lulled into complacency?

It may be damp and muddy underfoot,
But flowers blooming as if it is summer?
Squirrels scurrying here and there
As if it is the month to find a mate.

It is too mild, far too peaceful,
Something's up? What's about to happen?
Whatever comes, the now is restful,
The calm before the storm arrives.

AS BEAUTY PASSES

[9.49pm, Wed 19th November 2014, Denham]

Do I still have the will to say
The lovely words that she wants to hear?
Or am I void of all endearments,
To talk only of my own sad decay?
For if I dwell upon her beauty,
Not the wrinkles that I perceive,
Her façade would surely be
The Taj Mahal of all my days.
For if by some brief encounter,
I chanced upon her some thirty years ago –
I would have taken her beauty,
Trapped it in a world of my own –

For such is life as beauty passes,
I need to praise her beauty more.

DRUNKS
for Ed
[1.05pm, Sun 23rd November 2014, Denham]

Watching drink ruin the lives of others
Is like watching water going down a drain.
It's a waste of time cleaning the water,
Preparing it for everyone to use.

Likewise drink ruins the drinker,
Wastes their bodies better than worms,
Half-way to the grave they continue
To kill themselves with their habit.

I am no saint, and I like a drop,
But knowing no limit is the want of some.
Children cry, and spouses quiver
Before the terror of the drunk.

Diseased, these bums lumber on,
Leave their wake of self-destruction,
No words can halt or make them change
The course of their own oblivion.

TASKS UNDONE
[9.05pm, Wed 3rd December 2014, Denham]

The hurly burly of the day is over,
Evening eats on what is left,
Scraps of moments litter my leisure,
Make me doze in recollection –
But only in the tasks undone,
Those remaining for tomorrow.

YOU ARE THE ONLY READER
[9.24pm, Wed 3rd December 2014, Denham]

The alternative to reading is to write,
Create your own book to read,
Discover the truth of who you are,
Uncover the lies you tell yourself.

Why falsify your own inner-story,
The one place others cannot view?
Yes, show that you may be clever,
But deception is mere conceit.

Honesty of thought is hard to sum up,
It is easier to spin a web of tales,
Conform to an awful notion,
Write what people want to hear.

The point of writing for yourself -
You don't have to entertain others,
There is no audience to please –
You are the only reader.

WE TOO ARE WATCHED
[9.55pm, Sat 21st December 2014, Denham]

The outdoor man, once so wildly active,
Lies on his bed sipping beer:
The movies play in one long continuum,
Flashing through images of his times.

Where was he when Vietnam ended?
Where was he during the Miners' Strike?
Where was he on Nine Eleven?
For now he's idle every night.

Life is not about great moments,
Time is not about being there:
Reflections in our history's mirror
Should not be our measured worth.

Individuals, linger, always wear out:
We can't recall what we have done:
Our skins are scarred from adventures –
That's all we notice as we wither.

We are watchers as we age,
Wrinkled with each setting sun,
We view each dawn in wishful thinking
Knowing our time has overrun.

The outdoor man drains his beer,
Flicks his wrist in search of worlds,
New connections with his past,
He did not know walked his path.

SLEEP LIKE YOU HAVE NEVER DONE BEFORE
[11.40pm, 13th January 2015, Denham]

Between the winter and the shadows
I will look for sunshine –
Brightness in the wasteland of rocks

Under which hides the unknown,
That part we hide from –
That fear we shrink and cower before.

There is no shaft of light round corners
That leads towards the sun –
Waves roll like earthquakes,
Sands shift like a black volcano,
Ash obscures our vision of Elysium -
The land beyond our woes.

Great parks outlive the largest monuments,
Skeletons tell of lives –
Evidence is the body of our truths,
The dark secrets buried deep,
We slumber like granite monoliths
Perched on the edge of a cliff.

Light. The craving of the damned
Chained in dungeons –
Shut the door and enter freedom.
Discover the path across the mountain,
Find the circle of enlightenment –
Sleep like you have never done before.

TOW PATH

[5.17pm, 24th May 2015, Hillview, Denham]

Canals and life in flight –
Why talk now of wildlife?
Curiosity in the mayflies,
Wonder in moor-hen wakes –
What now fills the void?

Apathy is the world of old age
And days lived to the max –
Where now are the new kicks?
Walking blindly into each day
Without a lover at my side.

IVER GROVE

[12.50pm, 15th August 2015, Iver Grove, Bucks]

The clock counts the cunning pass of time
Stolen from us like candy from a child –
We're left in tears for what might have been
And angry that we wasted what we had.

ALIENS ARE STALKING OUR STREETS
[6.32pm, 18th August 2015, Iver Grove, Bucks]

The darkness that descends upon the world
Is not my world, it is alien –
It is the nightmare of others,
It is the dream of the rich and empty,
The purgatory of the slaves to religion,
Those who … those who you know.

Everywhere there are traitors, puke-balls,
Snakes rustling through the average day,
The snails leaving trails of slime.
You see them in their black cars;
You see them hiding behind menus;
You see them looking in estate shop windows,
Envy burning up their eyeballs.

Heaven knows nothing as it does not exist,
Just as haven from harm is an illusion –
For those aliens feed on every fear,
These aliens feed on other's illness,
Supply them with their cartels of drugs,
Fill their cabinets of despair.

For out of the darkness comes the evil
Seeping into every fissure,
Filling every sinew of weakness,
Taking over, sinking all resistance,
Draining blood out of everything –
These aliens are stalking our streets.

POSSIL GIRL
[12.18am, 7th September 2015, Earls Court, London]

Knock down the walls, throw out the piano,
Break up the sofa, and bin the kitchen sink -
There's a Possil girl at my front door,
and I'm going to let her in.

Lunch is her dinner, and dinner is her tea,
Give her a jeely-piece, cocoa for her supper -
There's a Possil girl in my bedroom
And she's kissing me.

Let the thunder roll, the rain piss down,
The rough tempest roar, the seas run wild -
There's a Possil girl making out
And we're on the floor.

The drums are beating, the pipes skirling,
The churches are empty, the chapel bells silent -
There's a Possil girl dancing naked
And its still not dawn.

INTO THE DARK
[11.30pm, 19th Sept 2015, High Wycombe]

Vikings raiding through the night,
Cycles wheeling on to nowhere,
Children lost and always crying,
Reckless trains speeding westwards,
On and on into the dark.

No-one knows what is right,
Planes crashing into Babel's towers –
Mothers weeping, never smiling,
Thunderballs rolling onwards
Out and out into the night.

Hordes migrate, slip the barbed wire,
Zombies wield empty power –
Chaos reigns and anger triumphs,
Danger dances with the lonely,
Spins them off into the dark.

HIGH WYCOMBE
[5.43pm, 20th Sept 2015, High Wycombe]

I live in a town where the rivers are brooks,
The woods as tame as a parrot –
The trees are filled with the voices of children,
The breeze as fresh as a daisy.

It is a town of back to back houses,
Pristine and smart like show homes –
Kerbs for skateboards, ponds for minnows,
Cars straight out of a sales room.

Kites crest the crowns of misted heights
Rising up, hiding golf courses –
Trains depart every quarter of an hour
To carry the folk to the Big Smoke.

On the edge of town hypermarkets sprawl
By the ramps of the superfast highway –
Escape is easy, arrival a slow crawl,
But time goes by very easy.

It is a town of alms houses and learning,
Proud of its past and the new –
A town where Sundays are always Sundays
As quiet as a cat in a dream.

It's the town my childhood once was,
Family life and everyday happenings –
A town that knows its place in the world,
As suburban, proper and clean.

BACKWARDS IN TIME
[5.57pm, 20th Sept 2015, High Wycombe]

I live in these times, backwards in time,
Traveling by foot on pathways …
That lead somewhere ahead of me
On the wind along with the kites.

I know where all these byways lead;
I worry that I've come to an end –
The storm has ended in a dead calm,
But I will fight on, my friends.

Renewal comes from getting good rest,
A door to lock, a bed to lie in –
The suitcase put away in the cupboard,
A sofa to put your head down.

Open the curtains, watch the sunset,
Open the windows, feel the air –
The way to the west waits, of course,
But I'm in no hurry to tramp there.

WAITING FOR NEWS
[7.19pm, 28th Sept 2015, High Wycombe]

Waiting for news for our ship to come in,
Loaded with cash and goodies and good times.
Who would take poverty and ill-health
As legacy for living out their last years.

SOMEWHERE SOMEONE IS WRITING GREAT POETRY
[8.52pm, 20th Sept 2015, High Wycombe]

In Stornaway, someone is writing poetry
About the stones of Callenish, the clouds,
The rocks beneath his feet, the red moon,
Eclipsed by the earth on a clear night.

I am too weary to rise at three a.m.,
In the dark to look for rivers on Mars –
Whatever the tick that tocks in my heart
Is the beat of a drum that is silent.

Try as I may, I am worn by events,
By comets, and stars I can never reach.
The excitement of youth, the sparkle of space
Is a glass of wine, and a broken sleep.

Somewhere someone is writing great poetry,
Words to inspire, to change who we are;
Once he was me, youthful and angry,
Not an old man searching for peace.

How we all turn into our fathers,
Into the men we once railed against –
The pigeons will fly to the crow's nest,
The eagles will plunge to the sea.

Change turns full circle as scriptures foretell,
The meek indeed inherit the earth –
The angry die or run out of anger
'till all that is left is the shell of oneself.

Cry as we may in our sad lonely flats,
Our empty houses harbouring time's shadows –
We older ones are the survivors of anger,
We've come to know passion as ignorance.

Had youth shown me much better purpose,
Guided me better to use my time well,
My pages of poetry would be as void …
As the blank eyes of an owl.

ALL OUR LIVES WE WAIT
[11.54am, 1st Oct 2015, High Wycombe]

All our lives we wait, we try to do,
But thwarted by the procrastination of others,
We wait, and wait.

Life is far too short, too short to wait
For others to get their lives together,
So we wait.

Try as we might as we try to do,
We are blocked by the inertia of others,
So we wait, and wait.

NEVER TODAY
[1am, 9th Oct 2015, High Wycombe]

Never today, never tomorrow,
Dwell on sorrow, never be sorry,
Always reflect, never fret.
Always be sure, and don't regret.

THE FLAKE
[11.59pm, 16th Oct 2015, High Wycombe]

Three times I waited like a young man
For an older woman who was a flake –
Eager in her desire to date me,
Three times I waited to be snubbed.

Tis easy to make excuses in hindsight,
To brush aside the actions of the flake –
So earnest was her pressing desire,
Three times I lingered to be ignored.

Three times is enough for any man,
No matter how humble his expectation;
No words can ease the wounding –
Three times stood-up by a flake.

THE MISSING COAT
[11.07am, 20th Oct 2015, High Wycombe]

Where's my coat? Where's my coat?
Its raining, its cold out there –
Find my freakin' coat, sonny,
now get out of my face.

Listen, sonny, you little tosser,
I'm going to slap ya! There I've done it!
Where's my coat, you tiny prick …
Find my coat, you wanker.

Don't touch me, mate, I'm warning you,
Get your face out of mine –
What? Get my coat, you dickhead.
You want me to punch you out?

Okay, biff! There you go –
Don't ever asked to be punched.
Now find my coat, you little cunt,
Its raining, and its cold out there.

MARY OF THE STAG
[10.31pm, 27th Oct 2015, High Wycombe]

In the quietness of The Stag,
Two days before the workers get paid –
There is a moment with the barmaid,
Old as the pub, and Scottish,
A stoic lady from Dundee -
Called Mary.

Many's the time in that pub,
A walk away from Pinewood Studios,
Mary has poured me a welcoming pint,
With her lovely Dundee smile,
Her soft Albion nature,
Her convivial warmth.

Whatever the hustle in progress,
The night's raising to the rafters,
Mary's had time to say hello,
To engage and exchange,
Smiled and made welcome,
One of her own.

THE DOOR TO THE GARDEN
[11.09pm, 27th Oct 2015, High Wycombe]

Try as I might to do things right,
Getting things wrong is being mortal –
Life ebbs away towards decay
Of everything once that was fine.

Try as I might to make things stay,
Things change, are never the same –
Wrong things bloom, right stuff fades,
All that is black is now grey.

Now as I hope to somehow cope,
To turn the dark into light –
Somehow I hear the creak of time
Closing the door on life.

LONDON
[15.44pm, 1st Nov 2015, High Wycombe]

From the smallest to the grandest,
They are all greedy for gain ...
People and politicians alike,
They all act falsely ...

Declaring all is well,
When nothing is well at all.

RETRIBUTION
[3.53pm, 1st Nov 2015, High Wycombe]

Every nation oppressed when freed
Cannot resist becoming the oppressor –
It is the nature of us all,
To seek retribution formerly denied
By slavery.

Apartheid breeds long term hatred
That is never vent 'till the oppressed
Triumphs over the oppressor –
Then the barbarity of the barbarians
Is outdone by the savagery of the victor.

This latent inhumanity is everywhere,
Dormant in the consciousness of us all –
Directed at our bitterest enemies,
It extends beyond our borders
To all our foes.

I AM SILENT
[12th Nov 2015, High Wycombe]

I will remain silent.
Many questions have been asked,
answers given on my behalf
while I have remained silent.

What news from me – nothing
about the hollow promises of peace,
the shattered lives and the untold dead
whose voices echo across the Aegean;
baby corpses float like flotsam;
shell-shocked misery, lines of fences
erected by their saviours.

What peace is this? Detention camps,
tramping innocents of the destitute -
forced marches of the hungry,
angry anguish midst callous apathy.

Others have spoken for me,
self-interest has overtaken charity -
I remain silent.

Who then speaks in my name?
Which hero can I trust?
Which heroine has made me believe
that we are governed fairly?

Our times are dominated by weakness -
moral force has no moral basis,
perverse greed and avarice ...
glass edifices, and sharded structures,
the epiphany of all that's wrong,
all that's built, the epitome of our times.

Corrupt ... or not at all, but amoral,
the surface seepage of the Arab sands
finds its way into private pockets -
through the holes, deep caverns of influence
drip down the leg of capitalism,
soak the thirst of bankers,
loosen the tongues of judges,
water the gardens of politicians
who speak for me, my conscience,
while I remain silent.

And I will remain silent ...
I will go with the flow of time,
I will bite my tongue ... choke
on the meat on my plate,
drown on the wine in my glass,
but I will not worry ...
for others will speak in my name.

Yet I will not sleep soundly,
nor dream of some reached utopia,
for there is no comfort in silence,
in my blindness to the hurricane.
I will rise, shower in hot water,
eat my warm cooked breakfast,
go to my heated, tidy office,
do my work, make my living,
and remain silent.

For I will owe nothing to the world,
or be owed by the world -
I live as I please, how I want,
say what I like, go where I choose,
have no corporal restrictions placed on me ...
for I answer to no-one ... others
answer for me, and I am silent.

Can this be the way life is?
Missile firing drones, online videos,
entertainment, modern war games?
Silent war games, never a sound,
always done in our name, for us.

For us? If we are not for ourselves
then who is for us? If not for us
then they must be against us?
Just one more enemy, just one more,
and always in my name -
for I am silent.

I need not fear my future ...
it is being secured for me -
by stealth and prudent use of weapons,
I am protected from all invasion;
safe from all loss of freedom,
I am free to sleep soundly,
free to dream of utopia.

For I am silent.

IT WAS NOT A GOOD DAY
[12.44am, 14th Nov 2015, High Wycombe]

It was not a good day for the world.
Paris blown up – the coffee massacres;
Jihadi John eviscerated by a drone,
Russian athletes banned from all competition;
A murderer convicted for dismembering his sister.

The world in a violent turmoil –
The devil turns the soil as we watch.
A dark night precedes a dim dawn ...
The candles burn for all our wrongs.

THE SMOKE FROM THE FIRE
[4.34pm, 15th Nov 2015, High Wycombe]

The smoke from the fire engulfs Paris.
Who started the fire? Who will put it out?
The arsonist cannot turn up in disguise,
Be allowed to throw oil on the flames.

Madness takes the form of sainthood,
Self-interest comes in the cloak of charity,
Debt is hidden in the supply of weapons.
And fear makes the unwilling collude.

Yet the fire still burns brighter,
The smoke goes half-way around the world,
No-one tackles the blazing inferno –
As we choke on the acrid smell.

PRAYER FOR SYRIA
[12.51pm, 28th Nov 2015, High Wycombe]

Shoot down the plane, behead the pilot,
Throw grenades at the wall –
War zips over broken glass.
The jagged edge of our horizon
Filled with smoke and screaming,
Our eyes burn – in the name of what?

Cut down the meek, slaughter the lambs,
The wolves are baying at our door,
Cast the babes to the lions,
Feed the vultures their rumps of meat,
Make no mention of God.
In our name – revenge or what?

Scatter illusion, shatter the mirage,
Place laurels on the victors' heads.
Shoot the vanquished, bomb the cowering,
Tear down the mosques and minarets.
Destroy all light, return to dark
In our name, or that of God's?

DREAMS ARE BEING MADE
[1.23am, 29th Nov 2015, High Wycombe]

Gone are the nights of the broken man,
The destitute lost in the defeat of his past –
Death is not the career of his future,
Failure is not the sum of his all.

Long were his days, beaten and down,
Until there was no further to go –
The lonely times with not much help
Except a friend offering shelter.

A little voice whispering 'quitter',
A nagging pain laying him low,
A languor making him hide away,
And a despair eating his hope.

Gone are those times, he never surrendered,
Never gave into the terrible doubts,

He never gave up on his own self-belief,
Never gave up on his life.

Out of misery, through his hard work,
Given the chance and a barrel of luck,
Success once more within his grasp,
His sadness changed to a life of laughs.

There is no number to life's chances,
No matter how many times they fade,
The sun comes up every morning,
And dreams are being made.

MY WONDERFUL LOVE (song)
[12.32pm, 13th Dec 2015, High Wycombe]

When the sky is grey,
And the rain comes down,
Despite the wind,
Despite the storm,
I think of you ….
My wonderful love.

When the sun comes out,
And the rays are warm,
I'm full of hope,
I'm full of joy,
As I think of you …
My wonderful love.

When night-time comes,
And you are here,
In my arms,
Close to me,
I think only of you …
My wonderful love.

YOU ARE MY PEARL
[10.08am, 14th Dec 2015, High Wycombe]

You are the pearl in my oyster,
The bit of grit I can't get rid of …
I secrete my love in you …
As you become more valuable.

The risk I run is incalculable,
How precious you could be to others …
I fear you will be discovered …
And I discarded.

So I hide you, my darling,
Shed no light on your beauty ...
Have you trapped, covered, smothered ...
I keep you guarded.

A FISTFUL OF BEER
[21.48, 15th Dec 2015, Uxbridge]

I used to believe - sitting in a pub
with a girl when I was twenty two -
that I was wasting my life.

How stupid I seem in my lonely years
watching nervous lovers -
envious of their youth.

Passion is an evil worm that wriggles,
makes the young man believe
that out there is a better world.

Over my pint, and my solitude,
I tell that young man -
seize what you can with both hands.

A fist full of beer and liver spots,
watching the lovers laugh -
youth is so wasted on the young.

GOZO SPARROWS
[15.56pm, 22nd Dec 2015, St.Lawrenz, Gozo, Malta]

Sparrows stalk the evening light,
Chase the dying of the day –
Their chatter fills the fading heat,
Then fades with dusk to silence.

GOZO
[22nd-30th Dec 2015, Gozo, Malta]

Down beneath the clean cut stone,
Under layers of ancient living,
Deep within the cysts of ages
Dug away, exposed to daylight –
There lies the truth, the past,
The sum of all endeavours,
The anchors and the vases,
The jewelry and the day tools,
The clay, the flint, the bronzes,
The fragments of Gozo's tomorrow.

Citadels rise on every escarpment,
Churches stand on every hillock,
Terraces run along every slope,
Houses perched on every road.

The sun goes down into the sea,
Red into the dark blue Med,
Black isles of cloud, wisps of mist,
Silver glints of distant stars –
Cool night settles on the pines,
The palms quiver in the winter solstice.

The sandy soil turns on the plough's blade,
Eases over like good earth should –
Into the ground goes the seed,
The future of all that is to come.

Twisting ancient roads descend,
Yellow-walled, cut-stone hemmed,
Pathways lead over cliffs,
And step-ways end at hanging rocks.

Into deep chasms gullies race,
Into fissures, rain filled pools,
Age washed limestone, fossil pock-marked,
Pitted and ragged, serrated and jagged,
Caverns cut into sandstone walls,
Grottos wind-gouged with every squall.

Hidden bays and sea-cut harbours,
Shelters from all wicked storms –
Caves etched into the landscape,
Dwellings abandoned by Egyptian times,
Phoenician traders of oil and wine,
Passing galleys and marauding tyrants,
Running after dark, - the curfew
In the cellars of the church,
Refuge found on the hardened floors.

What life was this? Slavers chains,
Pirates raiding at a whim –
The knights of St. John as saviours,
Their fleets fighting off the Moors.

From east to west ten miles long,
North to south five miles wide,
Africa a day's sail away ...
Sicily a half day the other way ...

Mighty empires have come and gone,
Left their ruins on Gozo's soil –
Punic, Carthaginian and Roman,
Aragon, Sardinian and Sicilian,
Turkish, French and British –
gone, all gone to history,
Lost in the yellow stone, sandy fields,
The memories dripping with the rain,
Into hidden caverns, caves of wonder.
The sub terrain beneath the normal.

Giant monoliths, and stone circles,
Grand edifices, smashed and crumbled –
Osimandi's world found, and buried,
Not more knowledge, just more questions.

Christmas Eve's bells ring loud,
Deafening the café drinkers in the square –
The children's choir before the altar,
The priest placing baubles on the pulpit,
Holy water pressed against a forehead
Under the tenth station of the cross.

And outside everywhere – ruins,
Land lent to rubble.
Hillsides strewn with history's dereliction,
As the ringing of the church bells
Summon Gozo's children from their dwellings
Into the sanctuary of the Lord.

2015 - THE YEAR OF THE DAMNED

[11.40am, 30th Dec 2015, Golden Sands, Malta]

Another year comes to its conclusion,
A footnote to the calends of history;
Many think it a year of misery,
Wars, displacement and ugly death.

Yet, are we not cruel to ourselves?
Injustice breeds insurrection and chaos;
So we reap the wind of time,
And cry for the wrongs committed.

But we cry for ourselves, not for others,
For the shame of being the culprit,
For being the perpetrator of hatred,
For being superior to the unfortunate.

We are not absolved by our aloofness,
While distant from the woes of anger,
We were the root of the problem -
We paid for the year to be damned.

AS STORIES GO
[12.50am, 24th Jan 2016, High Wycombe]

So as stories go, this is another one.
It begins with a fur coat on a chair,
Ends with a dryer tumbling damp clothes,
Wet streets and memories of football matches,
A girl with a dog, and face cream –

There is no order to this never-ending tale.
The middle is a jumble of mathematics,
A car journey down a long straight road,
A music box meant for outdoor playing,
A guru in training on my mobile phone.

So I will start again, finish off –
The sound of laughter in the night,
A letter waiting to be posted last week,
A lost hat never to be found,
A yarn mined from this mind of mine.

WORDS HAVE LOST THEIR DOMINANCE
[11.15pm, 28th Jan 2016]

While the world goes round …
Somewhere in India a theatre troupe performs
Romeo and Juliet to a student crowd
Who squeeze backstage to praise -
The foreign actress who has been in films.

If Shakespeare were alive, or Tagore …
The candle in the wind would flicker -
When the lights went off, no power plant
Could provide the playwrights needs –
Darkness put an end to his imaginations.

Is sound a greater frightener than light?
Listen to the words, the tales they show,
The wonders of the past, the fancy concepts,
The cache of ages caught in syllables,
Not with moving images, nor snapshots.

The language of telling has morphed –
Now made for the eyes, not the ears,

Blindness renders the story intelligible,
We listen but we cannot see –
Words have lost their dominance.

IF I'M IN LOVE
[12.21am, 4th Feb 2016, High Wycombe]

Is love a state of being, or a state to be in?
As big as a county and as wide as our memories,
Emotion plays with the spinning of the world,
Endless 'takes' on the bundle of our wealth –
What is really going on with my brain?
Am I wired to self-destruct?

Want is coupled with a desire for need,
Help is something that we all can give,
Acceptance is a novelty constantly cherished,
Apology the foil to deflect the strong –
Give me half an hour with honesty,
I'll give you ten hours in return.

When minds meet in an equal understanding,
No earthquake can shake the firm belief
That down the line, created by encounter,
Only good can come from such commitment –
Worry then as if there is no tomorrow,
And comprehend there is none to heed.

Selfless we may think we are progressing,
Yet endless we recede into ourselves,
Passion flares and lights the room for seconds,
Smoke lingers longer, but will disperse –
If I'm in love then love has no answer,
For the question will give answer to itself.

MY COAT ON HIS KNEES
[11.41pm, 4th Feb 2016, High Wycombe]

It's never too late to dream before dawn,
To stumble beyond your allotted departure,
The time set by the sum of your past,
Or by the will of your thought.

I'm not professing that I am immortal,
Or I will outlive all of mankind –
But perhaps by holding on to my dreams,
I can put off the inevitable knock.

Life is full of unfinished business,
And I'm not ready to get up and go
Out of that door and into the darkness
Without completing the last of my goals.

And every day I dream up new ones,
Schemes of thoughts, and plans of ideas,
Things that keep the devil waiting,
With my coat on his knees.

THE ITALIAN GIRL
[10.02pm, 28th Feb 2016, High Wycombe]

She said she really liked me,
Her eyes were dark and deep,
She looked into my shallow heart
And touched my crippled soul.

She slid her hand into mine,
Pushed her head on to my breast,
She spoke with Italian words,
Then took me to her bed.

Her hair curled about her head,
Her almond skin lit the night,
On never-ending sheets of silk
I traveled on her lips.

AS WINTER DEPARTS
[1.10am, 2nd Mar 2016, High Wycombe]

As the winter passes warmly,
As the future fills the mornings,
As my hopes open doorways,
I am on my journey.

Others wait on the morrow,
Friends believe in only sorrow,
Workers search for their saviour,
As I take their burden.

Life is but a bag of dreams,
Breathing's such a simple scheme
For getting through a troubled day
Is but a common theme.

Let the clouds grey the sky,
Half the world is in the black,

I am feasting in the sun,
But hungry in the dark.

Spins the world to its end,
Life is but a nest of eggs,
Dare we break with our past
To progress to our end.

Canter on the muddy track,
Do not take a backward glance,
Ahead is all we need to know
As winter now departs.

OUR DREAMS
[12.57am, 4th Mar 2016, High Wycombe]

Our dreams are but fairy dust,
Willows in the wind –
Headlong we rush on our whims
With hope and love –
Our faith like bubbles blow
Us out to sea –
We bob upon the deepest depths
Looking at the sky –
Waiting for the night to fall
To catch a star.

AROUND THE CORNER
[2.14pm, 3rd April 2016, High Wycombe]

Never is life so fraught as
When success is just around the corner
That you cannot see beyond.

Look all we want but still
The unknown better life is a step
Too far to reach just yet.

Try as we may to quicken
All ourselves towards that place
We cannot yet achieve it.

Left to ponder our own folly,
We take each painful hour
As our dose of poison.

FRUITLESS JOYS
[10.05am, 10th April 2016, High Wycombe]

How we waste our lives
In pursuit of fruitless joys.
How we wander off
The path of barren hope.
How we wish and wait
In our fields of idle time –
To reap no laughter,
Nor joy of any kind.

MAIDA VALE
[3pm, 16th Apr 2016, Maida Vale, London]

In the depths of Maida Vale,
Drinking wine with gusto –
Gone the day into night,
We look towards the morning light,
To have our moment in the sun.

A BELL TOLLS IN THE FOG
[10.36am, 19th April 2016, High Wycombe]

I try to look forward,
But I want to look back,
For the future is shrouded in mist,
While the past bathes in sunshine,
And rings out in laughter –
Ahead a bell tolls in the fog.

I want to see into the future,
Beyond the trees in the way,
But as I put my foot forward,
There is no light falling ahead,
The path is dark and dead –
I hear only a barking dog.

LITTLE ENGLANDER (JOHN BULL)
[12.35am, Tues 26th April 2016, High Wycombe]

Run, John Bull ….
Run and hide your face in shame,
The world watches your brexit posturing
As refugees remain … rotting in vile camps
While you don your whites,
Play your games.

Curse all those with foreign names
Marching on your cherished lawns –
You vote to keep England English,
You huff and puff your racist cant
For all to hear loud and clear ….
You selfish twat.

THE LONG NIGHT INTO DAY
[12.51am, Thurs 5th May 2016, High Wycombe]

The long night into day comes slow
Through a dark narrow endless tunnel,
At its end a meagre breakfast,
A cup of tea to wash the sorrow.

Daylight breaks upon my labour,
Sleep deprived I stand and shiver –
I shift the burden from my knees
To feel the weight of my existence.

Chained to notions above my station,
I seek escape and exultation –
There is no haven for the troubles,
Nor peace of thought for the restless.

The darkness brings on many doubts,
Sleep is but a fitful lull –
The narrow tunnel binds me in,
Leaves me hostage to the dawn.

GOING DOWN TO GLOUCESTER
[12.32am, Tues 10th May 2016, High Wycombe]

Broods the Brecon bluebell vales,
Castle straddled, dark and ruined –
Deep rut scarred to Offa's Dyke,
Tintern Abbey barren stands ….
Broken fords, lost Roman roads,
Every step steeped in time.

Black coal glaciers bleakly spread
Along the vale from Ebba's hell –
There is no music in the hills,
A stalking kite sails the blue …
Battered cliffs hedge the valley,
Thin haze hangs above the highway.

Brazenly the land upturns its dead,
In blazing shafts, joy returns …

The Severn slithers like a snake,
Smooth and brown to Gloucester –
As dragons race to beating drums,
The choir soars in sunset song.

VANISHED KINGDOMS
[3.55pm, Sat 28th May 2016, High Wycombe]

Broken skin split in broken dreams
Pounding on the sands of silent screams –
Blackbirds parade the promenade,
Kiss and tell their tarty tales …
Slip between the sodden sheets,
Sing their songs of freedom –

While tired, the old soldiers march
To the trumpet tunes of old,
Tell their tales of tawdry tarts,
Their priggish lusts and honky pasts,
Beat their breasts like wild apes,
Wail for their vanished kingdoms.

MORE TEASE THAN CAKE
(for Angela)
[11.02am, Sunday 29th May 2016, High Wycombe]

She flashed her eyes and showed her breasts,
Warm, inviting, but hardly chaste,
She teased me with her puckered lips
But did not give me cake.

I smiled and focused on her eyes,
I did not look below her chin …
No matter what she offered there,
I was not going in …..

She downed her whiskey with a gulp,
She pranced and danced into the dawn,
She led me to her plush abode,
But I could not bridge the gulf.

Life offers many tempting treats,
The best sometimes over tea …
But in the night with drunken belles,
The cake can be a tease.

THE COLD LIGHT OF DAWN
[10.33am, Sat 11th June 2016, High Wycombe]

What is this life we live?
A dance around the maypole ...
Making love in the long grass,
Wrapping scarves around our necks
And hiding from the cold in bed.

What is this merry dance?
A long walk in the woods ...
Holding hands in the afternoon,
Kissing under a full moon,
But empty by the cold light of dawn.

GREAT NATIONS
[12.29am, Sat 1th June 2016, High Wycombe]

The greatest nation in the world,
Is the nation that does not know its great –
The people who do, not only talk,
Who give, and think giving is normal ...

No bombast, trumpeting, or grandiose fanfare,
No beating of drums, no parade of arms –
Immense with humility, small with pride,
Greatness is by acclamation, not by shouting –

Thus the great nations of the world proceed,
Ahead of all those nations bent to conquer.

THE ARTIST
(for Agata)
[11.23am, Monday 13th June 2016, High Wycombe]

The artist danced her hands into the paint,
The music played a Maltese rag –
The colours poured like summer rain
Down her fingers to the floor –
Drenched her canvas with her art,
Showed the door into her heart.

BREXIT
[13.35pm, Sat 25th June 2016, circa Preston]

What tears and lamentation ....
Dragged into the abyss by demons,
Beasts and ugly monsters screaming,
Grins that show their yellow fangs.

Innocent of their vile world,
We become the new inhabitants,
Immigrants to their foreign ways,
Hostages to their ravenous destruction.

ANIMAL FARM
[14.01pm, 25th June 2016, near Carlisle]

Our new days start with introspection,
Anger, pain and disbelief –
Snatched from our land of Eden,
Deposited on a huge dung heap –
I do not like the smell of it,
Nor standing in it ten-fold deep.

Packed-in with the dispossessed,
Twenty-seven different tongues,
We look towards a distant shore,
Beyond the fence, beyond all harm …
Instead we stand in the rain,
Trapped inside this animal farm.

A NEED FOR GOD
[17.01pm, Tues 28th June 2016, near Locherbie]

The rancour and enmity,
The anger and the ache,
Nothing heals a broken heart,
No beer can make the mind forget –
Folk who embrace the devil,
Make God more needed every day.

BREXIT 2
[17.07, Tues 28th June 2016, train – Carlisle]

This is no Dunkirk,
It's the end of Empire,
The death throes of a nation
Totally obsessed with itself.
Fly the flag – empty gesture –
Mob rule at its worst.

OUT OUT DAMN SOUND
[13.00, Sun 24th July 2016, High Wycombe]

Distant times chime in my mind,
crash in on my present state,
discord with my inner self
and my majesty of grace.

Out out damn sound!
The pounding of the waves -
leave me with the butterflies,
my birdsong summer days.

THE GREAT WHEEL TURNS
[12.21, Mon 1st Aug 2016, High Wycombe]

The great wheel turns ...
burns the evening sky -
how my eyes carry into the sunset,
my back to the eastern blackness
as each night eats my days,
shortens my mortal coil,
fades me out, blocks my light
from this wonderful life -
propels me over the horizon
to bring on the inevitable dark.

THE SAND IN MY HAND
[01.07, Fri 19th Aug 2016, High Wycombe]

The sand in my hand -
I strain to understand ...
why God made my brain
so small that I struggle
with faith and beliefs.
Where is he?

Each day starts well -
the sun brings us light ...
and light is good,
without it I am cold,
left in the dark
would I meet the Devil?

One speck of crystal
turning in my palm ...
holds my ignorance of life,
contains my fears,
why am I here,
how did I get here?

Facts are not enough -
sand is just silicon ...
glass-like it sparkles,
where did it come from,
how did it end up
mixing with my sweat?

I cannot fathom it,
get to the bottom of it ...
as hard as I stare
up at the Milky Way,
plot the arc of the stars,
the sand remains.

Smash it with a hammer,
it will multiple in number -
if I heat it up,
it will turn to glass.
I can't make it disappear,
how did it get here?

God is the only answer,
God is everything -
yet still I ask myself ...
Is God a grain of sand,
the sun, the universe
beyond the void out there?

What is in between?
I have no answers -
no quantum mechanics,
no wishful formula,
no simple logic can explain
the sand in my hand.

I CAN SMELL THE PACIFIC
[17.05, Sun 21st Aug 2016, High Wycombe]

In the breeze today is the Pacific -
Alaska fireweed, forget-me-not,
tall pine trees touching clouds,
wild rivers of thrashing salmon.

The scent of moose in the wind,
hot springs and sulphur bubbles,
lone bears crossing glaciers,
rotting kelp on the tidal fringes.

Brown fern, blackened bracken,
blueberries ripe on the slopes,
bark-sap carried on an updraught,
carried to the furthest shores.

The day turns cold in the shade,
four quarter chimes, four full bells,

as I stroll an English park
of rose, yew, fresh cut grass.

Old age does play tricks with me,
makes me switch between the decades,
yet I swear I can detect ...
the perfumed wild Pacific.

AUTUMN EQUINOX
[23.52, Thurs 22nd Sept 2016, High Wycombe]

Day and night in equal measure share
in equal balance hold the turning tide -
summer lingers in the humid haze,
autumn tints the cool bright stars;
on the edge of change we hang ...
to wish for time to be suspended.

RAGS TO RICHES
[22.07, Wed 28th Sept 2016, High Wycombe]

I am obsessed with my days left,
not the days gone, or my glory years -
I look ahead with the same dreams,
the same hope I've always had.

I know others – with their lottery bets,
artists with visions of discovery;
none give up their inner faith
that life will be fair before they go.

With optimistic hope of success,
mankind is naive like an animal
seeking to find a winter store of food
to stay life's eternal struggle.

Some pray to their chosen God,
others to messianic over-lords,
many simply bank on stars and luck -
yet believe they will have their day.

Likewise I keep my dreams alive,
won't give in to what's gone before -
the present is where I make my plans
to win my riches, shed my rags.

LIBERAL ELITE
[22.41, Tues 4th Oct 2016, High Wycombe]

Those who do not wish to change their way of life,
hope that things will last their time -
after that let happen the tragedy that will come,
for they are blind to the chaos drawing near.

LOVE OF POWER
[22.04, Thurs 6th Oct 2016, High Wycombe]

Love of power does not go with goodness,
in all its aspects, it is pride, cunning and cruelty;
but to rage against a regime that is violent
is to replace one set of tyrants with another.

IF WE LET DAYS PASS
[00.48, Sat 22nd Oct 2016, High Wycombe]

If we let days pass without recording them,
then – we have never been here, not existed
for ourselves, nor for our memories of ourselves,
- we are only the persons we are now.

Who can see themselves in the mirror
without the shadow of time behind themselves
contrasting the false image we project
that obscures who we are are, and who we were.

I AM WORDLESS AGAIN
[01.04, Sat 22nd Oct 2016, High Wycombe]

My own silence baffles me -
empty of anger or burning passion
to rage against the world's woes -
I sip my coffee, eat my cake,
sit warmly in my neat abode
numb to all the distant killing,
detached from all the fleeing migrants.
The world is awash with chaos
and I am wordless in response.

WHEN THE POET DIES
[10.50, Sun 23rd Oct 2016, High Wycombe]

When aged forty the Poet dies,
the passion spent, the cynic born,
his anger changed to selfish rant,
all writing but a heap of kant,

rubbish piled upon himself,
his inner-soul lost to verse -

now lost in self-importance,
pinned by such to his past,
tied down by dogmatic lines,
chained to his clichéd lines,
the echo of his former truths,
on every page the dullest thud -

liberty once the gleaming goal,
truth the target of his barb,
when no coin could buy him,
when no romance could tie him;
free in thought, deeds and wants
living life with a God -

causes filled his wakeful hours,
his rage waged against the times,
his work flowed like the tide,
swept the beach of his mind,
drifting words made him distinct,
timeless in a wasteful world -

now – all washed up,
soiled by his own survival,
the cynic as the status-quo,
seeks approval from his foes,
goes to bed every night,
basking in his own betrayal -

so the burnt out Poet dies,
drops his pen to join society,
accepts corrupt immoral ways,
condones untruths for personal gain,
backs wars as doing good,
behaves blind to all injustice -

better then that he dies,
lets the mantle fall on others,
that we forgive his latter failings,
remember his poetic railings,
his anger, angst and accusations,
the truth of his youthful penning's.

I HAVE LOST NOTHING
[00.33, Sun 3rd Oct 2016, High Wycombe]

When I reflect on what I have lost,

I have lost nothing -
I may swat a bug with my finger
but there is no memory of cruelty.

Many have not found what they are seeking -
I cannot say that I am wanting -
along the path I have taken,
I have collected my dreams.

I have never exiled myself,
turned my back on the things I love -
I have never abandoned my vocation,
though many friends have been lost.

I don't pretend to be short-sighted
in order to cut out painful reunion -
I just quicken my pace to distance
myself from untimely encumbrances.

Regrets only come with reflection,
yet changes nothing, cannot undo -
loss is not a thing to dwell on,
there is more to find than lose.

ELEPHANTS
[00.14, Thurs 3rd Nov 2016, High Wycombe]

What cruelty there is in man -
greed, avarice and self-survival;
civilisation is just a game,
the cunning ringing our territory
with brick walls and wire fences.

Not so our big-eared beasts,
roaming their ancestral plains,
making their elephant walks,
towards their elephant graveyards
to be visited by us.

SIRENS ALL DAY LONG
[14.53, Mon 7th Nov 2016, High Wycombe]

What is wrong with the world?
Accidents and incidents,
heart attacks and crashes,
lights flashing on and off!
It makes my pulse race,
my blood pressure soar.

TEN MINUTES
[14.55, Mon 7th Nov 2016, High Wycombe]

I have ten minutes ….
should I write a poem
or should I exercise?

I'll do both …
have a cup of tea
and find ten minutes more.

NO TWO DAYS
[23.47, Thurs 10th Nov 2016, High Wycombe]

No two days are the same-
its river deep, river high …
storms rage every hour,
news pours on us like a deluge;
who is Noah in these times
with the foresight of the flood?

WE WILL DEPART BY DESIGN
[00.56, Mon 14th Nov 2016, High Wycombe]

Life has no answer to anything.
It comes as a gift ….
Ahead of it is the taking away,
but who can grudge the departure;
we have arrived by accident -
we will depart by design.

TO LOVE TOO MUCH
[00.02, Thurs 17th Nov 2016, High Wycombe]

To love too much, but not too well
is like gambling everything on one horse -
odds to win, but no sure bet
that its going to be first past the post.

CRISIS YEAR
[00.50, Sun 18th Dec 2016, High Wycombe]

No snow falls on this crisis year,
no cosy fires or jugs of warm wine -
little cheer to bring in joy,
looking back – an anguished task.

Yet forward pushed we will proceed
at our rate, not that of others -

we will falter all along the way,
marching to the tune of robbers.

What becomes us will be sorrow,
every day, and every morrow
until we house, feed our brothers,
sisters, children and our mothers.

These careless times will excel
a cruelty beyond our reckoning,
we now must bear the screaming
of our own distressed reasoning.

HAPPINESS IS NOT GUNS
[00.34, Wed 28th Dec 2016, High Wycombe]

Happiness is not guns -
firing them … watching them fired,
people being killed,
animals, birds … killed.

How can death be fun?
Or violence joyful?
Or mass murder give pleasure
in real life?

Spear, bows and arrows, swords,
bombs, weapons of mass destruction?
I cannot see the good times,
nor the benefit.

THE WINDOW IS OPEN
[00.58, 28th Dec 2016, High Wycombe]

The window is wide open -
every possibility exists.
Will the sparrow be lured
or a robin tempted?

Roll up the blind,
pull back the curtains -
anything can happen,
the day may rain.

Nothing foretold, nothing expected,
anything imagined may occur.
December may melt,
replaced by May blossom.

RAGE AGAINST THE LIGHT
[2nd Jan - 23rd Mar 2017, Bucks]

It began with a big bang,
an almighty roar, not a whimper,
no stifled sobbing in the night.
The sound was clear, distinct
like the roar that thunders,
like the beat of the Parana
falling on the mission rocks below.

How then did it start ...?
This epoch of uncertainty and violence,
this age of deafening chaos,
this time in which we live
with its wailing and shouting,
the endless cacophony of noise
disturbing our restless sleep?

The answers rest in the future,
that place ahead, that quiet zone
given to the babbling of brooks,
the listening to bird song bursting
on the gaggling of beasts,
the snorting of surface creatures
cruising off the coast.

There ... in that heaven ahead,
the solitude of certainty awaits -
all transgressors who trespass
shall find a rock to rest,
shall take the sun ...
shall shed their naked guilt,
re-find their days of innocence.

The present presses on the chores
that wastes the waking hours of thought,
garbage fills the streets of reason,
sewage seeps disguised as wisdom,
rubbish leaves a littered conscience,
fills it with a heap of nonsense,
exhausts the mind beyond all logic.

The epoch marches to a tune,
in step strides, does its duty,
no tearful sorrow for its actions,
unlike Arjuna in his chariot -
his bow slung, his arrows quivered,

questioning the choices given
and his own existence.

Reflection in a placid pool,
the snapping of a selfie image,
Narcissus lurks in the background,
few can see beyond the mirror -
Aristotle perceived the worth of idols,
little more than human folly
dressed up as art and drama.

The door of perception opens
out into a plain of grass -
this idle life of grazing,
foraging with the huddled herd,
Elysium shimmers in the distance,
crickets mix with the wind chimes,
chirp into the dawn.

Forests cover up our history,
plough-shares slice up our past -
once there was a city here,
over there stood a temple ...
Avebury now a line of rocks,
a wisp of what it once was
to a God.

Pagans plod through every age,
star-ward gaze with their dreams,
their feet planted in the soil
preventing them from flying off.
Beam me up! their eyes implore,
seeking more from life than this ...
earthbound erstwhile, just the same.

On the plains of poor Albania,
Ilyria lies beneath the dust.
Lost in ancient Latin texts,
locals know where it exists ...
point to where the ruins lie;
yet who has time for the past
when time is in short supply.

And fly it will, all too quick
until we find our sand has run,
our moon is full of shifting cloud
blotting out the evening star -
the steps worn, the way steep,

we'll slip and slide very stride,
stumble, just to stave the journey.

Thus each day becomes more precious
as we horde the hours we have -
yet we waste the one resource
that will depart, escape our grasp,
leave us silent in the dark,
without a hint of what to think
or what comes next.

Through each day we will slog,
tied to our pagan rituals -
routine as a vital virtue,
companionship as a constant vigil,
loyalty an essential ethic,
truth a fundamental element
of who we are today.

The fog comes down ...
the ice crackles underfoot,
dim lamps yellow in the mist,
pines stand on the ridge
drenched by the swirling dew
an owl wits its evening tune
above the traffic.

In the Okovango swamp,
rhinos wallow in the mud -
a river flows very slowly,
snakes its length to Mozambique.
Who can stem the predetermined?
Who can pause all momentum
or halt the inevitable?

Marked by time, scarred by fate,
tempests hurricanes and gales -
forced by forces beyond our know,
no man of science can explain,
no priest of thought can declare,
no argument, no simple faith
can unmask the mystery.

The polar ice breaks away,
drifts, melts, fades to nothing -
rain drops, seeps, then dries,
till it seems it never came -
sun heats, warms, cools,

dissipates to leave us cold,
to wait in the dark alone.

Solitary in our skins we sleep,
lonely in our minds we breathe,
snow drives on the mountains,
ice coats the city side-walks -
and somewhere a president is sworn-in
against the will of the people
he will divide.

This is the time we endure,
rock-an-roll a sideshow drug,
movies in staggering violence
splattered in expansive scope -
refuge behind new Chinese walls,
lessons never learned, bottles thrown,
smashed against urban sprawl.

Where is the eternal hope ...
the child with the open arms,
the parent with the loving smile
masking out the looming world.
Can innocence be preserved,
can goodness be untouched
by the doubts of age?

Life takes its turns ....
anger comes and goes -
the tide of passion wanes
then returns again to haunt
each waking second, and in sleep
the worry builds its walls
against its troubles.

Such seas swell each storm
bearing on the coast of angst,
no rest from the howling wind,
no shelter from the constant blast -
the light burns to the wick,
the heat turns to freezing cold,
sweat wets the pillow.

Terribly we live like this
in constant torment, fevered fear
of all there is to lose -
Has progress come to nought
but ticky-tacky little boxes

stacked in terraced rows
like lines of Lego?

Once three score and ten
is now four score and five -
the lengthening span of sorrow
increased by five thousand tomorrows.
Has this brought more joy?
Should we sing ecstatically
at our fortune?

Time will tell with each tick,
the liver spots marking age,
aches in the tender parts,
creases on the weathered skin -
yet inside the child hides
blowing bubbles at the world
with a wicked smile.

Slumbering lies the secret eye
beyond the sight of natural vision -
wisdom flirts from soul to soul,
knows no limit to its visit.
Somewhere in the Himalayas,
somewhere in the human jungle,
there is an answer.

For most, the days stretch on
without a clue about existence -
give us each our daily bread,
we shall breathe, give our thanks,
trespass not upon our brothers,
our sisters, or on any others
if we are righteous.

Yet, we fail, flawed we fall,
don't reveal our foulest sins -
in the dark we flail and flounder,
shut away our filthy deeds -
as fickle to our foulest thoughts
we deceive our better selves
and die alone.

Who is that inner struggling self
so tiny in this universe?
Frustration vent as modern art,
reveals little of this vital spark
of life, of being, this individual

trapped within the cosmic whole
without a reason.

To bear the pointlessness of existence,
too many end their engagement early,
burn up in one great rush
to get to their own Nirvana -
youth becomes a blaze of light,
ends as a martyr's life
or as an icon.

Victor or victim, it is the same,
they are gone from our presence,
perhaps to a better sphere -
we are left in our rotation
around the sun uninterrupted;
we wake, we sleep, wake to weep
at our existence.

Then the light through the window
whitens the black dog night -
I am alive, I am breathing,
I am joyous in my fortune
as I travel into the dawn,
the curtain drawn morning
of glorious day.

Down to the sea I go,
down to where the travelers sail,
to exit off to sweltering lands,
to lie beneath languid palms -
lost to cocktails on the beach,
lost in many lapping waves
washing me.

Simple sultry senses simmer,
contentment gives to deep desire;
lust fills the flickering mind,
each and every waking hour -
longing enters every bone,
want weighs every thought,
erodes all moral.

There my imagination stays,
lingers on a fresh corruption,
enters into darkened hollows,
descends into deeper chasms,
chases shadows into caverns,

catches air in clutching spasms
all for nothing.

The hunter soon hunted is
pursued until he finds the light -
the dark dog howls his fright,
the child knows no delight,
the adult in us seeks perversion,
the sinner in us tries coercion
on the weak.

No escape from inner dreams
tearing at our selfish selves -
we sip our tea, gulp our gins,
take a spin in our cars -
beat to some secluded place,
bask at some beauty spot
and seek redemption.

And still we try to laugh
at the absurdities, the banal,
the pointless and the pitiful,
at those who pontificate, seek
certificates for some knowledge,
or affirmations for some talent
or insecurity.

The wrongs of this world
cannot be healed by sociopaths -
politicians are merely policemen
maintaining social order -
they can't fix our illnesses,
mend our broken hearts,
or heartless minds.

Televisions cannot feed us,
nor books dress us warmly;
art is a drab distraction
meant to dull our dissent -
music is the people's opium,
movies a corporate commercial
selling pizza.

Then life brings love so pure
it need not speak its name;
love that is silent in its stealth,
so overwhelming in its honesty;
beauty in the dark lit eyes,

lips lightly pursed in laughter -
there is no crying.

Souls meet in distant circles,
entwine in unknowing worlds;
there is no reason to such connections,
it happens without plan or purpose -
eyes meet across a crowded room,
attraction draws each together
without restraint.

We wait for something to go wrong,
the bubble always bursts somehow,
yet love transcends corporal things,
survives somewhere beyond ourselves,
takes root in our deeper being,
saves us from our own deception
and inner evils.

Then death strikes like lightning,
no warning, a flash, a nephew gone;
the noise that follows is anguish,
anger that he was in his prime.
There is no time to lose -
each day must be taken now,
not wasted.

And though the times are hard,
the chores are dull and tedious,
there is hope in the smiles of strangers,
laughter in the face of bad news,
endless joy in the eyes of children,
calmness in the walk of widows
and their carers.

There may be cloudy times ahead,
but through the damp swirling mist
there is the longed-for open land,
where opportunity has no fences
nor barriers to advancement -
where dancing is the stimulus
to burst into song.

Destiny drives its own car into town
and parks on double yellow lines -
there are no rules or stipulations,
no limitations to its boundaries;
the predetermined waits to happen,

will come about come what may
for certain.

The tired wait with the condemned,
have nothing else to do but linger
between this world and the other;
between sleep and the suffering,
they flit between the light and dark
uncertain of the way ahead -
the lonely journey.

The sunny upland hills are waiting
to ring with the call of youth -
long strides atop the ridges,
bounding steps in gladed woods;
clear streams to quench a thirst,
long grass to rest and dream
of things to come.

As time presses on each day,
gnaws away at our conscience,
chokes and stifles all contentment,
strips the essence of existence -
duty bound to serve survival,
commitment eats our *raison d'etre*,
our *joie d'vivre*.

We march to different kinds of tunes,
the piper plays for all of us -
the soldier home, the traveler safe,
the flowers fresh on their graves;
we mourn the valiant and brave,
as we reflect and stare upon
our own mortality.

The sun sets on the cold horizon,
the crisp air turns to chill,
a calm descends on the churchyard,
the village clock strikes six times -
time is marked with precision,
marked by means so familiar
we lose count.

But count by count time runs out,
pours away, drains to empty -
we are done, spent of force,
we cannot change or fix our course;
no magic word can will our wish,

our want to somehow carry on
beyond our hour.

We face the truth in our mirrors,
in our friends lost to us -
yet we want to fool ourselves
that we are somehow made immortal;
we put off all our dreams,
put off all our best endeavours
until tomorrow.

We hear that ticking ebbing sound,
ignore it as an irritation -
paralysed by our own deception,
we blindly drain our inner doubts;
today will never come again,
tomorrow will never come at all,
the past is dead.

Truth is for the brutally honest -
when mothers die there are no lies,
all the wounds once so hidden,
now become bare and healing;
scars buried in the psyche,
secrets locked in the memory
told to all.

What of that mother gone to heaven,
her shame also gone with her?
Why she felt she had to hide,
hold her tongue all her life -
love can be a cruel deceiver,
love can be a vain protector
of our dignity.

Still the rivers flow on freely,
each new rain washes wisdom,
knowledge lost with the aged
finds new lodging with the young -
a child soon a mother is ...
a mother shields her precious child
from pain.

How big the cosmos wheels about
above our heads beyond our reach;
what joy there is in the stars,
where man for sure will never go -
God is safe from our greed,

God is safe from our desire
to conquer space.

Happy then, content to prosper,
I conclude that I exist;
I march through my final days
with a limp, not a whimper -
I will not go with a bang,
I will not go with a song
but with laughter.

A PICTURE OF ISABELLE
[14.14, Fri 20th Jan 2017, High Wycombe]

She had my mother's name -
Hair golden in the winter sun,
Her eyes sparkling in the frosty hoar -
Her voice free in the forest light.

The artist in her shone brightly,
Radiated from her excited thoughts,
Glowed against the darkened wood
Set against a clear blue heaven.

She sometimes trembled with emotion,
A glimpse into another time .....
But most, she jokes, simply spoke
About her love of life.

She painted her own picture ...
A snapshot, a blink of an eye;
In profile she was Hellenic,
Full faced – curious as a child.

In a click she was gone,
Back to her other world .....
Where beauty tries to blossom
And escape becomes a joy.

ANOTHER DONKEY ON THE ROAD
[14.30, Tues 2nd May 2017, Kalahari, Botswana]

Another donkey on the road.
Another elephant waiting to cross
to a distant waterhole.

The Kalahari stretches forever,
flatter than the Indian Plains -

the bush is lush with rain,
the season near its end.

TODAY WILL NOT BE RECALLED
[19.50, Sun 14th May 2017, High Wycombe]

Wet the British Spring dowses hope -
loud voices drown out the birds,
an argument over nothing but pride,
a chorus of unrepented shouting.
The quite of Africa so far away,
the heat of the setting sun -
tomorrow will be but a memory,
today will not be recalled at all.

THE BALLERINA
for Henrietta
[noon, Mon 29th May 2017, High Wycombe]

She appeared from nowhere ....
I looked up and she was there
sitting in the soft light,
her warm eyes fixed on me.

She offered out her hand -
and as I accepted her approach,
something inside opened,
a lotus blossomed.

How these things are mysterious -
We are not prepared for surprise,
moments counted in one hand
that last forever.

IT WOULD BE HER
[00.54, Tues 30th May 2017, High Wycombe]

If heaven sent down an angel
to remind us of all our wrongs,
to let us gaze on perfection
to gauge our own ugly forms -
it would be her.

If art drew on all beauty
to sculpt the perfect form,
to paint the perfect picture,
to express art's high ideals -
it would be her.

If the eye saw no blemish,
the ear heard no flaw,
our fingers touched the skin
of the smoothest of them all -
it would be her.

For when love is blithely blind
and hears no evil from itself,
that love is perfect love
a love that has no end -
that is her.

AND STILL SHE IS SILENT
For Teresa May
[10.55, Sun 4th June 2017, High Wycombe]

And still she is silent ...
We will turn the other cheek
and reiterate our superiority
over the tenets of another faith.

But we will still sell arms
and bomb the shit out of others,
though not in our name,
for she is silent.

Life will go on, the election -
she will defeat the enemy,
she will lock up the innocent
in case they are guilty.

Oh Sunday Sunday, pray for us,
that she is silent on the threat
we are to others far away -
blown up every day by our bombs.

Weak and wobbly we continue
into the abyss in silence -
a silence that does not work,
a silence that does not become us.

Silent we stand waiting for leadership,
but silent she remains,
as silently she turns her back
and dwells on her own silence.

A TOWER OF TRAGEDY
[1.07, Fri 16th Jun 2017, High Wycombe]

A tower of tragedy burns
into the souls of everyone.
A single spark ignites anger
and dismay at its enormity.
No words can describe pictures
that will haunt until eternity.
We weep for those now missing,
and cry for those in agony.

THE SUMMER OF OUR CONTENT
[17.07, Tues 17th July 2017, High Wycombe]

This is the summer of our contentment
caressed by our days of sunshine,
long afternoons of perfect bliss,
short shrift given to our cares -
short shadows cast on our past,
our talk is of the future.

PASSCHENDAELE 2017
[09.28, Wed 2nd Aug 2017, High Wycombe]

A hundred years on and Hell on Earth,
the dead still lie where they fell.
Ypres haunted by Australian spectres,
shadows on the old town walls.

Miles of rows, and rows for miles,
the white gravestones scar the ground
where half a million men lay down
and never rose to stand again.

Sombre, silent, poignant, sober,
a city lies beneath the soil -
there are no streets, only trenches
that house soldiers far from home.

Lest we forget, lest we forget
the names etched on all the walls,
the gate to Hell is open still
for whose who march to war.

23,163 DAYS
[08.33, Thurs 24th Aug 2017, High Wycombe]

Born on a Thursday, today is a Thursday,

three thousand, three hundred and nine weeks old;
I stumble on towards my glorious future
knowing the number of days since I was born.

Seven hundred and sixty months or so,
sixty three years with sixteen leap years,
one hundred and fifty two days added on
to get to today – a fine summer morn.

How many weeks, how many months,
how many leap years remain to be counted?
My days are numbered in various ways -
I live each one as another day saved.

YOU JUST HAVE TO SAY GOODBYE (Song)
[01.44, Thurs 16th Nov 2017, High Wycombe]

He said I was an angel,
but I have a brittle halo,
and everything he gave me
turned to bad -

sometimes when you're in love
its just not enough
you just have to say – goodbye.

Now he's gone I'm empty,
no-one else can tempt me
to cross myself, and
pretend I'm good -

for when you lose your lover
and sadness overcomes ya',
inside you die, you cry.

No angel, I've not fallen,
I have my inner calling
and everything I've got
will come good -

for though I'm on my own
once my tears have gone
I'll get over all my woes.

CHORUS
Oh lord, how I miss him,
his sweet talking whispers
and his kind of loving
every night -

sometimes its not enough
when the sun comes up
you just have to say goodbye

ANOTHER BOOK OF NOTES
[17.06, 19th Nov 2017, High Wycombe]

And so to another book of notes,
of poems penned between the light
that exists squeezed from the dark
of sleep and dreaming.

DITA AT KEW
[17.29, 19th Nov 2017, High Wycombe]

We walked round Kew in the sun,
the golden brown of all the world
at our feet, crisp and dry,
the canopy of autumn's cull.

We took our tea and almond bun,
we talked about our recent past,
she produced a tin of sweets,
I a birthday card.

The hothouse left far behind,
we wandered in the Himalayas,
squeezed down a Chinese path
no monkey ever favoured.

Until at last, three hours gone,
we left by the turnstile gate,
she went to buy some fish,
I, to drive away.

WHERE ARE MY FRIENDS NOW
[27thNov-26thDec 2017, H Wyc-Marbesa, Spain]

The hour is late, I am alone,
given time to quietly think,
to dwell upon my nine lives,
my passing through many towns,
places where I made friends
in countries where few travel,
but also here at home.

Where then to start, to tell,
when memory plays all its tricks,
makes us want to fondly think

that every friend we have found
was someone lost along the line -
but is this so, maybe not,
I'd like to know.

My early friends were my cousins,
Hughie, and his brother John;
I lived my youngest years with them
in a small council flat -
as children do, children play,
get to know each other well,
too well some would say.

At nursery in Pollokshaws,
Muriel MacDonald was my friend,
in later years her brother John
became my early teenage mentor;
Muriel, shy, coy and sensible,
I, wild, bold, unreasonable,
we parted at the nursery gates.

Then with John, aged thirteen,
a summer spent playing cards,
I teased Muriel about her breasts,
growing out, firm, erect -
tried to kiss her, did just once,
but she was younger by four months
and not as grown up.

In nursery there was also Linda
who next I saw aged sixteen,
she sided up to me at school,
stated boldly, I was the kid
who'd been to nursery with her
and changed his name.
I denied it.

Why, oh why, did I lie?
What arrogance ruled my heart!
For she was such a lovely lass
in a lower class than me -
I was such an awful fool,
we had grown up together
in the same slums.

Years later, when I went home
to live and marry yet again,
Linda lived along the street
though I did not get to see her

my daughter knew her youngest one,
through her passed the message on
to say hello.

How could I not have visited,
made the effort to make amends,
taken the chance to reminisce
about our times at nursery -
Too late now, the years gone
to renew the friendship bond
made in infancy.

How we waste our worthless lives,
blind to our own shortcomings.
What have I squandered thus
by being so un-empathetic?
I cannot turn back time,
I cannot reclaim the friends
I've thrown away.

Let this not be a reminiscence,
not a tract to make amends -
I have no reason to regret,
no grounds to frown upon events
that shaped my life, that of others,
whose I've met along the road
of my existence.

The pages turn on all us mortals,
on those we knew now passed on -
we each retain a part of them
in our own conscious self;
a special part we might recall
or feel it is a point of truth
we touched upon.

But to the present – my current
friends who populate my being,
my being here, present in my mind,
in my daily actions, there,
here and now, not back then
when such friends are mere stories
not now so real.

Is it polite to name these souls,
those dearest ones close to me,
when they are still around, about
me in my daily deeds and chores?
Should not I be respectful, churlish

in revealing such faithful friends
to my foes?

There rests my deepest reservation,
to let loose on my many secrets,
the things once told, never mentioned,
the whispered words, the tiny actions
that make for lasting friendship -
the greatest stories ever told
lost to history.

So safer then to recount the past,
to dwell on those lost acquaintances,
for this is what they become,
shadows on life's long wall,
flickering lights dancing in the mind,
leaves rustling in the breeze
that time blows on.

Neil Dickson, what a boy -
lost in my childhood smog,
aged seven, taken, just like that,
his desk empty, my tears dry,
to have your best friend killed
without a single goodbye
is a travesty.

How I have dwelt on this loss,
fifty odd years of bereavement
for my closest, dearest friend,
still not replaced, or dislodged
from the core of who I am,
of who we were together
at school, invincible.

His friendship taught me that
together two can conquer the world,
whilst alone we can only wish
for better days ahead, better times
than we currently get by on -
that man is an island of misery
without companionship.

And so, my friendships thereafter
became a competition, a rivalry,
a need to be better than my peers,
not their friends, but their leader,
not their equal, but their master,

with no need for love, just respect
through dominance.

Such admission, such woeful sin
to have led a life of pride,
to have lauded my being thus,
over those on whom I triumphed,
not out of love or friendship,
but out of loss.

This may seem a retold fabrication,
but no, the loss of master Dickson
so affected me – no-one knew,
no-one understood the deep bond
young lads place in one another
as they build their house of adulthood,
stone by stone.

At seven the man is made -
the child has begun to depart,
leave behind the crying for good,
to get on with being a boy
who cannot wait to grow up,
find adventure, seek his dreams,
and leave home.

With Neil's death, friendship became
transient in every friendship made -
Was I to lose again a friend somehow?
Would he be taken, gone too soon?
I learned to break friendships off
before the pain of separation
left me bereft.
[Unfinished]

SCOTTISH SUMMER
[15.52, 24th Dec 2017, Marbesa, Marbella]

It is a Scottish summer sun
though it is Christmas Eve -
in six months the Earth will spin,
turn some forty six degrees,
and bring back again the warmth
I know as Scottish summer.

Meanwhile here in Andalucia,
Scottish sun rages with its breeze,
its crashing waves on the shore,
the cool character of the shade,

the evenings of overcoats, some hats,
but dark, not light like Scotland.

There lies the Spanish difference -
the night time sky is black,
the moon is not behind a cloud,
there is no rain coming down,
there is no eternal twilight
to run free with friends on open hillside.

CHRISTMAS LUNCH
[13.34, 25th Dec 2017, Marbesa, Marbella]

What a feast! What joy!
Lunch – avocado, salami, cheese
on wholemeal bread, a glass
of Tempranillo as my champagne.
Palm trees drooping with rain,
the clouds shifting like pirates
in the wave-laden sky -
How dear is life so cheaply
paid for on Christmas Day.

HOW FAR MOROCCO LIES
[13.44, 26th Dec 2017, Marbesa, Spain]

How far Morocco lies is not far,
a mere gulls fly, a dolphin's swim,
yet for us it is an ocean's width,
a stretch too far for weary legs.

The day turns on its usual axis,
the idle sit and drink their coffee,
labour labours on it's chores
on numbers few, serving many.

The clouds drift like desert sands,
shade the sea, shift its hues,
the sun hides in the southern sky
beyond where far Morocco lies.

REFINDING WHAT IS LOST
[17.03, 27th Dec 2017, Marbesa, Spain]

What new is there to learn when
most knowledge has been forgotten.
It seems that nothing will be discovered
unless we re-find what is lost.

WITHOUT THE SUN
[17.24, 27th Dec 2017, Marbesa, Spain]

Without the hot Sahara sun,
I am in Nicaragua or Dunoon;
the winter shore shed of light,
a wild stretch of breaking white,
at my feet the thrown shells,
the pebbles wrenched from the depths,
my footprints in the dampened sands
unbroken for a thousand steps,
the wind in my weathered cheeks,
my lips closed devoid of speech -
how, now so like other times
I find myself retracing life.

MARBESA IN WINTER
[18.14, 28th Dec 2017, Marbesa, Spain]

How slow it all seems to be -
nothing but the sound of the waves,
the rustle of the wind in the palms.
It is cold now – no hot tiles
radiating their evening warmth,
no crack of the settling timbers,
no wet mist on the night lawn,
just a biting southern draught
swirling about deserted balconies,
empty wrinkled pools of blue,
colourless in the twilight hue.

MAIJA
[18.25, 28th Dec 2017, Marbesa, Spain]

It started with a zing, then a pop,
a simple tick, then a quick hello,
now its blossomed into a long exchange,
pics, and talk of art and children.

How easy it is to be open to strangers,
those we have never met, may still not -
we have no fear, for they do not exist
as real, but fantasies of our making.

Distant voices that we never hear,
we will never really know for sure
until we have proof they are flesh
and blood, and there before us stand

real after all, and full of frailty,
with flaws and everything we imagined
and hoped they would not be
mere mortals just like ourselves.

THE BULL IN THE FIELD
[12.36, 29th Dec 2017, Marbesa, Spain]

The bull in the field chased the chicken,
the goat and the sheep watched on,
the chicken clucked, jumped a fence,
the bull stopped short with a snort.

The goat turned, made eyes at the sheep,
the sheep looked back vacant eyed,
then started to twitch as the bull turned,
the chicken crowed at the fun.

The goat took flight, climbed a tree,
the sheep found a hole in the fence,
the bull fumed, circled the field,
the chicken stuck out its neck.

The goat bleated from a high branch,
the sheep ba'd stuck in a hedge,
the bull wallowed in a pool of mud,
the chicken made off for its shed.

The farmer came, just shook his head,
rescued the goat, untangled the sheep,
gave his prize bull one of his frowns
and collected from the shed his eggs.

THE IDLE LIFE
[14.58, 29th Dec 2017, Marbesa, Spain]

Why do some do all the work,
while others shirk, lay about?
Is there something wrong with this
or can the worker learn to live?

Live to work and die too soon,
work to live, enjoy life's fruits?
Busy hands make busy lives,
empty hands enjoy life's spice.

So what are you, my dear friend,
a worker or an idle wretch?

Wait you until the day is done,
or sit you all day in the sun?

MANDY
[00.23, 12th Jan 2018, High Wycombe]

Mandy had four fingers on her right hand,
four toes on her right foot,
but her smile was six fingers to the world,
and her eyes six feet deep with warmth.

She was small but boiled with life,
childless, but full of joy and spirit,
normal in a pub of freaks and clones,
more unique than all of them combined.

COME BACK INTO MY LIFE
[23.18, 12th Jan 2018, High Wycombe]

I want someone to come back
into my life to complete the circle.
The girl in the polka-dot dress,
the son of the mysterious secret agent,
the nurse who I could not fulfil,
the bigamist I loved despite his flaws.

Where are they? How I wonder,
how I search when memory returns -
a name is not enough to reunite,
friends must want to be found
or all the searching of the world
will uncover nothing of what remains.

It is the saddest of ironies that
we sing of - don't know where,
don't know when, but someday
we will meet again somewhere,
knowing not *ca sera sera*,
or the words of *auld lang syne*.

I am of an age of wanting closure,
a tying up the ends of friendship,
the need to know how life works
on those who once were close -
so close I cared, care still
for them to come back into my life.

WHAT HAPPENED TO ME (Song)
[00.39, 5th Feb 2018, High Wycombe]

My lips need time to recover,
my legs are like rubber,
what happened to me?

I was pulled out of my bubble,
and now I'm in trouble,
'cause that girl got to me.

My head's in a tail spin,
my heart's been done in,
what happened to me?

I'm free falling with no chute,
its not looking too good,
she was too cute for me.

I'm a dodger and weaver,
I'm an artful deceiver,
what happened to me?

It was just that one look,
I was totally hooked,
how did she do it to me?

My lips need time to recover,
my legs are like rubber,
what happened to me?

EXCHANGING TIREDNESS
[00.07, 13th Feb 2018, High Wycombe]

That moment the eyes close ….
I am tired, worn out by repetition,
witness to mundane happenings.

I just want to shut life out,
fall asleep, float off in dream,
flee every day routine -
exchange it for jumbled fantasy,
make-believe nonsense -

in exchange for the desire
to wake rested, renewed.

BACK FROM AFRICA
[22.30, 18th April 2018, High Wycombe]

I am back, but knowing not
what I am back to.
A month in Africa has passed,
and so too has my past.

I am no longer that young man
so eager for adventure and risk;
the old man has arrived
and the rocking chair beckons.

THE HOLE IN THE HEDGE
[08.01, 25th April 2018, High Wycombe]

I am told 'just knock it out',
but its been knocked out of me,
the stuffing, the omph, the substance
that makes me, me.

Through the hedge backwards,
I feel I've been thrown, landed
not on my feet but my neck
in a head-banging heap.

'Pick yourself up' I'm told;
I need a wheelchair today,
and someone to shove me back
through the hedge hole.

MY RUSSIAN SPY
for Lana
[23.02, 25th April 2018, High Wycombe]

I spoke with my Russian spy,
it was a distant voice,
but she spoke sweetly -
I forgave her all her flaws.

I urged her to get a suntan,
buy dresses for the summer,
told her to rest her mind
and ignore the FSB.

She was on the Riviera,
being chatty and carefree -
I loved her for her boldness
and her time for me.

APPLE
[21.55, 29th April 2018, High Wycombe]

The little Chinese dancer moves
as a flicker in my eyes.
Such beauty in a perfect form
of movement that is joy -
emotion and understanding
that straddles all divides
and cultural differences.

TAO GIRL
[23.30, 20th May 2018, High Wycombe]

She speaks with symbols,
she sings her song,
moves without a shadow.

No plum petals fall,
no weeping stains the earth
through the bewilderment of life.

No left-over consequences,
every step is traceless,
a bird darting in the night.

CHINESE IMAGES
[23.50, 29th May 2018, High Wycombe]

I'm all words, not pictures,
the sounds I make, not images,
the crude sentences of ink,
do not paint, do not colour.

All I write is black and white,
characters with little character,
a repetition of plain information,
transcriptions to be interpreted.

If only I could draw Chinese,
use a sweeping brush, not a pen,
real images, not mere letters.

TWO SIDES OF LOVE
[00.02, 30th May 2018, High Wycombe]

What can another person offer,
give of themselves you cannot take?

In reverse what can you give
that you do not need returned?

Love is two sided like a coin,
it has an edge that can be rolled
until it falls flat to reveal
which lover has the upper hand.

A RIVER NEVER FALTERS
[23.50, 8th June 2018, High Wycombe]

My life runs its course -
like a river that knows its way,
edging past fields containing shadows
that I wave to as I pass.

It is not too late to extend
a hand towards the bank,
to take hold of a lover
and float onwards together.

We will part on the journey,
I will surely float on alone;
my river is running swiftly
and I detect the nearing shore.

It is as it should be,
I am at peace with myself -
a river never falters
on its journey to its end.

A KISS ON THE LIPS
[23.56, 8th June 2018, High Wycombe]

Can love exist as words
without touch or scent or sight?
Can the object of desire be real
without a kiss on the lips?

MY LITTLE APPLE
[00.08, 9th June 2018, High Wycombe]

She is beautiful, just perfect,
there is no need to look for flaws,
she is human, has her moments,
don't we all doubt our actions?
My task is to love her, need her,
make space, let her into me,
make changes to my being, soul,

throw off my ways, my reservations,
say things I've never said before,
pack my bags and be prepared
for the journey along love's road.
For ahead lies joy and laughter,
a life better than the old.

JANET PRICE
[00.37, 11th June 2018, High Wycombe]

And so our good friend Janet Price
passed away today, aged ninety five,
a child hood friend of Richard Burton,
a poor boy who came to her house
to receive soup and bread from her mother,
the doctor's wife.

We will clearly miss Janet Price
who only put champagne to her lips,
who lived on the sunny Riviera,
who knew everyone who knew her,
a favourite of the mayor of Cannes,
her confident.

The Valley's will remember Janet Price,
the Welsh girl with her Chanel style,
who took in artists and poets,
who befriended stars and princes,
in Monaco and Nice, on radio
with that Valley voice.

I will remember dear Janet Price,
a true friend in hard times,
a true friend in every sense,
a wizened soul wisely wise,
a saint to all film-makers,
a blazing star.

MY BODY HAS CLIMBED MOUNTAINS
[13.58, 18th June 2018, High Wycombe]

My body has climbed mountains,
crossed deserts, sailed oceans,
trekked jungles, faced elephants.

It is still my temple,
the house of my Gods,
the home where I reside,
the library of my thoughts,

the dwelling place of my being,
where my soul is imprisoned,
unable to escape yet.

TEXT MESSAGE
[01.27, 15th July 2018, High Wycombe]

Its the little things, the little thoughts,
however short, however brief,
that brings joy, brings happiness.

I want for nothing more, nothing,
for the little thoughts are enough,
they fill my weary days with light.

Bless the sender, bless her again,
bless every little thought expressed,
I am blessed.

LAKE VICTORIA
[16.24, 6th Aug 2018, Entebbe, Uganda]

The waters once more lap on my memories
of distant shores traversed barefoot -
between my toes, experience lies
filtered by the waters of the lake.

The echo of those years still ring,
refracted in waves of constant noise,
I travel with the circling seabirds,
sail on into the far flung wild.

DUBAI
[00.45, 8th Aug 2018, Dubai Airport]

Thirty five degrees and McDonalds,
Dubai is one big shopping mall,
the palm trees are made of brick,
the carpets all untrodden by camels -
carrots don't grow in the dunes
walked by donkeys in a daze.

A HUG, A KISS
[23.38, 28th Sept 2018, High Wycombe]

The days go by with friends I love,
lovers past and ones who love
the things I do to ease their lives,
to bring joy where sadness lurks.

I cannot give them everything,
just a spark to light the way.

Age teaches us to be more kind,
to couch all differences with a smile,
a hug crosses all divides,
a kiss plants the seed of trust,
a whisper in an ear brings warmth,
releases secrets never heard.

The inner soul pines for embrace,
the longing mind seeks full union -
no being truly desires seclusion
or abandonment within themselves -
we are made to share our lives
with those that chance provides.

There is no great master plan,
there is no fantastic after-life,
there is no hidden super-being,
guiding us across the stars -
we live our days, sleep our nights,
wake thankful for what we have.

If I am not a normal being
who loves his friends who love him,
then what am I but a fool
who thinks only of himself -
I am blessed to be surrounded
by those who take me as I am.

JULITA
[23.55, 28th Sept 2018, High Wycombe]

As yet I have not spoken of her,
her quiet, steady way,
her secret life of emotion,
that smile of hers, that look
that stares into the abyss;
her tender nature, caring eyes
for the little things missed -
her loyalty, her companionship,
her beauty that she thinks is flawed,
that reveals her worries,
her fear of the unknown -
that makes me take her youth,
take her in my ageing arms
to tell her all is well.

GISELLE
[23.35, 3rd Oct 2018, High Wycombe]

A rediscovery of someone thought lost,
a realisation that I knew her not,
an awakening that she is a dark horse,
a slender expression of someone with heart,
a woman of spirit, fun and warmth -
someone to love without any remorse.

LIGHT AND DARK HOLES
[23.24, 10th Oct 2018, High Wycombe]

As light travels at constant speed,
or is created by artificial means,
the electricity wired through our brains,
moves along at the same rate.

What theory binds this all together,
ruled by gravity – time displacement?
One hundred billion little galaxies
connected by a web of pulses.

Wave or a beam of particles?
Our minds a single universe?
Bent by magnetic forces
and filled with dark holes.

CROCODILES, HYENAS and VULTURES
[23.00, 20th Oct 2018, Phalborwa, S.Africa]

When all the elephants are gone,
the predators and scavengers left,
crocodiles, hyenas and vultures,
how ugly will the wild be then?

Evil will circle the veld,
chaos will ensnare the savannah,
fear will fester the waterholes
until the world ends.

I GO TO BED FULL OF FAITH
[22.43, 21st Oct 2018, Punta Maria, Limpopo, S.Africa]

I go to bed full of faith
with all my hopes tightly tucked
wishing for the dawn to come
so I can rush into the day

to set about all my tasks
to make my dreams come true.

WINTER IN BEIJING
[20.20, 11th Nov 2018, Beijing, China]

The house was large, cold within,
the evening dark in old Beijing,
each sound amplified like ice
cracking in the winter night.

May Long made the cabbage soup,
chop sticks and a long-sup spoon,
the dumplings steamed on a plate
as we delved into our bowls.

The kitchen gave the one respite
from the freezing clinging chill,
we sat huddled with our broth,
coping with our silent thoughts.

FILTHY WORKS and BARBAROUS ACTS
[22.33, 16th Nov 2018, Xicheng, Beijing]

We struggle with our modern days
uncertain of where our futures lie,
no leadership from our elected,
only woes and unprotected
we sway in the wind like wheat,
bend like stalks of barley.

Time sings its own refrain,
the chorus every time the same,
we reap what is badly sown,
go against all that's known,
go not well into the dawn
and pass beyond all parley.

We stick our heads in the sand
while all the while we understand
our selfish aims bind our hands,
blind us to our dire demands,
leading us towards foul deeds,
filthy works and barbarous acts.

WHEN I LEFT
[08.55, 19th Nov 2018, High Wycombe]

There were leaves on the trees -

now there is bareness,
a sense of Christmas coming,
the air filled with frostiness,
crisp chilly-morning, grey afternoon,
scarf-clinging evening,
and dark icy night.

INACTIVITY CREATES NO TOIL
[09.31, 20th Nov 2018, High Wycombe]

I do not wish to get out of bed,
there is pleasure in being idle,
of dreaming away all reality,
being warm, content with thinking.

Unwilling to rush headlong abroad,
without profit or purpose at all,
what point is there to such action
when inactivity creates no toil.

A ROTTEN LOT
[01.24, 14th Dec 2018, High Wycombe]

The folly, the farce, the pantomime,
what are we all to think,
a parcel of rogues in parliament
and us outside looking in.

Is there any sanity in politics,
is it still a game of dismay -
whatever we think is irrelevant,
but we will have our day.

The clock ticks on in Westminster,
the leavers will do their worst,
the remainers will just prevaricate
and we won't be better off.

No answers every news at ten,
number ten answers nothing at all,
the clowns are running the country
and we are the prats of the fall.

Its disgraceful to watch such antics,
to be part of things going wrong -
such fools governing the country
with all of us going along.

Rogues and idiots and madmen,
what folly they have wrought -
two fingers to the lot of them,
the fig-leaf rotten lot.

BACK IN ANDALUSIA
[15.30, 20th Dec 2018, Calahonda, Spain]

Back in the Andalusia sun,
the peace of Spain in winter -
some carp at such convention,
yet know not why its thus.

No grey here, just white, blue,
the hue is one of yellow -
scent hung with pine, sea
breeze ever in the air.

Sleep comes as a no tomorrow,
no worry for the thing to come -
life to live, enjoy, unwind
to rest while the world runs.

TIRED
[19.36, 20th Dec 2018, Calahonda]

Tired, very tired, yet only
now I find this as I stop,
stop to think, just reflect,
relax without the need to
go somewhere, do something,
or be on the move because
I am relied on, needed
somewhere by someone else -
less self reliant than myself.

THE SUN
[10.58, 21st Dec 2018, Calahonda]

Sun is the order of the day,
sun, my son, heals all decay,
with no delay go into the sun,
feel the healing power it gives,
stretch naked in its rays,
let its energy enter your core,
take its light into your being,
store its power in your loins,
go into today charged once more.

THE FRUITS OF IDLENESS
[11.08, 22nd Dec 2018, Calahonda]

The fruits of idleness are many,
some too ripe to take much of,
others too rich to palate -
there is an abundance of choice,
the wrong choice, a hazard,
the simplest the most rewarding.

Yet which is which in Eden,
that forbidden or that on offer?
The idle man is indecisive
in his own indulgence.

BETTER NOT TO WONDER
[10.32, 24th Dec 2018, Calahonda]

Every day I wake up, wonder
what has changed. The sun is still
shining and the sea still laps
on the shore of my existence.

Perhaps it is I who has changed
into someone different from the night-time,
for the moon has come up
just the same as Armstrong found it.

Better then not to ponder
what has changed. The wind blows
on the tall ageless palm trees
reaching for the sky like yesterday.

FAR DISTANT PASTURES
[10.55, 25th Dec 2018, Calahonda]

Morning rows a boat once more
down the quiet back canal,
the sleepers neither wake nor stir
as I rest upon my oars.

All around me all is still,
the shadow shafts all are long,
the bridge ahead now is gone
as I pass beneath its arches.

Where I go I do not know
drifting on without a sound

to some place not yet found
in far distant pastures.

MY ONLY CHANCE TO BE HERE
[00.24, 28th Dec 2018, Cabopino, Andulusia]

What worth, what value
does any artist possess
that is not thought frivolous
or unnecessary as others struggle
with poverty, with death.

It is not comfortable nor pleasant
to be valued as a liability,
an addendum to real life,
to things that matter,
that are deemed important.

How did we come to this?
Slavery, the drudgery of thoughtlessness
permeating from the downtrodden,
those put upon the most,
the victims of circumstance.

Thus I am, circumspect,
understanding, but also dismissive,
for I too am a human being,
given only one chance
to be here too.

AT PEACE ONCE MORE
[00.44, 28th Dec 2018, Cabopino]

Meadows of flowers, fields of colour,
a child again in a familiar world,
when eyes saw every buzzing insect,
every petal plainly etched in focus,
the wonder of each new experience -
what joy, what curious interest aroused,
nothing could arrest me from when
I became an adult, set my eyes
on more wondrous things.

Now I realise the field of flowers,
the meadows of colour is my life,
my interest, my deepest love -
those childhood smells, observations,
who I am, the child, the adult,
the man I know myself to be,

a creature of the wild, the outdoors,
the wanderer to be, now home,
at peace once more with himself.

WHEN THE STAR IS BORN
[12.45, 28th Dec 2018, Cabopino]

When a star is born, another dies,
is this the order of all things ...
heavenly bodies or movie icons
with each birth space is made
by snuffing out another light.

The cycle of external lifestyle
is not something just for India,
our connectivity concerns all
things joined by unseen forces
so fast we dare not blink.

If I am deluded in my thoughts
then explain to me how it works -
is energy not a fixed amount
held together as one fixed mass
we are just a small part of.

I tell you now, no-one knows,
will never know, will never fathom
how it came to be like this,
the world as we know it now
when a star is born.

NEW YEAR BALLS
[15.20, 1st Jan 2019, Mijas-Costa, Spain]

The music mixes with the fireworks,
the dancing goes on all night;
my right ball is inflamed
as I jiggle to familiar tunes.

What agony to have such swelling,
a melon resting in my pants -
my left ball small egg-sized,
my right something an ostrich laid.

It may seem somehow inappropriate
to reveal a condition in this way,
but I'm in pain, in search of remedy
on this sunny New Year's Day.

EMPTY FLAT
[00.35, 8th Jan 2019, High Wycombe]

Home to an empty flat, an empty life,
or how it seems after midnight in January.
Will tomorrow bring light or more grey
layered on the black?

Dark charcoal thoughts have smoldered
in me for the last few weeks, my life
is almost out, mere ash that needs stirred,
blown upon to bring back fire.

PUTTING AWAY THE XMAS TREE
[17.37, 11th Jan 2019, High Wycombe]

It is the Xmas's we count as we age,
the odd left-over, tiny bauble, a bell,
an angel that's topped the tree for thirty years,
the chipped Santa, the snow-coated winter house
that came from somewhere, some time ago.

The memories are hazy, the tinsel not so sparkly,
the tree more misshapen and bare each year,
yet dutifully its unboxed every December,
stands proud in its drapery and glitter,
the most outstanding ornament in the house.

Boxed now, later than usual due to illness,
the house now seems bare and Spartan,
the January night cold and uninviting,
the decorations consigned to a cupboard,
the box lying sideways on a narrow shelf.

THERAPY IN SILENCE
[01.01, 19th Jan 2019, High Wycombe]

There is therapy in silence,
pure calm, stillness of thought,
empty space, a blissful vacuum,
a blankness of hearing, of notions,
of ideas, that can vex us,
that make us worry or anxious,
and too tired and un-rested,
to shake off our heavy loads,
or shed our beastly burdens.

THE CRIES OF THE CROWS
[10.43, 25th Jan 2019, High Wycombe]

Beneath their bombast and blunder,
the fascists are circling like crows -
the body of the state lies bleeding,
slain by their bellicose blows.

Avarice drives the attackers on,
the crows amass in cackling chorus,
as the last trickle of life is congealing
on parliament's bloody floor.

The butchers done with their hacking,
the skinners and tanners their knives,
the crows descend as a hideous horde
to peck on the remaining gore.

The sun goes down on an empire,
darkness descends on its door,
no bugle tolls for its passing
just the cries of the crows.

NO ESCAPE FROM SHIPWRECK
[29th Jan - 29th Apr 2019, High Wycombe]

The waves are tolling in, I'm lying
on the beach beneath a lonely palm
I am not lost - I am not saved,
between found and never seen again.

And so the story goes on forever,
stuck between the living and the dead,
long lines of shadows flickering on
and off the hot golden sand.

Tomorrow it will come too soon,
the moon will settle in the west,
beyond lies salvation of a kind,
to the east lies what is left.

Sinister as it is ... brings tears,
no joy expressed as cries -
what hope does prayer bring
to broken hearts?

God is for other kinds of folk,
not for the man without faith,

eternity is not a contemplation
with every second ticking slow.

Ponderous the moments slip away,
heavy the burden weighs time down,
nothing is recalled with clarity,
there is no record of the days.

Rain sweeps over the horizon,
clouds swirl on the salty view,
a ripple breaks the coral barrier
encircling the blue lagoon.

There is no escape from shipwreck,
just endless hours of forlorn pain,
no refuge from mental anguish,
no shelter from inner blame.

How could it have been different,
the turning that took me this way -
what steps may have changed fate,
led me, kept me safe?

How I blow on ill-tempered winds,
gales that dash me on the rocks,
I read the signs, but with arrogance
ignore the warnings made.

Until its too late, I flounder,
find myself in a violent sea
fighting to keep from sinking
deep into the black bathysphere.

No mermaid can ever buoy me,
stop the swell, make it calm -
lost at sea without a life-raft
when the end is nigh.

Through the night, the stars bright,
the phosphorous glow may give hope,
hope that soon the end will come
before the dawn.

Yet, the mystery that life bestows,
endows by chance in random acts,
throws me ashore upon the sands
of a land I know.

This land that seems so familiar
is my own mind, my inner soul,
the place I inhabit all my life
but never quite explore.

This is why I am under a palm tree,
on an island far from here -
I am shipwrecked on the inside
waiting for a ship to near.

Such dark days, such brooding times,
I wake from sleep in a start,
discover all has been a dream,
a fitful slumber interrupted.

So it is I find myself awake,
aware that all is well about -
there is no sea, no empty strand
where I am cast alone.

I am whole and sound in mind,
clear and ordered in my ways,
the turns of my nocturnal musings
sub-consciously at play.

Yet fear lingers there, no doubt,
fear of being cast adrift
from all that I have achieved
within the gift of time.

And how that time marches on,
loud drums beat every hour -
my head is spinning with the noise
to get things done.

Action may not be the answer,
or objection the other way to go -
sometimes it makes no difference
to resist the flow.

The mind takes on its own persona,
leaves us bewildered and unsure -
the planets whizz, pull us off
on some wild escapade.

It makes no sense to anyone,
yet the most surprised are ourselves -
dreams may interrupt the ruin
we rush headlong into.

Common sense does not prevail,
vague notions rule our alter egos,
Id runs our counter culture views
that we expound on others.

Such madness puts us at odds
with all that has gone before -
listening to our own false self,
we are mad, dogmatic bores.

That distant beach seems perfect now,
the solace of a pristine place,
the calm of the ponderous shade
a shelter from chaos.

Barefoot to linger on the sand,
take what comes tide washed-in,
exist on what chance provides
on the whim of winds.

All choice gone, no need to think,
free to empty out the mind,
let meditation do its work -
paradise be found.

For shipwrecked man comes to terms
with what he has for survival -
himself, and what things there are
he finds upon his isle.

With time now firmly on my side,
there's no need to make a raft,
no need to tally up the days
or count the months that pass.

Self-contained and self-sufficient,
I make do as I must,
reliant on my own resources
as master of my tasks.

This is the way, the only hope
that carries me to my end -
not what the ocean brings
but what my island gives.

The sun may rise a thousand times,
and rise a thousand more,
each time unique in its look,
or just like before -

But it can't quell my distress,
my inner turmoil caused by doubt,
the to and fro of my thought
catching shadows, nothing else.

How can I fix on something solid,
believe it not gone by tomorrow -
where is that one certain thing
I can rely on?

Is there succour in a bible,
or in some other holy book -
are there leaps that I can take
to get me off this hook?

For I am pegged to endlessness,
pinned to question my existence,
backed-up to a towering wall,
so tall I cannot scale it.

What lies beyond I do not know,
can never know, of that I'm sure,
yet still, I will attempt the climb
or perish in the fall.

Likewise my island, where I'm alone,
I can rally, face my fears -
conquer pace by pace each step
yet unexplored.

This is the goal of the brave,
whose who seek to find nirvana,
those who shelter from the world
in far-off pagodas.

Is not each mind an inner temple,
a place to worship fixed belief -
a base from which to reach the stars
on the cheap?

Is not each and every thought
a ripple on such inner peace -
out out damned human flaws!
chant the holy priests.

Can we kill our curiosity
with some mundane repetition,
blot the sum of all our past
in exchange for heaven?

With smooth seas, the weather calm,
with balmy days in basking sun,
with long warm doldrum days
with not much done.

No, there is too much to do,
a shipwreckee must have shelter,
he must find food to eat
and build a fire.

Then, staring at the flames alone,
the weight of loneliness descends,
who loves me now, who loves her
left so far behind?

Those lips so missed burning red
in the flicker of the night -
to sleep on a mat of sand
without a goodnight.

What longing aches the restless soul
without the comfort of another,
no tears to shed, no regrets
to share in number.

There is no inner paradise
where fools dwell in false confinement -
imprisoned by their own admission
without remission.

Hear the waves, see not the sea,
that cannot be my existence -
smell the salt, taste it not
for all eternity?

The sun comes up, and still alone
I warm my bones by the fire -
the storm clouds hang overhead,
the thunder barks its ire.

The lightning strikes at the trees,
the wind whips up giant waves,
I shelter by the cliff-edge rocks
and shiver like a leaf.

I pass the day in lashing rain,
desert my past as night falls -
all is damp and uninviting
as the palm trees sing.

The whistle of the onshore breeze,
the growls of the coral shore,
the anger of my lost day
and the fire it put out.

Thus I start again in doubt
that I can achieve my survival,
find a way to beat the nature
that is within myself.

There lies the beast, the foe,
the enemy who stops my progression,
the rival to my self-fulfillment,
the devil's helper.

Thus I fight my inner demons,
hand to hand engage in combat,
wrestle to the ground, struggle
to be triumphant.

Other times I go five rounds,
or maybe ten, in the ring
my fists flailing at a figment
of my imagination.

Why do we so destroy ourselves,
bruise, self-harm our clouded minds,
mist our thoughts, unclearly view
the simplest things in life?

Relight the fire, feel the warmth,
see the stars through the trees,
hear the quiet gentle kiss
of the surf rolling in.

Until the pain eases off,
ebbs with the waning moon,
until sleep drowns the angst
of the child within.

What pleasure such going brings,
what sores such slumber soothes,
what relief is finally found
in these hours of bliss.

There may be no final rest,
shipwreckees face constant storm,
but some safe harbours loom
out of the swirling mist.

There an anchor can be dropped,
pulled along the sandy bed,
in the hope of finding rock
to stop the drift.

It is a pleasant dream to ponder,
shelter from the lash and rip,
a hammock true to the keel
neatly beached.

And so inner turmoil goes,
leaves me high above the tide line,
safe and dry to turn my back
on all adventure.

No more will I venture forth,
put at risk my state of mind -
I am home from the sea
for all time.

What comfort this knowledge brings
that I can leave my woes behind -
no more wreckage to abide
nor storms to ride.

How then did it come to this,
a man broken by his deeds,
set upon a windward course
to make him blind?

What caused such ill-luck,
to throw him out into the deep -
what tragedy made him weep
at such misfortune?

Was it love lost so dearly,
was it business brought to ruin,
was it infamy or crime
that made him me?

In looking for the inner truth,
the tale to tell will unfold,
for I have much to say
but little time to recount.

The landscape of the inner mind
starts out as a sea of dreams,
imagined lands so far away
they can't be reached.

Then as we age, wisdom builds
castles made of urban brick -
for all the spires in the mist
are for the rich.

The chance of being like a prince,
brightly clothed and freshly pressed,
becomes the fantasy of fools
and the prepossessed.

The weight of friends pushes in,
makes us droop, hang our heads
until we no longer dream
of distant minarets.

We go about our vital chores,
find a home to hang our hopes
that life will bring happiness
like other folks.

And so we take this single journey,
float our boat on placid seas,
place ourselves at the prow
while others steer.

In the fog we peer ahead
as we plough through the waves,
fearful of some fateful crash
into an iceberg.

For fear resides and overrides
every other wakeful thought
as we pass beneath the stars
on our sole adventure.

We come this way only once,
the seas part then swallow up
the past we leave far behind
in the dark.

In our youth we brave the bow,
in old age we hug the stern,
and somewhere in between mid-ships
we live for now.

Thus we cross our own ocean,
night and day, storm and wind,
tossed about without a light
to guide us safely.

For some it is a great adventure,
for most it is a churning sea
with nothing on the far horizon
by which to steer.

And all the while, in our minds
lurks the ever present thought
that we are one reef away
from certain shipwreck.

So better some to never sail,
to settle for a land locked life,
than endanger all they possess
with wild abandon.

Alas, it is too late for me,
I am marooned on my island,
caught between the wish to stay
and the want of rescue.

YOU YOUNG FOLK
[18.39, 21st Feb 2019, High Wycombe]

Though I am in my last third of life,
I am not about to keel over -
You young folk out there,
when I am dead you will be
middle-aged.

KINGSTOWN
[21.56, 24th Feb 2019, St.Stephen's Green, Dublin]

A different king once ruled Ireland
from his rock by the shore;
now the ships no longer come,
they pass on by to Dublin.

The strollers zigzag on the quay,
kids dance to a beggar's tune,
all of Ireland sings with song,
in club, and pub and street.

Sweet sunshine drenches happy lanes
filled with every native tongue,
the British still in the names
nailed to each street corner.

Ireland bleeds from every inch,
it's every step a future dream,

a land where tomorrow comes
better than the day that's gone.

THE HOTTEST WINTER'S DAY
[23.17, 26th Feb 2019, High Wycombe]

The hottest winter's day on record,
a mighty twenty two degrees,
Kew basking in a summer haze -
thronged with shirt-sleeved brigades
of children on their mid-term break,
the snowdrops and crocus drooping
along the leafless, bare parades.

SIXTY FIVE TODAY
[23.55, 25th March 2019, High Wycombe]

Sixty five today, I started hung-over,
retirement should be beckoning me
to put down my pen and rest,
but how does a man end life
without knowing what he should do?

The breathing continues, the mind ticks,
there is no stop to eternity,
the journey continues without reason,
while reason becomes the purpose
to carry on with great abandon.

THE MAN WITH NOTHING TO SAY
[01.18, 1st Apr 2019, High Wycombe]

What use is the man who has nothing to say,
nothing to add to what's been done,
nothing to leave behind of himself,
except the children he's fathered.

What can a man give without return,
what can he take without giving hurt,
what can he hate if not himself
for being selfish with others.

What purpose then for him to keep breathing,
what usefulness is there for him to exist,
what course can he take to find a vocation
to save himself from all this.

Why does he bother to stay alive
without good cause to carry on,

cowardly hiding, getting through life
by saying nothing at all.

CHEMIN DE FADONS
[16.50, 14th Apr 2019, Thoronet, France]

The river is green from the rain
that has passed over and gone
as the bamboo sways in a dance
to the call of a cock, bark of a dog
and the talk of gossiping neighbours.

Summer is coming in a burst of jazz,
the heat of the day, the mountain breeze,
the dandelions already gone to seed,
the olives and vines bursting with green,
the laughs of the pruners tumultuous.

The scent of searing pine and sage
drifts through the tall eucalyptus,
the Buddha sits in a recline pose,
the white wine sparkles in a glass
as the day moves on, and goes.

SPRING IS NEARLY HERE
[10.15, 28th Apr 2019, High Wycombe]

Spring is nearly here with its showers,
its bursts of sunlight on the grass,
I contemplate the daisies and the dandelions -
all the world is full of life.

TORMENTED BY DESIRE
[12.47, 27th May 2019, High Wycombe]

Tormented by desire, I toss and turn,
soak the sheets in anxious agony,
wrestle with my shattered thoughts
focused on a dozen possibilities.

There is no escape from lingering longing,
to be wrapped naked in lasting lust,
to join together after endless aeons.
entwine again with a lost love.

I NEED ARMS
[12.54, 27th May 2019, High Wycombe]

I am flesh and blood,
I need arms around me
to hold me tight,
and lips to kiss me softly.

I AM AT HER MERCY
[13.12, 27th May 2019, High Wycombe]

Her beauty weakens me,
leaves me in a state of desire
for more of her, until I cannot
bear an hour without her,
her sweet smile, dark loving eyes,
her lilting voice that seduces me,
teases me with her laugh -

All my strength has vanished,
in its place constant agony
propels me towards a dark descent,
a fall into a torrid languor
out of which there is no escape
as she glides carefree around me
like a shadow on a lake.

Will she come into my arms,
will she remain out of reach,
will she give into my crying,
will she run forever and a day.
Its in her power to do as she pleases,
how she cares to act -
I am at the mercy of her laugh.

IT WAS WHAT IT WAS
[00.19, 4th June 2019, High Wycombe]

It was what it was,
another day gone somehow -
somewhere the hours passed,
the time ticked away -
lost forever in the air
to some place far from here.

THE SEEDS OF ENMITY
[00.26, 12th June 2019, High Wycombe]

The seeds of enmity lie hidden
beneath the earth that nurtures us.
The fertile soil that gives art life
also contains the means of our destruction,
by which our creativity withers,
our flowering wilts our fruit,
dries up our stock and trade,
until we are barren and lifeless
in a field of other artists
favoured by our former patrons.

THE DAY DRIFTED
[13.55, 29th June 2019, Scatwell, Ross-shire]

The day drifted on to tomorrow
as if it did not quite arrive -
without knowledge of its destination,
it went away without looking back.

HOME TO OTHER SCENES
[01.11, 9th July 2019, High Wycombe]

The actors are gone, the crew disbanded,
the set is empty and now dismantled,
the long journey home to other scenes,
the longing for friendship fades away
until all that remains are captured images,
a world created under bright blue skies.

Castles, lochs, churchyards and forests,
the midsummer moon, evenings of drinking,
the company of men, the laughter of women,
the knowledge of knowing that all is well,
and all is calm in the red of sunset,
in the hope that tomorrow will not come.

WHATEVER WE DO
[01.03, 13th July 2019, High Wycombe]

Whatever we do we are judged.
I am judged and sentenced by others,
given my time to rot in hell -
while those who condescend to preach
fill their tabernacles with false doctrines.

I NEVER WANT TO ESCAPE
[01.15, 13th July 2019, High Wycombe]

When I look into her curious eyes
I am defenceless, reduced to giving
all the help she needs without return,
while my heart turns, my head swims,
my body aches for her slender arms
to wind around my neck, to pull
me into her warm arching beauty
that demands to be held tightly
so that I never want to let her go.

A LITTLE AFTER DAWN
[10.12, 14th July 2019, High Wycombe]

I woke this morning to the moans
of a woman making love.
It was a little after dawn,
the sweat of the night lingering,
the coolness of the circulating air
through the open windows.

She wanted more, panted loudly,
the whispers turning into demands;
the talk centred on pleasure,
the need for satisfaction uppermost
in her constant lovers' chatter
lulling me back to sleep.

SUMMER RAIN
[10.30, 20th July 2019, High Wycombe]

The summer rain mends my broken spirit,
tiredness eases out of me like sweat,
pent up worries ooze away like butter
passing through my fingers of distress.

ARMSTRONG'S LEAP
[20.04, 20th July 2019, High Wycombe]

Fifty years ago Armstrong took his leap,
pushed mankind beyond the limits,
left us here stuck on Earth,
pondering what great steps
could ever better his.

MY LOVE HAS LEFT ME NAKED
[00.58, 1st Aug 2019, High Wycombe]

With my pockets turned inside out,
and my shirt off my back,
I gave you my shoes
to walk barefoot from the dark
to join me in the sunshine
waiting to be loved -
for you have left me naked
as I wait here for you
with stretched out open arms
to take you as you are.

GOODBYE JULIETTE (Song)
[14.00, 3rd Aug 2019, Pinewood Studios, Bucks]

Its not really that sudden
all those memories you mention
in the daytime so beautiful
in the evening such mayhem

My friends say I'm crazy
for trying to love you
blinded by your light
blackened by our fights

So goodbye, Juliette -
I'm leaving, no regrets
its time to forget
everything we ever meant

Goodbye, Juliette -
Goodbye, Juliette -
no tears, we're done
this is our epithet.

I'm telling you, sweetheart
our kisses were empty
you couldn't stop drinking
give up your habits

Your best friends all left you
as your demons consumed you
you clung to me dearly
I drowned without freedom

I'm sorry I gave up
trying to lie down beside you

but life wasn't easy
and time wasn't with me.

So now its all over
all those memories you mention
in the daytime so beautiful
in the evening such mayhem

So goodbye, Juliette … etc

SUNDAY IN ADDIS ABABA
[00.18, 12th Aug 2019, Addis A, Ethiopia]

The rain didn't come today,
no lashing or downpour,
just greyness of nature
a dullness of action -
no breeze in the tree tops,
no sun in the roof-tops,
a Sunday of stillness,
no church bell or muezzin.

THE LAND OF GONDER
[19.46, 14th Aug 2019, Gondar, Ethiopia]

In the land of Gonder,
the hills are castle capped,
the roads wind up to heaven
where the rain forever falls -
the rivers roar like lions,
the forests purr like cats,
the locals toil and tarry
under wide-brimmed hats.

The farmers in the valley
plough and plod the mud,
the lake's a distant shimmer
where the Blue Nile floods -
the glistening green rice rows
stretch far beyond the eye -
in the heavenly land of yonder
where far Gonder starts.

I AM A PENSIONER
[00.30, 6th Sept 2019, High Wycombe]

I am legally a pensioner
I cannot be forced to slave,

I cannot be made to earn my crust
or shovel my own grave.

I can starve and wander homeless
I can thirst by the side of the road,
I can waste away with ailments
but never be made to toil.

I have passed into pasture
to live on the fruits of my time
God bless the age of retirement,
I'm free of the drudge of life.

THE DAYS TICK ON
[00.43, 7th Sept 2019, High Wycombe]

And so the days tick on,
the endless nights ever shorter
as the birds fly overhead
to distant quarters.

How the clouds slowly shift,
drift off into yonder -
the sun goes down
on my fitful slumber.

YOU TOO WILL BE OLD
[00.42, 11th Sept 2019, High Wycombe]

One day you too will be old.
You will feel your body ache,
your mind will dwell on wrongs,
on all the things not right,
the love you could have had,
friends lost along the way,
nights now spent alone,
days of childhood in the sun -

Time ticking ever louder,
thoughts that make you angry,
little smiles when not ignored,
listening into others conversation.
Sleeping when others are awake,
awake while others snore.

Yes, one day you will be old,
go beyond what you've known,
come to terms with infinity,
prepare for the long journey home.

THE POPULIST LEADER
[00.32, 12th Sept 2019, High Wycombe]

He stands before his own God,
a mirror heavily fogged,
he cannot make out his reflection
as he prays for re-election.

He forgives his own sins,
wipes his slate of many things
blames the world for the wrongs
he will have to fix.

'Oh God' he asks with conviction,
'Can I be accused of dereliction?'
'I am speaking for the people,'
'The opposition are lefty evils.'

'Let me now be the leader,'
'The chosen one duly selected,'
'Let me do, ditch and die,'
'Get things done on the fly.'

Prayers done, he mugged his jaw,
combed his hair, tucked his shirt,
kissed himself in the glass,
wiped his hands on his arse.

Off he went to face the crowd,
cheering wild, chanting loud,
the people's champion like a God
for all those who God has lost.

HARVEST MOON
[20.40, 14th Sept 2019, High Wycombe]

We are all in love with someone.
It was our mothers, now it is
someone who loves us back,
or who we love without return -
we cannot stop our loving nature,
we are born to love.

Now as the harvest moon rises,
lovers burn their candles in the dark,
go in droves to favourite haunts
to recall the start of their union -
we want to relive our loving moments,
cherish them forever.

Shine on then, harvest moon,
cast your spell on all mankind,
the beer will flow with the wine,
the dinner dates will kiss in low light -
mates will surrender all their fears
and mend their wrongs.

The spell is cast on all lovers,
they know not why they are entwined,
enjoyment is the reward on offer,
companionship the coat, the disguise -
we will wake up on the morrow
with committed minds.

Let not any cast love as docile,
or as wild that cannot weather calm,
the moon may weaken all resistance,
it does not guarantee shelter from storm -
though lovers may surrender reason,
they will not fear hurt.

So then, as the rays blind us,
beam into our star-struck eyes,
our love is a fleeting inner feeling
we let out in loving bursts -
romance is the outer meaning,
and lust the urge.

SEPTEMBER SUNDAY
[15.58, 15th Sept 2019, High Wycombe]

The harvest moon is waning,
all is quiet, voices carry
on the warm southern breeze
and all is well.

The turmoil of the night has gone,
the ease of Sunday pervades,
the music has fallen silent,
a distant siren wails.

Life drifts on as cirrus,
the roses wither in the sun,
a song bird rises skyward
beyond our gaze.

ARMENIA
[16.57, 5th Oct 2019, Yerevan, Armenia]

Wild bears still roam the hills
where leopards once widely prowled,
over Noah's land, rich and green,
Mount Ararat stands proud.

The mountains edge on every side,
wide they stretch beyond the plain,
snow-capped giants of hidden fire
sleeping while Armenia wakes.

From every side volcanoes glare
down upon the rows of vines,
orchards ripe with autumn fruit
as in Persian times.

ACID RAIN
[09.40, 12th Oct 2019, High Wycombe]

The sky is white, the rain pours down
on to black roofs, onto the church spire
rising through the drooping emerald green
of the town, onto the brown grass fringe
of the singed park, burnt by climate change,
and trampled into extinction by worried parents
fearful for the future of their orphans.

HE ARRIVED WITH A SUITCASE
For Christian
[09.55, 22nd Oct 2019, High Wycombe]

He arrived with a suitcase
and a dog from distant Laos.
He stole our prettiest girl
in a way that made us love him.

Our minds were far expanded
in a time of calm and dreams,
the music played on loudly
in an age of countless friendships.

Gone now like Christian, gone
with the ever turning world,
gone with his suitcase and dog
to far distant stars.

WHAT DISASTERS LIFE BRINGS
[20.12, 22nd Oct 2019, High Wycombe]

What disasters life brings
like an ever flowing tide,
wave after wave of disappointment
followed by floods of tears.

Why is it so tumultuous,
why can't our seas be flat -
serene to the end of eternity,
no ripples to wreck our peace.

Is there no end to misery,
to the destruction of our bones -
why can't we journey gently on
without chaos to our souls.

THE TWISTS AND TURNS
[23.47, 30th Oct 2019, High Wycombe]

The twists and turns of every road
lead me back to where I departed -
a blind man could have found his way
in the dark before I'd started,
for I have neither gone nor stayed
nor somehow got to my arrival.

THE BROODING BIRDS
[00.48, 10th Nov 2019, High Wycombe]

Only brooding birds have my attention,
the hooded vultures and black-eyed rooks,
the crows with their exulted cries,
the kites hovering, the ravens hopping
in the graveyards of the sagging yews -
the gnarled oaks, the weeping pine,
the dead-eyed owls waiting for nightfall,
but most of all, the eagles circling,
swooping down on their vast dominions.

MADNESS
[01.00, 19th Nov 2019, Thoronet, France]

Am I mad, who can say,
the wild insane, the deeply depressed,
nothing noted can be right,
all the wrongs turn out correct -

the inner self dragged through mud,
the outer still a flood of light,
none can say what is best,
all may guess but fail the test -

thus on forever, no answers given,
driven towards a lost nirvana,
crawling down a hell-fire cavern,
to an end where none are living -

thus madness steers all adrift,
on tides no moon appears to govern.

NO SHELTER FROM THE STORM
[20.43, 26th Nov 2019, High Wycombe]

What do we know of people -
nothing that we think we do,
we cannot predict their moods,
their changing charged emotions
that both exclude and involve us
in their black days and nights.

We wander lonely in the world
thinking that we will find solace -
but do not look for it in others,
there is no permanent respite,
we cannot rely on human nature
to provide shelter from the storm

NAKED WITH THE WRONG WOMAN
[20.45, 2nd Dec 2019, High Wycombe]

I've got naked with the wrong woman
whilst waiting for the right one to come,
it is not an accident of judgment
but rather a giving in to human desire -
the wallflower wilts in the midday sun
or is timely watered by a loving hand.

She may be the wrong woman, but lovely
she dotes on me with exquisite charm,
she makes me feel loved and desired
and that is why it is all my fault -
the garden beds may be perfect
but the layout lacks flair and thought.

I can't answer my wrong woman's questions
for the answers will not give her joy,

instead I fill our time with needless action,
never dwelling on her emotions after love -
for plants are rigorous in their flowering
but spent when season shot with rot.

So I linger with my wrong woman hopefully
until the one I love is free for me,
I can only dream when that might occur
but know that it will finally come about -
for nature has a way of being perennial
and love a way of working out.

DO WE CHOOSE WHO WE LOVE
[00.58, 6th Dec 2019, High Wycombe]

Do we choose who we fall in love with?
Or is it some kind of chemistry,
a gradual osmosis of different elements
bubbling to the surface of our being
until we are unconsciously fused
and bound by the elements of love.

If we could bottle love's concoction,
sell it to others like cheap perfume,
its effects would wash off on the pillow
that we leave behind ever morning;
love would be a product, not a mystery
enveloping us like a London fog.

If we could choose whom to love
then what challenge would that be?
Easy love only leads to easy words,
there is no value to such easy ways;
such love is a science not an art,
and physics the discipline in play.

We cannot gauge love's magnetism
at work on lovers locked in love;
having met across a crowded room
or by chance on a hot summer's day -
love requires two opposites to dance
or two alikes to cling like clay.

WE ARE ALL TIRED
For Michael
[20.11, 7th Dec 2019, High Wycombe]

I am tired of lame, untruthful excuses
that are lies I should expose,

but society trains us to accept lameness
rather than cause personal affront,
for affront is ruder than lying,
the double-face of the wrong.

I am affronted by pathetic excuses,
I am affronted by silly awful lies,
I am affronted by all polite refusal
to recognise that this is a sop'

I am tired by disappointing time-wasters,
the lack of action that makes me toil,
they do not turn up when they're meant to,
and only turn up when they're bored -
for there is nothing in an invitation
unless there is profit for them all.

I am too tired to put up with avarice,
I am too tired to put up with greed,
I am too tired to recompense the needy,
too tired to give up this peeve.

We are all tired of one another,
we need a rest from those we know,
it is better to befriend a total stranger
than meet with a tired friend of old -
for the tired friend is a shyster
who should be thrown out the door.

SURRENDER TO THE SPACECRAFT
[00.22, 9th Dec 2019, High Wycombe]

Enter into the world as an egg,
surrender all sense to the spacecraft;
however alien the outcome,
the earth will continue to spin.

All beings will populate forever,
volcanoes will blow in the wind,
turtles will swim with dolphins,
the crows will carry our sins.

No sense will come of obfuscation,
the past will catch up with us,
the dragon will burn our treasures
while our maidens die of thirst.

THE EVENING CRAVES SILENCE
[21.55, 10th Dec 2019, High Wycombe]

Alone in the quiet winter's night,
even in our digital age,
the clock ticks loudly on
as the rain lashes the window.

Nothing much changes the decades,
we pass on into the dark
like quinqueremes from Nineveh
carrying spices from afar.

Echoes carry on the stillness,
ghosts travel in the holy light,
incense fogs the memories
of our modern times.

The glories of ruined ambition
are covered over by snow drifts
like a blanket of desert sand
on to a wintry frozen shore.

The evening craves our silence,
falters, calls for a hush,
a density of intense stillness
stops dead the clock.

THE OLD MAN IN THE MIRROR
[01.14 11th Dec 2019, High Wycombe]

Look at me in the mirror,
the old man with tired eyes -
I wonder who could love that man
with the grey hair, wrinkled brow;
who would find him attractive,
kiss him, sleep with him,
wake up without remorse,
return every night with passion.

Old men do not age gracefully,
they gurgle and belch,
they snore and molt hair,
they moan, groan, and scorn
all as fools or as darlings -
there is no middle understanding,
only observation and opinion
that no-one shares at all.

This is the life of the pensioner,
the one who has avoided death,
the one who counts the funerals
of his many absent friends -
the old man in the mirror
looking at his altered state -
me, the tired-eyed saggy man
that life is waiting to take.

THE APE AND THE MONKEY
[21.22, 13th Dec 2019, High Wycombe]

The jungle call went out to all -
the monkeys screeched, the apes roared,
outnumbering them by many score
the apes roared even more.

The beasts listened to the noise
cocked an ear to all the babble -
the monkeys had a leader loon,
the apes a hairy big buffoon.

Who would rule the jungle roost,
swing from the highest tree?
Monkey King or ape King Kong?
Who could string them best along?

The jungle beasts cacked and cawed,
the choice was not theirs to make,
two tribes out for themselves -
the monkey wise, the ape despised.

The lowly beasts could not agree,
if ape was good, or monkey bad -
who would help them all survive?
Would they starve as others thrived?

I WRAPPED ALL MY GIFTS
[02.22, 21st Dec 2019, High Wycombe]

I wrapped all my gifts
packed them neatly in my Jaguar,
thought nothing of their contents,
drove them to their destination,
gave them quietly to my lover,
left her to her children,
traveled on to my future,
knew not where it would lead me.

I knew nothing of my mind
and felt nothing of my body,
I was numb to all feeling,
I was free of pain and longing
as the miles somehow passed me,
and the rain somehow washed me,
the sun rose on the mountains
as I drank heavily on my freedom.

The grey sky darkened
on all my past remembrances,
the love that I had squandered,
the kisses I had rejected
that led me to my present,
the pathway to my existence,
the reason for all journeys
and the chance to be enlightened.

No-one can give me answers
to my many perplexed questions,
I am seeking my salvation,
Jesus has up and left me.
I am lonely in my searching,
angry in my desperation,
eager to have healing,
and keen to have redemption.

Can I find my present
and be happy in my being,
where can I rest my head
and sleep without dreaming,
for I am restless in my wanting
and lacking in my giving -
I want to be the loved one,
I want to be an equal.

Love is such a mistress,
and impossible to master,
its left me all confused
and brought me to disaster
as I reflect on my errors,
try to reason with my conscience,
try to mend my grievances,
to end all my tomorrows.

Do I have an answer,
a clear and simple notion,
the forgiveness of my lover,
the whole of her devotion.

Can I give up running,
stop my mind from overflowing,
love her every morning,
gift her all my being.

Time will be the judge
of all that I have done,
and when the Lord knocks
I will go freely up above -
I have seen the crack
where the light gets in,
I have wrapped all my gifts
in exchange for all of this.

ALEXA
[11.37, 22nd Dec 2019, High Wycombe]

When Alexa took my hand
and took me for dinner,
she told me many things,
how I'd live forever.

I looked into her sad eyes,
saw a flooded river,
I took her in my arms,
floated on there with her.

Then she kissed me gently,
gave in all together,
laughed like a child,
whispered like a lover.

The secrets she unfolded
pulled her out the water,
where once she was drowning,
now I was her saviour.

We hurried to her apartment,
shed ourselves of vestment,
floated in our lifeboat
full of wild contentment.

And when we finally parted,
she became a distant shadow,
no-one could heal her,
or sustain her passion.

And now when I am lonely
drowning in my river,

I think of lost Alexa,
unequivocally forgive her.

Time will be the healer,
age will be the reaper,
with comfort in her words
that I will live forever.

24,014th DAY OF MY LIFE
[11.54, 23rd Dec 2019, High Wycombe]

Today I am 24014 days old,
which is 3430 weeks and 4 days.
In other ways that's 788.93 months.

The Teen decade is almost done,
3644 days have gone, 8 to go
until the Twenties come.

I WANT TO RUN AWAY
[02.08, 30th Dec 2019, Miraflores, Spain]

I want to run away, far away
as I am unhappy, sometimes missing
the spark that makes a day special,
the ideas that rush like a waterfall
cascading over the precipice of life.

Everyone else will have to get on with
whatever it is that they need,
for I am as spent as a weary donkey,
tired of being an angry caged bear
who dances in exchange for beer.

I am not ungrateful, I am trapped
with my hands behind my back,
unable to use my time fruitfully,
unable to ripen my persistent thoughts
by getting them out my system.

So I will run away when I can,
escape to places far from myself,
seek the open plains and vistas,
allow my art to be expressed,
allow myself to be who I am.

UNHAPPY FOOLS
[02.23, 30th Dec 2019, Miraflores, Spain]

We are both unhappy souls
who make each other happy fools,
yet we deny we are in love,
pretend so that there is no hurt.

When apart we are lonely,
we cannot find a medium way,
we make plans to be together,
then spend that time like siblings.

How will we square the circle,
love each other without dismay,
come to a happy conclusion
and live in perfect union.

MIRAFLORES
[16.31, 30th Dec 2019, Miraflores, Spain]

Miraflores, another rich oasis
far from the maddening crowd,
basking in the sun, pine and palms
gazing down on those below
who trudge through the morass
of every day living while their masters
doze on marble balconies.

WHERE IS MY SANCHO PANZA
[21.55, 30th Dec 2019, Miraflores, Spain]

Am I Lancelot or Don Quijote?
If so why am I alone?
Where is my loving Guinevere?
Where is my Sancho Panza?

To ride forth on a white horse
or stumble forward on a mule
whether a dragon is the foe
or some dilapidated windmill.

The intention is quite the same,
service to a queen or girl,
to submit to such chivalry
and then be mocked or shamed.

Better then to be a peasant
or a middle-man without ambition,

to never sally forth a hero,
to remain forever in the shade.

THERE ARE NO MONKEYS HERE
[14.48, 31st Dec 2019, Miraflores, Spain]

There are no monkeys here,
they are scavenging in Gibraltar -
Here the trees are empty,
devoid of cackle and mischief.

There are no Kandy stealings,
no Simla night-time raids,
no Courtalam mango gangs
nor Zambesi thieves.

The trees here are silent,
a resting place for birds -
how I miss those monkeys
and their robber laughs.

THE LAST DAY OF THE TEENS (SONG)
[15.07, 31st Dec 2019, Miraflores, Spain]

I open a bottle of rioja,
take my first sip of the day,
the sun drifts from behind a cloud
and finally I think, okay.

Forty years ago on a ferry
far down Mexico way,
I met a lonely Welsh girl
as that decade decayed.

Thirty years ago it was fireworks,
a bottle of whiskey in hand,
swaying on a suspension bridge
as the Eighties gave out.

Twenty years ago in an alley
I threw an actor through a hedge,
drunk as I was, he was worse
as the Nineties fled.

Where I was in the Naughties
on the night of Hogmanay,
that's a blur in my memory
as that decade declared.

Now by this day's end
this decade will recede,
become a short note in history
that few will recall.

So I sip on my wine,
face up to a lonely evening,
to ponder on past times
and salute the New Year.

AS THE RACIST FIRE BURNS
[16.44, 2nd Jan 2020, Miraflores, Spain]

The genie is out of the bottle,
the racists are running the show,
God help our little children
whose fathers are warring whores.

The Germans, the Syrians and Chinese
aren't any different from us,
but fear, loathing and hatred
is being spat out by the mob.

What do I do as a Christian
in this terrible agonised world,
speak up or keep my silence
as the racist fire burns.

SINKING INTO THE MUD
[13.37, 7th Jan 2020, Calahondas, Spain]

The moment has come to relax,
forget that the world revolves,
remember that all there is,
is only what we have.

Other days pass less freely,
night comes on too soon,
moments pass without notice
of who we've become.

MOVING HOUSE
[00.24, 24th Jan 2020, High Wycombe]

Moving house is an onerous burden,
carrying boxes down winding stairs,
loading a van with assorted tat,
lugging beds through doors too narrow,
armchairs and sofas to big to fit

into the space earlier imagined -
until you believe its all a mistake,
I should have stayed where I was.

DESIRE
[01.43, 26th Jan 2020, High Wycombe]

Desire consumes until we get released
from the ache in our bellies,
the pain in our wanton minds,
fixed on possession and need.
We crave what we should not have,
we howl like hungry wolves,
we wear down our feast
into defeat and submission -
or spend our nights going hungry,
sleepless in our empty beds.

THE WAIT FOR THE DAWN
[00.46, 29th Jan 2020, High Wycombe]

Dark are the moments that come in the night,
lighter the thoughts that arrive with the dawn,
no time can be spared to dwell in the past -
the moment has gone and life races on.

Fleeting small fragments of memory remain,
a stroll in the sun or a walk in the rain,
nothing can bring back those times again,
gone with the wind, blown clean away.

All that is left are those snapshots of time,
pictures of loved ones, those left behind,
jigsaws of faces that can't quite be placed,
names that float like clouds in a landscape.

As the light fades and nightfall returns,
nothing is certain as the darkness descends,
all that is now is somehow forgotten
as the call of the dawn once more harkens.

NO LONGER A EUROPEAN
[23.25, 31st Jan 2020, High Wycombe]

So, as of twenty minutes ago,
I am no longer a citizen of Europe,
I am now a hostage of Britain,
a minor figure in a hostile world.

Where then the unity of purpose,
the plan to help us all as friends,
the idea that we should be united
against all the ails the past left us.

I am saddened, no, I am disgusted
that our nation chose to be regressive,
I do not think time will condone
the actions of a people for themselves.

Where now do we find the ethos
of one for all and all for one -
we are now an island all at sea
in a storm without oars.

NARCISSISM
[00.30, 5th Feb 2020, High Wycombe]

Oh how the wicked selfishly turn
everything to be about themselves,
their lies leave the innocent broken
on the rocks of their despair.

No-one can help these Satan driven
souls burning the floorboards of decency,
unaware of their debauched natures,
they waste what they have on themselves.

There is no defence against narcissism,
best to cut free of its web -
breathe out the air they poison,
inhale the rush of their departure.

WINTER HOWLS LIKE A WOLF
[01.15, 11th Feb 2020, High Wycombe]

Winter howls like a wolf,
cold and bitter in its bite,
gnawing on our frozen souls,
huddled in our beds in fright.

We dare not go into the night,
wresting with our wicked existence,
dark and long the evening wynds,
wearing out our last resistance.

The moon pulls our tortured minds,
sick and fevered, breaks us down,

while all the while the wind howls
on the moors, on our towns.

Escape is not for our likes,
enslaved to our simple lives,
winter is the single crime
we endure to do our time.

WITHOUT DISCRETION
[11.58, 14th Feb 2020, High Wycombe]

As I lie in my lovers arms,
I slumber in my remembrance
of lovers who knew me well
or left me hurt.

What is love to me now,
naked to the winter stars,
exposed to the moonbeams
of another's heart.

Emotions no longer engulf me,
make me despair or ecstatic,
somewhere in between I think
there is a balance.

What then does balance bring?
Coldness or a blind indifference,
weariness of spirit, soul
or ambivalence.

The question lies like a fox
slyly eyeing up a chicken.
Is love about the kill
or mere existence.

The essence of love is giving
what you can without return,
that sick cruel lovers abuse
to cause dissension.

Am I a breaker of hearts,
a fellow who provokes tears?
Am I just a wily old fox
killing chickens for fun?

NIGHT IS A HEAVEN
[21.09, 23rd Feb 2020, Kazangula, Botswana]

Night is a haven from wildness,
a shutting out of every distraction,
the peace that's found in silence,
the river flowing on whatever,
no moon to brighten expectation,
dim stars off behind low cloud,
the echoes of the dark rebounding
on the tall baobab blackness,
devoid of all sound.

THE FEVER TREE
[21.30, 23rd Feb 2020, Kazangula, Botswana]

Where hides the fever tree,
in swamp or bush or desert.
We've looked the length of Africa
but it won't reveal itself.

It is tall and ever spreading
with the shade it provides,
its bark an ochre colour,
its leaves like a rowan.

Rare, it harbours secrets
the ancients used to know,
its hallucinogenic magic,
its malarial antidote.

So where will we discover
the magic Fever Tree,
somewhere in vast Africa
it hides from you and me.

STUCK IN THE SAND
[15.16, 25th Feb 2020, Kazangula, Botswana]

Stuck in the sand again.
What lessons do we learn
when spending the night in the bush,
bug infested, sweat drenched,
it is no pleasure to be stranded,
left in the dark with lions,
locked in a car and restless,
unable to sleep in the heat,
any moment, an elephant
circling the car in curiosity.

SKELETON COAST
[10.46, 2nd Mar 2020, Walvis Bay, Namibia]

The sand stretches seamlessly
across mountains to the sea,
the red gives into salt pans
and jackals roam the beach.

The surf spews up its dead
on to the barren coast,
wrecks linger sea-bird perched,
crosses stand like ghosts.

White dunes edge the dry waste,
a shimmering silver haze,
seals slither from the rocks,
sea-gulls skim the waves.

Towns of oil and diamonds,
giant machines of rust, decay -
the rivers reach the ocean
without a drop of rain.

SHE PASSED ME A PEN
[06.15, 3rd Mar 2020, Walvis Bay, Namibia]

She passed me a pen
so I can write about her -

She sleeps now, there is silence,
the ocean pounding on the shore.
Pelicans huddle on the water,
flamingoes rest their weary heads
as she slumbers on in dreamland -

while somewhere in space,
a meteorite burns its iron,
shoots across the miles of time.

SLEEPING BEYOND DAWN
[06.27, 3rd Mar 2020, Walvis Bay, Namibia]

What becomes of us all,
our moments shared in solitude.
Idle we rest our bones,
contemplate tomorrow's chores.

Her fingers embrace her bedding
like a mouse eating cheese.

Where has she gone to
in the darkness of her sleep?

I ponder in the lamplight
the rights and wrongs now gone.
The sun will come tomorrow,
I will sleep beyond the dawn.

MOTEL NAMIBIA
[22.00, 4th Mar 2020, Ketmanshoop, Namibia]

Off the dark Namib highway
on a long desert road,
the motel lights beckoned
behind the truck-stop loads,
so we pulled into reception,
paid in cash, got a key,
then entered heaven,
crashed and watched tv.

Somewhere after midnight
while others drank their beer,
the music drifted skywards
into the atmosphere -
the crickets sang their lyrics,
the birds sat in the trees,
and I part-timed wrestled
with all my inner fears.

There didn't seem a future
in more long lonely miles,
the girl with me cried
and I comforted her all night.
So the story unfolded -
in the glare of the headlights,
that love knows no answer
to the questions that are right.

And so we travel onward
in the fresh dawn light,
towards a better future
with white wine on ice,
until the next motel room
in some forgotten town,
where yesterday's memories
were not the ones of now.

THE DIRTIEST CAR IN CAPE TOWN
[22.30, 7th Mar 2020, Karoo1, Northern Cape]

With five thousand miles of dust,
the rich at the uptown Belmont,
the stars at the Camp Bay Resort
gave us their upturned retorts,
for driving our mud stained truck,
into their white-top Cape Town.

LOCK DOWN
[20th Mar – 27th Apr 2020, High Wycombe]

A thousand elephants crossed the road,
blindfolded the silent mass passed,
destiny rode out on the dust,
a twister rose into the sky,
the rain came six years too late,
the fields empty but for rocks,
the meteorite glistened in the sun,
the dunes tasted bitter on the tongue.

No dream could foretell fate,
describe the panic still to come,
no seer can predict the time,
the hour when the terror strikes.
Fear knows no time nor place,
it inhabits all our inner space,
disaster in its man made form,
eats resolve, destroys our all.

The monkeys fight in the street,
the zoos empty into the wild,
as by decree the pubs are closed,
exiling us from all we know.
We stagger into the unknown dawn,
without direction, we soldier on,
wander down vast empty aisles,
empty shelved and empty minded.

Workers yearn to go to work,
children play while locked-up,
the sun shines down on empty streets,
a hoarder weighed down hurries home,
the shadows flicker here and there,
a black car runs an amber light,
the silence settles on the day,
curtains twitch in constant play.

The parks are barred, playgrounds locked,
coffee shops and cafes boarded,
hotels empty of all their staff,
offices brooding, shut and dark;
a gloom pervades every action,
despair declares an Armageddon,
while numbers rise on speculation,
the unknown blights our expectation.

Who will death finally snatch,
a sneeze, a cough, then fever wracked,
we stand aside to wait and watch
neighbours from our locked down flats,
knowing not who will survive,
knowing not how we'll live
or how long we can endure
the curtailing of our freedom.

Spring has arrived to spare our gloom,
the sun benignly warms our woes,
day two of our stay at home
is like a carefree summer Sunday;
slow and still, fresh and warm,
the calm before the coming storm,
children's hands tightly clasped
in their mother's clinging grasp.

In ones and twos and at a distance
folks are focused on their business,
a journey to a corner shop,
a jog along a country path,
deliveries of food and parcels,
hushed voices in cellphone rambles,
an old man wobbling on a bike,
carrying on to master life.

If there is an upside to this story,
and tragedy not the complete tale,
families so quickly flung together
rekindling love, not filing divorce,
not yet at least after two weeks
now that Spring has finally come,
there is hope and expectation
that all will finally turn out well.

Yet, what cost is there to incomes,
the means by which people live,
the unemployment rate is soaring,
the markets falling at a pitch.

Can life as we currently know it
survive the assault on our purse,
while politicians draw their stipend,
the people suffer debt and hurt.

What's new in history's progression,
who pays off the national debt -
always it is the poorest folk
who fill the pockets of the rich.
As we lament the rising death toll,
it is a blip on the Devil's chart,
common sense tells us so,
as fear runs roughshod in our hearts.

Yet all the while we are convinced
we're doing better than our neighbours,
in our zeal, and in our manners,
we'll survive no matter what;
The self destruct gene running wild,
overtakes our daily lives,
leaves us powerless, separated
as others prosper unabated.

The weeks droll on into months,
there seems no end to it all,
death stalks every home,
the old the worse in the toll,
no bells rung for the dead
placed in quick-dug holes,
no family to shed their tears,
no friends to bid a last farewell.

When will this specter leave us be,
depart and let us live our lives?
If this is God at his worst
then let the healing now begin;
let the children play again,
let their laughs fill our hearts,
let us meet, hug, embrace,
let these sad days depart.

We carry on in separation,
line the streets, wait to shop;
how can we endure such ritual,
is this the norm now for us?
Covered mouths, furtive eye-nods,
shuffling forward to step aside,
avoiding every kind of contact,
dehumanised by fear and law.

A FRIEND I CANNOT REPLACE
for Brian Howell
[00.47, 4th Apr 2020, High Wycombe]

Suicide should not have been
the answer to my dead friend's strife.
What were the questions that made
him take such worries on himself?
Childhood does not prepare us
for what is thrown in our face,
we cannot wipe away the anger
or rid ourselves of its garbage
then we sink into a whirlpool
and drown in our own despair.

We cannot comprehend the turmoil,
the inner boiling of our minds,
but we can try to cool our impulse
to rage against the dying light.
Adulthood prevents us from revealing
the emotions binding us to time,
our days are short and unfulfilled
by the trivia of our existence,
that leaves us too engaged to save
our dearest friends from extinction.

I will not ever know for sure
why he is gone on his journey,
to that place that I too will go
though I'm not sure where it is.
Faith is a precious thing to grasp
in moments of empty meaning,
yet I know there is no place
where friends will meet again anon,
so I must mourn my friend's loss,
for we will never meet again.

GOLDEN NECTAR ON MY LIPS
[15.18, 5th Apr 2020, High Wycombe]

What joy to sit with beer
and watch the world amble by,
no chores but eternal pleasure
in the passing of the day.

The breeze may blow in my hair,
the sun rest upon my skin,
barefoot and sleeveless on the porch
while other fishes swim.

There is no guilt when you're old,
your time to rest has arrived;
with golden nectar on my lips
I'm not about to die.

EVERY DAY IS SUNDAY
[20.09, 9th Apr 2020, High Wycombe]

Every day is Sunday -
the pubs are shut,
the cinemas are closed,
the shops locked and bolted;
our twenty four hour society
is a life in lock-down.

We clap halfheartedly
for those who are alive,
we pray for deliverance
from the terror of our times;
the singing carries far
and the fireworks bang.

Sadness pervades the evening,
the air still with grief,
a nightingale chirps on
as the echoes recede;
what is there to do
but eat and sleep.

Alcohol becomes solace
as the days number up,
the queues to buy basics,
the distancing undisturbed;
life is distant voices
and loneliness the norm.

THE OWL AND THE PUSSY CAT
[01.01, 20th Apr 2020, High Wycombe]

The lonely owl sat and woo'd
for who? For you in a yew
it eyed a cat on the prowl
between the churchyard headstones.

The air was deadly dark and cold
hung with a haunting moon,
shadows slithered through the trees
barely-boned, but blossomed.

The owl wittered his worn wisdom
down upon the dim-lit lanes,
a dog whimpered in his kennel
instead of at his master's feet.

Nothing stirred to snap a twig,
nor turn a fallen leaf.
The owl remained watchful-eyed
while the cat pretended sleep.

THE PIGS WILL ALWAYS RUN THE FARM
[02.49, 3rd May 2020, High Wycombe]

This is no time to rattle our chains.
isolated in our distant worlds,
we revolve in utter confusion,
knowing not when it will end.

There is no guidance on the future,
fear governs our leaders' minds.
I have no say on these matters,
I am a sheep in the crowd.

The pigs will always run the farm,
they make the rules to suit themselves,
we lesser beasts may bay and grumble,
but power is beyond our grip.

Thus we suffer their imposed misery
as if it benefits us all -
deep down we know it is their folly
we will pay for down the line.

For the present, we endure uncertainty,
hope for better times ahead,
the pigs will always run the farm
but their time will end.

IS THERE A MOMENT
[19.46, 23rd May 2020, Vila Bled, Slovenia]

Is there a moment when we are free
to roam the world without restriction;
locked in our rooms in every land,
caught in the panic of mass extinction,
the sensible always keep their distance,
the reckless bent on self-destruction,
we somehow manage to co-exist
without the joy of former freedom;

we now somehow live in limbo,
knowing not what is the future
or when to celebrate our survival.

THE FIGHT IS NEVER OVER
[20.35, 26th May 2020, Porto Roz, Slovenia]

It was over. Eight thirty-five
and the sun passed into the sea.
She bent her legs, her hands locked
between her floral covering.

The twilight crept into the villa
as she lay on the chaise-long,
her eyes were droopy, drowsy
for a day without photography.

She was cold before being old,
restless in the failing light,
the years sitting on her hips
as she rose to stretch again.

There is no stopping time,
we age as the sun goes down,
we wake with hope eternal
and sleep knowing no tomorrow.

But the fight is never done,
the halting of advancing age,
she stood in the gloaming,
a silhouette on the scarlet sky.

LIPICA
[22.40, 2nd June 2020, Lipica, Slovenia]

The horses stand unimpressed,
they fill the fields unperturbed,
nurse their foals as mothers do
without the worry we humans have.

The swifts nest in the yard,
dart to feed their crying broods,
the stable doors wide ajar
in the oppressive summer heat.

The thunder rolls across the Karst,
the limestone caverns echo loud,
ancient tracks wound round walls
that stone age men erected.

Black pines tumble to an abyss
topped by a lofty spire,
the meadows stretch speckle-flowered
as the rain squall passes.

THE SECRETS OF MONTENEGRO
[01.06, 7th June 2020, Bar, Montenegro]

Th rain lashed the windscreen
of their sleek black car
winding on the coastal road
of the sun baked Adriatic -
the apartment towers were shuttered
the beaches forlornly lonely,
the mountains grey and brooding
above the snaking road below.

They exchanged their anxious hours
for a sushi shaded terrace,
followed a power boat to Kotar
with their focused camera lenses
as it went between two islands,
a church and mosque opposed,
not knowing which side won
or when they'd been divided.

The black clouds descended
as the many towns receded,
the flood lights of the stadium,
the walls of lost imperialism,
the mysteries of history's making,
the masks of present living,
the road wound on southwards
to dispel their misgivings.

They held hands just briefly,
they hugged above the calm sea,
they exercised their surly manners
and forgave their moody reasons,
they were equal partnered vagrants
on a wild far-flung coast
that revealed its many secrets
while they concealed their own.

THE GIRL IN PINK
23.29, 9th June 2020, Igomentista, Greece]

The woman in black in Montenegro
is now the girl in pink in Greece,

she carries her phone like a javelin
to pierce the hearts of her lovers.

She presses the buttons of her menfolk,
creates pure joy out of the pain,
she never dances to any tune
nor kisses the lips of pure strangers.

Caught in the trap of independence,
she does what indy women do,
she creates chaos in a timely manner
and makes sense of the confusion.

Her politeness is a desire to please,
her smile the foil to all arrows,
while her javelin rests on the table,
her shield is the barb of her eyebrows.

There is no defence against such arts,
the flick of an eye, crease of a smile,
the girl in pink cannot conceal
that she is the woman in black.

CORINTH SEA
[10.33, 11th June 2020, Selianiki, Greece]

The breeze blew through the olive trees,
vines hung with a coat of salt,
a young girl carried her schoolbooks
towards the beach and sun.

The laughter of children echoed,
the waves lapped on the shore,
geraniums sat in their clay pots
as the sunflowers gave a nod.

Clouds thinly veiled the blue,
cafes closed, their shutters shut,
the smell of coffee faintly lingering
since the plague has struck.

DAYBREAK IN SANTORINI
[09.30, 14th June 2020, Fira, Santorini]

The dogs barked into the night,
blanked out the constant chatter
rising from the hotel below
before day broke on the cliffs.

Greeks flags merged with the sky
as the breeze turned onshore,
the church bell struck once
then broke into a roar.

The sun dried out the bikinis
g-strung on a pegged out line
as their weary wearers rose
from their dreams in paradise.

HYDRA
[00.24, 20th June 2020, Hydra, Greece]

I don't know if today should end
or that tomorrow should come,
whatever gap remains behind
will soon be only me.

The birds fly high in the wind,
the boats sail across the sea,
the harbour fills with travelers
but none are here for me.

The stars hang on the clouds,
the windows open for the breeze,
who knows if God will come
and let me flee.

The traps we make for ourselves,
the choices that divide our lives,
the sheets on our double beds
that shield us from our love.

No man can seek his truer self
than to find it in his lover's arms,
how fleeting all those moments are
as time turns on the tide.

No memory can ever savour
the seconds lost, the minutes found
when night is about to go
and dawn brings tomorrow now.

SILENCED
[22.45, 22nd June 2020, Belgrade, Serbia]

Silenced, the voice in my head
deserted me, left behind rubbish,
images that were never mine

floating on top of my memory
like plastic in the ocean.

Caught in the seaweed anchored
to the floor of my soul,
like a net of knotted debris,
I am trapped by the waste
that has ensnared my happiness.

To cut free I need help
to clear my endangered deep -
with a desire to cleanse,
to rid my once clear blue
of all the filth I've collected.

MY TORMENTED HOUR IN VIENNA
[22.50, 24th June 2020, Sussen, Germany]

In St. Stephen's church I wrestled
with the demons chasing me.
I prayed they would leave
and my answers would come clear,
but God somehow left me sitting
on a pew looking up,
the stain-glass windows shone
as the heavens drifted on.

I spent an hour in torment
as my girl sat in the shade,
she watched a child fall over
and get up, to fall again -
God still refused to reply
on my anguish and my lows
as I struggled with my conscience
in a crippled bent repose.

I sought my own redemption
as a churchman swept the floor,
the lofty fresco restorers
brushed on their leaves of gold,
while I in tearless abjection
wrung my hands in woe,
asking God for his guidance
as God only knows.

HALFWAY THROUGH THIS VIRUSED YEAR
[23.24, 1st July 2020, High Wycombe]

Halfway through this virused year
and all my dreams are shattered,
not broken and ready to be fixed
but fragmented and irreparable.

Such years come rarely in life,
most years drift by as time does -
but this year is one of misery,
woeful goings-on everywhere I look.

With heads down and no good news,
despair pervades into our souls,
the expectation of more bad tidings
steals the laughter from our lives.

The hidden war that is ourselves
as we are the carriers of death -
a bomb dropped from high-above
is something we could comprehend.

For the now we bear the silence,
the stealth that takes folks away -
the corridors of life are empty
and we are the shadows lingering there.

LOUISE
[00.45, 18th July 2020, High Wycombe]

Many people interested, none of them interesting
as we strolled the alleys of fame -
She told me of times madness struck
at her dreams of living a life -
free of the demons pulling her down,
shot of the whispers filling her mind,
rid of the lies rotting her brain
making her think she was insane.

Fear is a weapon used upon her -
the threats of a mother bent on death,
the whims of a father never at fault
using her guilt to get what he wants.
Tiptoeing between suicide and violence,
a ping-pong ball batted back and forth
in a backhanded spin or forehand smash,
the child is broken or learns to resist.

JULES (song)
[23.40, 30th July 2020, High Wycombe]

I love her like no other,
I cannot give her up,
I must have her forever,
or I will forever weep.

I love her like the mountains,
I love her like the sea,
I love her every movement
and I love her close to me.

I cannot bear our partings,
I cannot be alone,
I need to have her love
and kiss her all the more.

She is my only lover,
she is my sole respite,
she saves me from myself
and wrongs all my rights.

I cannot live without her,
I perish at such thought,
She is my only solace,
and she is hot!

FILM STARS
[01.52, 9th Aug 2020, High Wycombe]

In their heyday they are great,
young, athletic, in their prime,
glowing like a burning star
with no end to their brilliance.

Then life takes its payment,
tarnishes what it once promoted,
dulls the shine once so bright
to leave an empty black hole.

All fires must burn then die,
have their flames finally spent,
the warmth and comfort they provide
will as ash scatter wide.

Yet we still love these stars,
immortal in our own dull times,

blazing through our short lives
like Gods in ancient paradise.

THE FAITHFUL TEMPTRESS
[00.25, 12th Aug 2020, High Wycombe]

How secret are the secrets kept,
the dual world of the faithful temptress,
the flash of her flirtatious eyes,
a smile to quell pent up ire,
a way with words but not enough
to let the mask fall away.

How can a man deal with this dilemma
but to run away to Samarkand,
ride a camel into the storm,
hide in some far-flung hovel,
for nothing else will save him from
the temptress he cannot have.

I JUST GOT LUCKY
[00.42, 18th Aug 2020, High Wycombe]

Not a genius, just lucky,
the millionaire told me on the phone.
I was in the right place, right time
and the money flooded in the door.

There was no design to my actions,
no plan to get rich quick,
I just happened to be lucky
and now I am extremely rich.

HABITUAL SPEECH
[00.15, 21st Aug 2020, High Wycombe]

Over the top a century ago
was equated with death at the front,
now it is an online platform
delivering war films at a price.

As our language changes every day,
we are the victims of old age -
lines that were funny just yesterday,
now are the phrases of bigots.

Who can be certain of their vocabulary
that it will not fall into disrepair.

Ever watchful our tongues wag,
whisper the things we want to say.

Who can keep up with each new mote,
abbreviations or slick catchphrase -
all of us succumb to habitual speech
until we are part of a bygone age.

I WILL SLEEP WITHOUT HAVING DOUBTS
[00.06, 24th Aug 2020, High Wycombe]

At the centre of the universe is a black hole,
a darkness that no-one can describe -
a shooting mass of gas and heat
that has birthed the whole of the cosmos.

But who really knows if God,
that eternal being we'd like to meet,
exists in some parallel dimension
that will always be beyond our reach.

Always these same damned questions,
that the scientist nor preacher answers,
they give us their qualified viewpoints
but always fail to satisfy somehow.

So for the time being I will gaze up
and read my bible in the failing light,
thus armed with the tools of understanding,
I will sleep without having doubts.

A FUTURE TO POLICE
[01.59, 30th Aug 2020, High Wycombe]

Yesterday Julie went back to Poland
and when I arrived back from Heathrow,
my bus pass was lying on the mat.

How time has flown like pollen,
scattered are my years now spread
to leave my seed floating in the wind.

There is still a future to police,
a chance to order what is right,
to plant new ideas in nice neat rows.

NORMAL DAYS, AVERAGE HOURS
[23.19, 30th Aug 2020, High Wycombe]

Some days are just meant to pass
without any thought of remembrance;
these normal days, these average hours
of nothing special, or worthy of note.

BACK TO THE TREADMILL
[23.34, 30th Aug 2020, High Wycombe]

It is the end of summer -
the rain has stopped for now,
darkness has fallen on the town,
the streets are empty and silent.

Next week the schools reopen,
overcoats shaken and brushed,
the adults forced back to work,
lamenting the summertime lost.

Trying hard not to feel hard done to,
the treadmill mounted once more,
Christmas becomes the focus
before thoughts of some rest return.

NOTHING OF VENICE
[21.52,,1st Sept 2020, Palanca, Venice]

Whatever is said about Venice
has been said before in prose,
in poetry and in visual art.
I cannot add one iota
to works that fill libraries
and museums around the world.
Such is the knowledge on Venice
only a fool would add more.

Yet I will, as I am foolish
and cannot still my pen;
I must make mention of beauty,
of decay and views to die for.
But perhaps this short poem
is not the place to say a thing.
I will leave off here now
and not begin again.

MEMORY
[01.19, 10th Sept 2020, High Wycombe]

And so time goes like a freight train at night
to wake in the morning further down the line,
a bird on the wire chirping its song,
heard long after the rain has gone.

The eyes of a lover the following dawn,
the cries of a child moments ago born,
the feel of the wind on a bare back
bent in toil over newly dug soil.

The clouds wizz by like a galloping horse,
free like a tramp with no fixed abode,
the days gliding by like a boat on a lake
lost to our gaze in a fine summer haze.

THE WORLD STOPS TO SAY HELLO
[00.33, 30th Sept 2020, High Wycombe]

The world stops to say hello,
then it moves on, leaves behind
those who cannot step with time
to the march of history.

Thus standing still without a plan
gives no place to shelter from
events that make them unprepared
for the dance of destiny.

And so they wait ill at ease
in the hope of a chance
to carry on beyond their fate
to escape their dull reality.

TO FEND, MAKE DO, SURVIVE
[01.03, 8th Oct 2020, High Wycombe]

The warmest September on record,
the world burning up with fires,
the virus raging on unstoppable,
no-one knows when it will end.

Here the rain still comes down,
a week of storm, violent flood;
if Noah were alive just now,
he'd be sailing down the Thames.

Life seems to be so chaotic
without a steady guiding hand,
we are adrift, on our own,
to fend, make do, survive.

THE MANY HOURS TO HARBOUR
[18.35, 15th Oct 2020, Brindisi-Igumentista]

The dark falls on the windy sea
as through the swell the ferry rides
the waves towards the Grecian shore
still distant in the gloom ahead.

Onboard we sit in empty hope,
a ship devoid of any souls,
behind us now Italy's shore -
a hazy fuzz of night lights.

And so we pitch into the void,
the Adriatic chop and roll,
sip our coffees, chat or doze
the many hours to harbour.

OUR BAGS ARE PACKED
[20.52, 7th Nov 2020, Hydra, Greece]

Our bags are packed, our ship has sailed,
yet we are trapped in a raging storm,
the island soaked in winter sun
while we're marooned to walk the shore.

The world closes down around us,
the cafe chairs stacked, the tables bare;
the wind howls on the awnings,
whipped, lashed, and cracking loud.

Abandoned to a double fate of helplessness,
the curfew curtailing all our escaping hopes,
companionship's fraught hours of boredom
makes me hopeful, my companion full of fear.

Elsewhere a new president is elected,
the rancour of living a distant worry,
the solitude of our island existence
a contrast to the world's bitter woes.

Make-belief should be for film-makers,
not real life in this present unreal world,

the actors here made their timely exit
but we remain here to pick up the tab.

How difficult it is to end enjoyment,
to return to a norm that is not normal;
this paradise in Greece called Hydra
is rightly only half of what's required.

There is no place to find true salvation,
no place where the head and heart can rest,
for one pulls this way, the other t'other,
until discontent builds into strife.

And still the wind howls quite foully,
as if the roofs are going to fly;
the sea a black swell of darkness
and the sky a black void of hell.

The hours tick away as they dwindle
into the late hours of the wild night,
an orange light offering some warmness
as the humid cold numbs our sleep.

Ancient houses creek with every new blast,
floorboards crack and shutters bang,
the lanes ghostly empty of locals
except for the cats patrolling the town.

The donkey men have gone to their lairs,
the carpenter lathes are eerily silent,
the shops boarded up, restaurants closed,
the times we have are not the best.

This is life in these unfortunate days,
the plague compounded by a winter storm;
trapped we find ourselves for many hours
but always is the hope of dawn.

I LEAVE BEHIND
[23.59,19th Nov 2020, High Wycombe]

Every place I go, I leave behind
a thought, a deed, a footprint in the soil.
I leave something of myself each time,
on every pillow, on every sandy shore.
What I leave is in the air -
unexplained to others and myself,
there is no need to quantify or tally,
things that no words can describe.

Yet, something, is there left unseen,
something you could not put your finger on,
something your hand cannot touch,
yet your mind knows, senses the ghost
that has passed by, lingered there,
taken action, somehow changed the place,
just by having once been present -
a living being you have never met.

How many living souls, most now dead,
have walked the streets I trudge,
here trod the grass, the meadow-lands,
the mountain pathways of many foreign parts,
sat on chairs, in cafes and in bars,
drank and eaten, laughed like children,
left their palm-print on a door-knob
while walking through doors into oblivion.

Will I be discovered when I am gone,
my presence felt, my shadow detected;
will my thoughts be relived, experienced
by those who will be many after me.
Will they see what I have seen,
will they touch where I have been,
will they think like I oft do,
about those who walked in other times.

I have no fears, I've had my fun,
far-flung has my shadow fallen
into the shade of other's presence,
I'll let my being fade away.
For this is life, we are mortal,
passing though beyond such shadows
into the light, the warm calm place
where I can rest, and worry none.

POSITIVE
[23.42, 21ˢᵗ Nov 2020, High Wycombe]

My test came back positive
just as I am back on my feet;
eight days of fever gone,
the anguished dreams banished,
my stiffness of limb lingers,
fatigue grinds me to a halt.

Otherwise I am on the mend,
gone is my stifling cough,

I have survived the pandemic;
I pray for those who've not.

VACCINE
[00.19, 24th Nov 2020, High Wycombe]

I'm out the other side of Covid,
but now I'm itchy, covered in spots,
my right leg is stiff and limp -
how much more can go wrong?

The spots – its like having measles,
a rash across my back and midriff,
and that cough, still underlying
every time I think it's gone.

No chance of seeing a doctor,
they're still locked down and scared,
I'm waiting on the national vaccine
to get me back to any kind of norm.

THE DEVIL WAITS TO SEE HIM BURN
[00.27 6th Dec 2020, High Wycombe]

What now as the Trump years end -
that horrible excuse of a human being.
Has there been his like since Adolph Hitler,
he's not far off, he's full of hatred -
for all the sins of his father,
for all the pride of his mother,
he is a failure as a person,
despite his rise to being President.

Bringing his country to such division
by his inaction, his texting quips,
the damage goes around the world,
returns to wreck all moral code.
His lies, his barefaced bragging bouts,
his tongue tied tales he fabricates,
can such a man be made for heaven -
the devil waits to see him burn.

IMAGES
[01.11 9th Dec 2020, High Wycombe]

Sometimes when I think.
When nothing seems to fit -
a rain dogs, cycle sort of thing;
I love the one I'm with,

the villain and the kid,
the falcon and the dove all mixed.

I think I know myself,
but the heckles always hurt -
the dark side of heaven remains.
Finding fortune in my friends,
seven crosses as their end,
islands in a crab filled sea.

Inside I've got to run
from the number runner's sums -
so long to all that puppet stuff.
The rose has lost its bloom,
as the warrior takes the nude,
the hunter lays down to sleep.

The axe raider sails away,
the beast departs his lair -
fingers part the water for good.
The stone is going green,
the right bus leaves unseen,
as the sisters wave a sweet adieu.

HUMAN FRAILTY
For Neil
00.46 12th Dec 2020, High Wycombe]

Friends will always disappoint
as they are flawed and human
to the point that their existence
is more important than my own.

Naturally I must sometime be
a disappointment to my friends -
I do not see it, only feel it
when love goes out the door.

Too often it is our values,
our upbringing forming our view -
the disappointment our expectation
of how others should be.

However hard the hurt hits -
causes pain to hearts and minds,
acceptance of all human frailty,
a lesson Christ taught well.

GOD HELP US
[23.29 12th Dec 2020, High Wycombe]

When will the light shine bright again
so we can go about our business
with smiles, and joy, and happiness.

The politicians are playing silly games,
gambling our future for their ideals
while being paid from our taxes.

Is there a glimmer of future cheer,
a time for celebration and laughter
that for now evades us all.

I will not pray for our deliverance,
I will bring no superstition into play -
but please God, give us hope.

WHO KILLED THE ALBATROSS
[15.59 19th Dec 2020, Marbesa, Spain]

Who killed the albatross,
brought this time of bad luck -
someone shot it down,
watched it cruelly drown.

All our hopes disappeared,
sank with the albatross -
one moment freely roaming,
the next a frightful omen.

Fate is as predetermined
as the planets round the sun -
the albatross our conscience
of all we do wrong.

We all shot the albatross,
took part in its demise,
until left with a horizon
and a bare empty sky.

POTENTIAL
[23.18 19th Dec 2020, Marbesa, Spain]

Some say I have not reached my potential.
What would my parents say?
I believe I exceeded their expectations
and those I set for myself.

Yet others always want to push,
get me to go beyond my limits,
the limits I think exist within myself
that seem impossible to breach.

To excel without being dishonest,
lies, or the deception of others -
How do we reach our potential
if we don't know what it is?

TO HAVE SUCH PEACE
[22.15 20th Dec 2020, Marbesa, Spain]

The child skated in the moonlight,
drifted into the dark sultry night,
the streets deserted by the seaside,
the vacant villas all without light.

There was peace to be found there,
the waves lapping without fear,
the stars twinkling in the blackness,
the way the sky ought to be.

No human speech, just the shore fall,
the lapping waves on the beach,
the bliss of having reached there
to have such peace.

DRINKING CHAMPAGNE IN THE AFTERNOON
[15.14 23rd Dec 2020, Marbesa, Spain]

Drinking champagne in the afternoon
is not the socialist norm -
but at sixty-six such concerns
are merely for the birds.

Our politicians are morally bankrupt,
corrupt and mentally holed -
sheep are far better fellows
to follow than government blokes.

Reading Jean Brodie in sunshine
as the stock market goes up -
old age offers some hindsight
on how society works.

Now I've tumbled the methods
that always made me poor -

'Its up your bum, you wankers,
and fuck your Brexit too!'

The sun will go down as always,
come up again for sure -
lets hope for a better future
and a proper covid cure.

So I'll continue my drinking,
champagne in the Spanish sun -
don't judge me for my values,
I've done my socialist work.

THE ZOOM MEETING
[15.31 23rd Dec 2020, Marbesa, Spain]

Middle class and middle aged,
they cackle on in babble,
relieved that Xmas had arrived
and work was off the table.

Its no bad thing to take rest,
get all worries off their breasts,
sipping on their tipples,
gaggling on quite tipsy.

Talk of husbands, turkey roasts,
charades played with little cries,
shared confessions, little cries,
laughter breaking through the sighs.

Questions asked, answers given,
bonding in their tearful havens,
lonely, but somehow driven
to bridge the rules of lock down.

As Christmas comes at a distance,
the ladies have their little party -
sweet and kind and understanding,
the hours pass in part oblivion.

EVE OF CHRISTMAS
[12.32 24th Dec 2020, Marbesa, Spain]

The pancake sea, donut sun,
the hot bun sand, ice-glazed pool -
all is ready to consume
as party-time is with us.

But this Xmas is not cake,
not chocolate, not party hat,
no cracker jack, paper jokes,
no friends around us.

The pancake sea remains unswum,
the ice-glazed pool ripple-less,
the hot bun sand sandle-less
this year's eve of Christmas.

PROBLEMS
[01.21, 26th Dec 2020, Las Chapas, Marbesa]

Whatever problems people have
I have my own. Loneliness
is a disease that eats life,
makes ending life a good way out.

When you get to the end of the road
and find that it ends at a cliff,
you look in the mirror and decide
that you won't go back the way
you came.

The pain's too much,
its too full of pot-holes and traffic,
so you turn the engine off,
get out the car, walk to the edge,
stare into the abyss,
and jump.

LAS CHAPAS
[23.39, 28th Dec 2020, Marbesa]

Here the leaves do not fall,
scatter nor drift into a pile.
The day ends, the night descends,
with no sound other than the pines
catching the breeze inward bound
from the silent sea.

WHAT IS THERE TO SHOW
[00.29, 29th Dec 2020, Marbesa]

What is there to show for another day,
showering, shaving, the breakfast consumed,
the photos taken of my closest friends,
the beer drunk, the wine devoured,

the book bought, the forest walk,
the groceries bought home for tea?

THE DRUNKEN JOURNEY HOME

[29th Dec - 2nd Jan 2021, Marbesa-Malaga]
[5th Feb 2021, 25th July 2021, Iver Grove]

The moon was full of chaos,
on this cold Spanish night,
we drank to all the werewolves
and howled in wild delight.
We laughed into the marshes
with swaggering bottled hands,
we straddled countless ditches
and frog-jumped boggy land.

We took relief in a churchyard,
between the silver-frosted graves
we rested on a headstone,
and cursed the Devil's mates!
We did not believe in witches,
in goblins, warlocks, nor more,
we were high on vino tinto,
and free of nonsense lore.

We were men of the morrow,
not the type to cower in fear.
Our motto was 'Up them!'
to all who'd venture near -
until a chill came upon us,
stilled our bombast shouts
the moon obscured by a mist
descended like a shroud.

It covered the entire graveyard,
hid my friends from me,
and when the vapour lifted
I was alone in that lee
where not a soul was human,
alive, or able to say -
"Hello, my sweet drunken fellow.
How was your full moon day?"

For it was night and eerie,
as I sat with the dead,
I began to doubt and wonder
if I'd be home by first crow.
Can you imagine my bravery,
alone with the spirits of old,

some of them my ancestors,
but many my enemies' folk.

I swigged on my empty bottle,
threw it against a stone,
it smashed with a violence -
I wished I'd not done so
as a moan, and then a murmur
shook the frozen ground,
and a ghost appeared before me
and I was mortified!

My heart gave out – stopped -
as I died a hundred times,
the spirit eyed me sideways
then sank into the ground.
I gasped and gurgled loudly
as my life somehow returned,
I careered to my feet
despite my limbs being numb.

An owl wittered loudly,
a bat went past my ear,
a spider crawled up my leg,
I stood frozen full of fear.
I recalled the beers I'd drunk,
the wine I had consumed,
the spirits liberally poured for me
by my friends who'd disappeared.

What now could I imagine,
was it the drink doing me in?
Or was I in this graveyard
for all my dreadful sins.
I crossed myself threefold,
then again, three more times,
for when you call on God,
no-one is keeping count.

A wind got up, blew off my hat,
left me staring at the moon,
I was betwixt blue heaven
and the Devil's motley crew.
Was I now part sober
or caught now in a trance?
I knew not June from January,
nor October now from March.

Where was I now I wondered,
so close to home but far,
how many miles still to go
until I reached my hearth?
For now I had a vision
of my wife before the fire,
my dinner cooked and ready
and her welcoming loving arms.

Suddenly, a cold blast shook
this idyll from my thoughts,
as I knew my wife was angry
and nursing her vilest wrath.
That is the lot of the drinkers
who reject their wives for booze,
when they come home merry,
her tongue's their only muse.

How had I let it become so,
in love so long ago -
I'd traded in companionship
for the demon alcohol.
How now then to get home -
to plead my deep remorse,
my legs were like jelly
and my head a sea of words.

I would beg my wife's forgiveness,
pledge to give up drink,
help her with our home-life,
and pay my debts on time!
I'd seen the road I'd traveled
as a wicked wild highway,
led up the garden path by many
and down many broken lanes.

Done now! I was a changed man,
standing straight and clear in mind,
I looked at the glaring full moon,
and saluted the grinning swine.
I was not going to be seduced
by any celestial rays,
I was a man by my own rights
whatever my wife may say.

I staggered out of the graveyard,
left that ghost of mine behind,
carried on to my nearby village
where I came to the stile -

that long since had been broken
and required a difficult climb
over a fence, trailing a ditch
where a dead witch was found.

That was all just hearsay,
and well before my time,
but still when we were children
we never crossed that stile.
And as I stumbled, clambered
o'er that crooked fence,
my foot caught on a post
and I fell into the mire!

The stench was all country,
thick and caked on me,
I swore at all creation
and damned that wife of mine,
for had she not been home,
I'd have slept in the mire -
Now I was a scarecrow
covered in rural slime.

The rooks all laughed loudly
as I passed beneath the boughs,
onward then I staggered
without a thought of time.
For I knew when I arrived
I'd be tried for my crimes,
jury, judge and hangman
all in her combined.

So I tarried under an old oak
where we had first entwined,
and I recalled a little vaguely
where it had all gone wrong.
I welled with such emotion,
the tears poured down my cheeks,
great fountains of self-pity,
burst the dam on my deceit.

Perhaps I was not perfect,
the sort of man who's loved,
more the kind of fellow
well met but somehow shunned.
I'd had my share of hard knocks,
and times when things were rough,
but my wife had stuck by me
though I was often drunk.

I resolved to end my bad ways,
and somehow sobered up,
I bade the rooks a farewell
and set off for better luck.
The night light in the window
cheered my withered soul,
as I peered through the glass
at my wife on her own.

My love for her swelled greatly
as I strode through the door,
I bent down to kiss her
and she stuck me on the nose!
I went reeling off the cottage wall,
and landed in a heap -
and there I slept the whole night
until she broke my sleep.

She handed me a porridge bowl
and a mug of stewing tea,
she said it was time for me to go
to work in the fields.
I kissed her on her reddened cheek
she blushed and wiped her nose,
a little tear drowned her eye,
then she cried out loads.

And as I set off out to work,
I vowed to swear off drink,
I loved her more than all the world,
she believed me so I think.
With happy plod I ploughed a field
knowing all was well with me,
one drunken night behind me now,
it was the moon, not me.

MALAGA
[13.57, 4th Jan 2021, Malaga]

The beer glistened in the sunlight,
the soup warm against the cold.
Picasso left here for Paris's lights,
left behind this ancient town
the Phoneticians built so long ago.

The fountains babble in the squares,
the orange groves are everywhere -
the narrow streets marble worn,

the churches reaching for the sky,
bluer than the bluest eye.

HAPPY DAYS
[20.19, 14th Jan 2021, Iver Grove]

Happy days have returned.
Without happy days we are dead,
useless to the world,
useless to our friends
and everyone we love.

Thank God for happy days,
for when all is done,
happiness is the best -
it lets the heart soar,
the sad mind unwind,
makes friendship a bliss,
and each day a joy.

THE KISS OF A LOVER
[23.56, 15th Jan 2021, Iver Grove]

With a kiss on the lips,
we parted for the first time
in a way that was different
from all the years before.

The feel of her softness,
the sensation of her touch
that lingered long on me
as she smiled and left.

What had we just done,
we had not done before,
something different had occurred
beyond that we had known.

It was the kiss of a lover,
not that of old friends -
why is love so guarded
and a mystery without end.

THE ALLUSION OF LOVE
[00.35, 16th Jan 2021, Iver Grove]

I admit – I am in love,
but at my age I am guarded.

There have been many old fools
made to be mistaken by looks,
enamored wholly by youth,
taken in by guile and flattery.

I prefer then – to say nothing,
keep my feelings to myself,
show my love in small gestures,
collect gestures in return,
balance my hopes with caution,
keep my feet on the ground.

How age warps the emotions,
somehow, not worth the exposure,
playing safe to avoid commotion,
keeping the peace at all costs,
stability the guiding purpose,
and love a lost cause.

FORGIVE ME, FRIENDS
[16.20, 16th Jan 2021, Iver Grove]

For all those I've misplaced,
forgotten, or haven't had space -
forgive me for my disloyalty.

Better now to understand friends,
hard to find, harder to replace,
forget me not in your prayers.

Time throws egg in our face,
our actions can be a disgrace,
please forgo my many mistakes.

Dear friends, let us retrace,
find new ways to embrace,
I apologise for my past ways.

Signing off on gone days,
I ask you to retrace,
retake the path of our friendship.

So thank you for listening,
yours sincerely, R M,
this end is just the beginning.

OUR FUTURE IN THE BRIGHT BLUE SKY
[14.13, 25th Jan 2021, Iver Grove]

The snow was down around us,
Simon sang his song for America,
the sun flooded the stable eaves,
the music faded into memory.

All our troubles were beyond us,
gone without the smallest care,
hope was in the crisp air,
our future in the bright blue sky.

MY LIES CONCEALED
[00.11, 12th Feb 2021, Iver Grove]

Is truth the words I set out
here upon this cream page,
or is truth the lies I tell
somewhere further here below.
I cannot tell if I am deluded
or blinded by my own deceit.
Are my views somehow tainted,
somehow tarnished by my lying?

How can I remain truthful
on matters that are personal -
my ego will not permit my faults
to be revealed in their entirety.
Part of me remains unexposed,
covered by a blanket of words -
my truths are lies in disguise,
my lies concealed in verbose.

SPRING ARRIVED
[23.36, 20th Feb 2021, Iver Grove]

Spring arrived today with warmth,
the first glimpse of yellow spotted
in a shallow trough of earth
up against the old garden wall.

WE DANCE TO NEW COMPOSITIONS
[23.59, 20th Feb 2021, Iver Grove]

Dutifully we dance to new compositions
tailored and cut to suit our gait -
so we as cripples can take part
in the waltzes we try to imitate.

Into the dark, out into the light
we cruise across the uneven dance floor,
spinning our partners, whispering our worries,
listening for secrets, and so much more.

The music plays on, night follows day,
we find new partners to wildly spin,
until we are giddy, tired, exhausted,
we end our hoof with a parting kiss.

But the music plays on, an endless record
as the wallflowers wilt, and others get up,
the tunes fade from our pounding heads
and our dancing kicks are yesterday's licks.

CONSPIRACY OF SILENCE
[00.44, 22nd Feb 2020, Iver Grove]

When great men are greatly wronged,
condemned by a conspiracy of silence,
they carry the falsehood to their graves
with no reply to all who've shamed them.

Only when such men are buried,
and only once their accusers die -
does the truth emerge from the silence,
and others speak to clear their names.

Thus great men are often set up
by greater men seeking revenge,
and being greater, and in power,
false witness is at their command.

Perhaps the folly of all great men
is to put pride before common sense,
to have their honour on their sleeves,
so that their wounds don't heal.

For those who go along with wrongs,
knowing that a wrong's been done -
these are the lesser kind of men
whose silence tarnishes everyone.

ART HAS SHUT DOWN
[00.39, 23rd Feb 2021, Iver Grove]

Art has shut down like in Shakespeare's times,
the plague closing theatres, artists hungry

to feed themselves, not just their art,
taking labouring jobs to make ends meet.

When times are hard, food, clothes and shelter
are the means of survival, not plays,
not comedians letting off steam in hot rooms,
nor musicians blasting out their rock and roll.

Disease and death is about health and welfare
of the human body, but not the mind -
all effort goes into preserving tissue
with nothing spent on dreams of any kind.

This is art, the wasting of endless hours
by artists trying to make us all understand
that our bodies will succumb to disease
and our minds are indeed who we are.

When the plague leaves us, gets controlled,
audiences will flock to their favourite shows,
for they will want to lightly recap, recall
what they have suffered, to laugh at it all.

SHE CAME BACK TO ME
[00.39, 26th Feb 2021, Iver Grove]

My sweet friend, came back to me,
with a text, a warm loving note
that sparked, rekindled the fire,
relit the room, cleared the gloom
that had descended on our friendship.

THE HOBO'S PRAYER
[00.25, 28th Feb 2021, Iver Grove]

I've tried to forgive them,
her brother, her sister,
but I can't quite give in at all.
Though I pray to my saviour,
and do good without favour,
its just not coming along.

I somehow still hate them,
cannot quite face them,
they are the low, of the low.
But I do it for her sake,
try not to look fake,
yet she know's it's all a show.

And when we get gone,
and we are alone,
I wipe the tears from her eyes.
For her brother is cruel,
her sister's a fool, both
easy to loathe and despise.

We've said our goodbyes,
packed up our bin bags,
gone back out on the road.
Her family's a lost case,
there's no hope of some grace,
taking on some of our load.

I hold her hand tightly,
walk with her nightly,
looking for some place not cold.
Its not coming easy,
its not light and breezy,
the worry is making us old.

Its tough on our bodies
as we search for somebody
to rent us a cheap room.
When you're down on your luck,
and don't have that much,
you inhabit a world of gloom.

All the folks up against us,
I try to forgive them,
but its hard not having hope.
Lord, please answer my prayers,
save us from this despair,
for she's at the end of her rope.

But before I leave off,
though I want nothing as such,
don't leave us on the streets all alone.
For I've had enough
for a man sleeping rough,
without a home of his own.

BIG THINGS IN LITTLE PACKAGES
[22.44, 10th Mar 2021, Iver Grove]

Big things arrive in small packages
carefully wrapped, beautifully bowed;
expectation is in the content potential
as the outer coating is peeled away.

Now as I open what is concealed,
I understand what I have been gifted;
a priceless object I cannot describe
for I am dazzled by its richness.

And so it is with my little treasure,
my big gift in a small package;
lost for a time in misunderstanding,
feeling somehow she'd been wronged.

Not so, my love, not so at all,
time has a way of being cruel,
sowing discord instead of unity,
dividing souls, and causing wars.

Not us, never, friends for life,
we will love and never fight;
there will be no divide,
just kisses where hurt is found.

THE SULTANS SING IN THEIR PALACES
[23.40, 17th Mar 2021, Iver Grove]

The sultans sing in their palaces,
the dog-leap stairs lie bare,
money is free on the tv
as others nurse despair.

Days like these are not rare,
they are common average times,
local heroes so hard to find,
sip on gin, suck on limes.

The roses bloom in early Spring,
news of cancer makes us shrink,
fear is hidden in our dreams
while others turn to drink.

Bed is for the early starter,
while dark is the killer's heart,
some progress with their art
despite all that binds us.

The cars race into the night,
round the corner lovers fight,
comets whirl beyond our sight
as time goes on without us.

TILL DAWN BRINGS UP THE STORM
[00.25, 23rd Mar 2021, Iver Grove]

All is quiet in my western world,
the guns are silent in my house,
the clock is ticking like a bomb
but inside there is no dynamite.

The day departed with a whimper,
a barking dog at a window,
a whiff of curry in the air
and angry voices simmering.

All is now peacefully calm,
there is no sense of due alarm,
there is no fear of coming harm
till dawn brings up the storm.

AS OTHERS LEAPED
[11.15, 27th Mar 2021, Iver Grove]

I had many lovers,
very few chose to stay.
While the kites flew high
and the moles dug deep,
I carried on dreaming
as my lovers leaped -
fell to their fate
while I remained asleep.

THIS WASTELAND, MY HOME
[30th Mar - 9th Apr 2021, Iver Grove]

This wasteland, my home,
this place destroyed by many hands,
my village, ravished by greed,
demolished stone by stone,
made derelict by demolition.

There is no beauty in decay,
no stop for the eye to rest,
all is gone, removed
or left to fall down -
day on month on year.

Snow, rain and wild wind
do their worst on my memories,
replaced once, replaced again,

bulldozed into non existence -
my village I call home.

The river no longer stops,
rushes on without a flood,
the weir broken, long unused,
the mill now just a hut
for storing rust and debris.

Hope of lost things returned,
faith in finding new beginnings,
a roof put on the church,
the school children all returned
to their abandoned classrooms.

No such charity exists -
the fountain lies in pieces,
the headstones in the graveyard
lie sideways in a ditch
where derelicts piss.

That place that made me!
Is there no shame?
Are there no tongues wagging,
no wise heads shaking,
fingers pointing at the rot?

Is the decay like empire?
Tennis courts green-slimed,
bowling greens just puddles,
my memories of greater times
before the nation regressed?

The park swings gone,
the public baths demolished,
the chip shop boarded up,
the Italian cafe shuttered -
no ice cream for the young.

The pavements uneven, broken,
the cobbles coated in tar,
the poplars lining the road
cut down before the lime trees
gave up the ghost.

What shadows lurk there
in the lanes of the past,
the voices of congregations,

the chatter of infants
coming out of Sunday school.

All the laughter long blown
away on the south-west wind,
carried on to barren mountains,
scattered on the sodden moors,
drained and left to wither.

How can life return anew
when all is almost dead,
the village barely breathing,
its last cough a gasp
of trembling and shaking.

There is no place to rest,
nowhere to sit, to reflect,
no tree to put a back to,
no wall to wind protect
the weary and the old.

My home is a wasteland
made so by many hands,
the village that I loved
has left me homeless
in a bitter world.

CRITICS THERE ARE MANY
[13.35, 10th Apr 2021, Iver Grove]

Critics, there are many,
doers, there are few -
the critics in their armchairs
sipping on their wine -
while the doers climb their mountains
and chant their songs.

WE ARE WILD ONCE MORE
[23.00, 19th Apr 2021, Iver Grove]

The cage is open, we are free
to leave our narrow perches
and fly into the trees.

What joy to have our freedom
to drink the perfumed air,
chase the cherry blossom.

We can sit and warble,
make our nest the best,
hatch our little eggs.

No more bars, kept indoors,
left to trill and tweet -
we are wild once more.

WHY DON'T I HAVE A LOVER (song)
[from The Beehive, 24th Apr 2021, Iver Grove]

Why don't I have a lover
who has a great hunger
why don't I have a hundred
or thousand or so.

Why cant I have a lover
who has seven brothers
why do I have to suffer
til I'm wrinkled and old.

Why have I no lover
who's handsome and clever
why must I serve beer
to dirty old bores.

O give me a lover
who brings me flowers
O give me a true love
before I grow cold.

YOUR HUSBAND HAS GONE
[23.3, 10th May 2021, Iver Grove]

Your husband has gone, you are alone,
you are free to share your love at last
with me, for I have loved you always,
adored you in a hundred different ways
that you have pretended not to notice,
though I know you have suspected
that I have waited for this moment
to arrive, and now its come.

I MEASURE OUT THE ROPE
[23.59, 18th May 2021, Iver Grove]

Some people just take the piss,
try to get what they can while they can

without any thought for your feelings -
well, they're wrong and stupid!

They think they are God's gift to you,
stupid to believe that they are entitled
to tramp on your respect and morals,
and then get a way with it!

If you are meek you might whimper,
cower before such selfish tyrants -
but I quietly measure out the rope
I'm going to hang them with!

I CRAVE SILENCE
[00.22, 19th May 2021, Iver Grove]

I crave silence from the noise
that people make with their mouths
the roar of their wheeled-machines,
the rattle of their humdrum lives.

I want to hear the birds,
shut out the fume-filled skies,
close my tired sagging eyes
and listen to the rising lark.

What luck to have such sound,
the ecstasy of the moving air,
the pleasure of it on my face
with not a whisker out of place.

To lie still undisturbed,
to slumber with no ticking clock,
to dream like no dream before,
deaf to all the world's woes.

SUNSHINE
[23.32, 30th May 2021, Iver Grove]

Sunshine heals all our woes,
gives us life we had forgotten,
restores the lost and terminated,
revives the tired and irritated,
makes us forget our miscalculations,
renews us with determination,
provides us with exhilaration
to conquer all our trepidations.

NATIONAL BANK HOLIDAY
[23.42, 31ˢᵗ May 2021, Iver Grove]

Has summer come, I hope so,
the icy Arctic wind eats us up,
freezes all our good intentions,
makes us huddle in our misery.

Not so now, this day,
this national holiday enjoyed,
made use-of as it should,
meeting with friends from afar.

Taking walks by old canals,
breathing the freedom of rest,
lounging without counting hours,
making plans beyond tomorrow.

This is a good time -
the reason to be breathing,
the essence of existence,
the purpose of our lives.

BANNED FROM FOREIGN TRAVEL
[23.32, 3ʳᵈ June 2021, Iver Grove]

The misery of lock-up continues
to restrict our personal freedoms.
We are banned from foreign travel
out of fear of mutant variants.
God forbid that aliens will arrive
and zap us with their ray guns.

The Martians are here already,
the white men forbidding our futures,
the children of Empire immigrants
interning refugees and asylum seekers;
concentration camps in rural Kent,
and God knows how many other places.

Crypto currencies continue to tumble
as house prices rocket through the roof,
wages are stagnant and inadequate,
workers are too few to staff the schools;
the rich are running off to Cornwall
to live off their home-rental loot.

The Prosecco perches on the verandah,
the sun sets into the pristine sea,

the well-off stroll the shimmering strands,
eat prawns for lunch, sea bass for tea;
they have sworn off foreign travel -
they should be happy to let us leave.

A DAY GONE WRONG
[00.05, 8th June 2021, Iver Grove]

Not every day runs smoothly,
the bus is often not on time,
it rains while the sun shines,
with none to catch our falls.

Failure may be the only option,
the table may be bare at lunch,
but somehow, no matter the solution,
there is no answer at all.

GOING TO BED
[23.30, 22nd June 2021. Coalpits Heath, Glouc]

Eleven o'clock is heaven,
midnight is just right.
By one o'clock we are done,
two o'clock should be one!

COTSWOLDS COTTAGE
[23.47, 22nd June 2021, Coalpits Heath, Glouc]

The ash falls upon the table
as the laughter shakes the rafters
of the medieval Cotswold cottage
nestled on the chalky uplands
in a village near to Bristol
but closer to old Bath -
where the vicar is a nuisance
and her churches always barred.

The garden falls into the combe
like blossom on a summer breeze,
the pear and the cherry tree
offer shade from the Wiltshire sun.
A wooden chair, a rusty axe,
the bunting o'er the bower path,
the crunch of gravel underfoot,
exotic flowers and verdant grass.

IVER GROVE
[23.27, 5th July 2021, Iver Grove]

Back to the sound of rainfall
on the stable yard cobbles,
the running of the flood
down the internal wall drains.

Old buildings echo older sounds
once common, now long gone
with the clatter of the hooves
across the stony courtyard.

The rose petals wash away
down the cast iron stank,
as the rattle of thunder
shakes more rain from above.

ANNA
[14.01, 11th July 2021, Cannes]

We drank into the early hours,
danced to wild Irish songs,
planted kisses on our lips,
caressed with our finger tips.

As dawn came up we lay down,
slept beyond a decent time,
rose to find our two clocks
ticking to a different chime.

THE ACTRESS
[13.00, 13th July 2021, Cannes]

She came in her red robes
and filled me with long tales,
she lay on the white sheets
naked and longing.

She performed all her horse skills
and submitted to my will,
she moaned my name softly
into the pillow.

She passed into the evening
white robed and red scarfed,
held on to my arm firmly
then went up the red steps.

SILENT IN THE CORNER
[20.00, 18th July 2021, Le Thornet, Var]

He is invisible, silent in the corner,
sipping his red wine and watching
the night pass well into the dawn,
the revelers oblivious to his presence.

So time passes, silent in the corner,
the old man wrestling with his thoughts
with each sip of wine an old memory
returns to shadow his present existence.

SHE IS BACK
[23.44, 27th July 2021, Iver Grove]

She is back to haunt all my thoughts,
beguile me with all her charms,
engaging me with all her tales
of home life and adventure.

Like a fool I'm taken in -
entranced, bewitched by her smile,
tricked by all her little looks
that rip my heart asunder.

What hope have I against such arts -
the darting of her flashing eyes,
the pursing of her sensual lips
on words that hold my wonder.

Can I escape her web-like spell
that binds me like a coiling snake,
or are am I doomed to my fate
of unrequited blunder.

Time will tell if she succeeds
in keeping me so betwixt,
for such strokes can turn the tide
and sweep the swimmer under.

THE LIVING ROOM LODGER
[23.25, 2nd August 2021, Iver Grove]

She wears her red shorts to bed,
her black hair cascading on her skin,
her long brown legs stretched on the sheets,
her dimpled chin resting on her hand,
the bareness of her shoulders inviting kisses,

the arch of her back prepared for giving,
her smile full of warmth and longing,
her eyes full of life and living.

LIFE TAKES ITS TURNS
[23.10, 9th Aug 2021, Iver Grove]

Life takes its turns on the merrygoround,
the horses bobbing up and down,
the lights flashing at blinding speed,
the chatter of the crowd incredibly loud,
the senses all dazed and in a whirl,
all feelings numb, all emotions swirled,
the wurlitzer music drowning out
notions of guilt and lingering doubt.

TIN SOLDIERS ON PARADE
[23.44, 9th Aug 2021, Iver Grove]

The same circle drawn every day,
the routine that comes without thought,
the endless hours spent in ritual,
nothing changing but the clouds
passing overhead without influence.

This is the daily bread of God,
the repetition of all daily chores,
the never-ending tale to tell,
the ever-binding chain we wynd
link by link around our frames.

This same circle our fathers made,
the routine that our mothers taught,
the endless rules to be obeyed -
the everlasting commands we salute
like tin soldiers on parade.

There is no escape from such order,
tablets fetched, scrolls unrolled,
laws to make the circle whole -
no gap to somehow wriggle through,
no escape from growing old.

DAYS GO BY
[00.23, 21st Aug 2021, Iver Grove]

Days go by like pennies through my fingers,
spent on nothing much to remember -

then along comes a day of pound notes
and I find myself creating requerdos.

By surprise comes a fifty pound note,
a day that refuses to be cashed -
a day when everything is free and easy
and makes me happy to be alive.

TUMOUR ON MY BRAIN
[00.17, 28th Aug 2021, Iver Grove]

Today I was told
I had a tumour on my brain.
It was all rather surreal
and impossible to equate.

It was twenty months ago
I had my MRI scan,
Covid in between
and doctors on the run.

What will be the outcome
of this turn of events -
life will be the question
and my life the test.

DESPAIR AS MY ONLY THOUGHT
[21.59, 28th Aug 2021, Iver Grove]

I've had a lucky carefree life,
yet I've learned nothing of this life
except cruelty and a little generosity
to light up the world's wicked ways.

As life ends, surely as it will,
I take stock and chastise myself
for my ignorance of others' suffering,
my lack of compassion and my pride.

Even now as millions in Yemen starve
and thousands face Afghani persecution,
I feel sorry only for myself,
for my own self-inflicted misery.

How the weight of time depresses,
makes the world dark and foreboding,
casts the lonely down into hell,
leaves despair as my only thought.

SUMMER ENDS TOMORROW
[23.19, 30th Aug 2021, Iver Grove]

Summer ends tomorrow, will be gone
leaving us with autumn at our heels,
the return to thoughts of winter
that will in time approach.

It was not a great summer.
It contained too many unknowns,
the continuation of the plague
the orders to stay at home.

What kind of summer was it,
other than one we will forget,
short, and wet, and passing
and gone with no regrets.

EMPTY LONGING
[23.30, 4th Sept 2021, Iver Grove]

When the women you love like no other
leaves loving you more than ever -
the feeling inside is one of empty longing
that lingers endlessly until she returns.

ALL THINGS ARRANGED IN A ROW
[0.10, 6th Sept 2021, Iver Grove]

All things arranged in a row -
the car parked up in the bay,
the shelves stacked with the essentials,
the laundry washed and dried,
the plants watered, carpet swept,
the flowers arranged, dusting done,
dinner cooked, the bedding fluffed
and the day all run.

ANOTHER'S DIRT
[20.00, 22nd Sept 2021, Iver Grove]

I left school fifty years ago
to grovel, bow and scrape,
to make a living in a world
not made for me.

I've sweated, toiled and laboured
with nowt a thing to show

173

except my blistered knuckles
and my broken toes.

Had I been a smarter man,
what tales I may have tell't,
adventures on the high seas,
the wealth I'd spent.

But none of that transpired
in the life that I have led,
despite my dreams of respite,
God has held his breath.

This is not how I foresaw
all those years since I left school,
rising early in the darkness
and trudging home at dusk.

Now I'm old and luckless,
I have grovelled quite enough,
the dirt I've dug to live
is now another's work.

WHEN YOU ARE DRUNK
[00.17, 2nd Oct 2021, Iver Grove]

When you are drunk,
drunk as a skunk,
you don't see anything
except the spinning lights,
the stupid conversation
making your head light.

You make jokes and stuff,
try to pretend you're sober,
but the harder you try
the more you keel over -
even at my age
I can't escape closure.

THE DRUNKEN PHILOSOPHER
[00.31, 2nd Oct 2021, Iver Grove]

This month tells me nothing new,
though it tries to say – listen,
there is still much to learn
on this road for you.

I'm not interested in looking
at what's up ahead,
it may be pretty pictures
but I'm already dead.

Yet my voice is still whispering
'You cannot give up yet,
all that you have experienced
is the sum of all regrets'.

I may fight those opinions
as I want to come to rest,
but the doubts of existence
make me question what is next.

So if I want to tally
all that I've come to test,
then I reckon it is likely
being pissed is not the best.

DAYS LIKE THIS
[20.25, 4th Oct 2021, Iver Grove]

There are days like this -
when I want to get on my donkey
and ride off into the sunset.
To hell with responsibility,
to hell with the people in my life
fading into the night!

THE WHEEL I CAN'T GET ON
22.32, 9th Oct 2021, Iver Grove]

We play our songs, carry along
as if nothing is going wrong,
but underneath the cloak, the hope
has long gone, gone up in smoke.

It's all maybe a joke for some folks
with their life in order, free of bother
and all the little piddly things
that make life hard, disordered.

The grass appears greener, bellies leaner
on that side of the street, a cheat
of a place to be, to be seen
getting on in life, with no strife.

I try to be, but its not me,
its how it is arranged, displayed
before my face, the rat race,
the broken wheel I can't get on.

LOOKING FOR THE LIFE-RAFTS
[22.35, 17th Oct 2021, Iver Grove]

The winds of change are sweeping
through the corridors of our institutions,
our banks and our computing systems.

Nothing is the same as it was,
its all topsy turvy and awash -
afloat on a sea of chaos.

Politicians look for the life-rafts
they have thrown into the sea -
they are going down with the ship.

Holed with their recklessness,
they will drown in their own folly
and we will be left adrift.

FORGOTTEN ART
[23.37, 20th Oct 2021, Iver Grove]

Forgotten art, forgotten artists
who made a living from their craft;
their work moulds in damp attics,
turns yellow in the summer sun,
either hidden from the world
or ignored in frames on faded walls.

Brilliant colours once so dazzling,
bodies etched and superbly shaped,
gone now to hidden vaults
beyond the gaze of the public -
what tragedy awaits us all
when we view what's gone before.

Dwell then not on the future -
those artists lived for their time,
worked to please their paying clients,
somehow kept their souls intact;
for they have left a little something
many dreamt of having done.

ALL SAINTS DAY
[00.22, 1st Nov 2021, Iver Grove]

Halloween ends with an icy blast,
the arrival of November at its heels,
the turn of the clock back an hour
brings on night by late afternoon -
the memories of summer in the chill
of winter, laid bare before us.

I AM A STRATHCLYDER
[00.22, 2nd Nov 2021, Iver Grove]

It is said that I am a Celt,
but this may not be so.
I am from the Damnonian lands,
the Alba people of Strathclyde
where the Rock Kings ruled,
where the people dug the earth,
for coal - and smelted iron
to shape their swords.

There is nothing Celtic in this.
Daanan and their tales,
their four sacred treasures
they carried in their ships
through the Pillars of Hercules
and unloaded in fair Ierne;
which they easily conquered,
but not so in green Strathclyde.

Perhaps I have some Celtic blood,
but what part, what share
of me is that post-Milesian race?
For I cannot see it -
I cannot see it in my eyes,
in my statue or in my gait,
I don't fit the mould …
I do not look Celtic.

Perhaps some Roman intermingled
with my people two thousand years ago.
Some Norman perhaps, some Norse,
some Gael from the Highlands.
But I do not feel it …
I do not believe it …
for I am from Strathclyde,
it is in my bones.

Perhaps memory tricks our thoughts,
makes stories from our desires
to be that which we are not.
But not so with me -
I am a Strathclyder ...
I have my sense of belonging,
of knowing that my people
were the first settlers.

It is a fixed, inherent feeling
in a world of flux and chaos -
to know where I am rooted,
where my seed was spawned,
where my ancestors had laboured,
where my own kind has toiled,
where life has been continuous,
and that I belong.

IT TRICKLES AWAY
[23.32, 15th Nov 2021, Iver Grove]

It trickles away, no matter what,
it trickles every second, every day,
every moment of our existence,
it runs through our lives,
it passes through our hands,
it disappears followed by itself,
in a never ending trickle,
never stopping, just trickling on.

MOTHER
for Valerie Tucker
[23.41, 15th Nov 2021, Iver Grove]

She died of cancer -
quickly she passed away
as if life had gone,
the reason to live, departed,
the desire to see the dawn
not in her gift to have,
so she faded quietly,
went without a fuss,
so no-one would notice.

THIS LONDON LIFE
[18th-19th Nov 2021, Iver Grove, Train to Penzance]

This London life, what life is there
for those living on the streets,

for those who live to pay the rent,
for those who struggle with their health.

Where are the mountains & the seas,
the fresh green uplands, golden beaches,
the places where normal humans heal,
where eyes lift up beyond the concrete.

This London life of toil and greed,
this town of anguish and broken dreams,
this place that offers no relief,
that shakes the core of self-belief.

Lost, not found, in every borough,
the city oozes wealth and power,
eats the soul each languorous hour
of all who live and work there.

Lured by riches beyond the grasp,
seduced by fame that never lasts,
sucked in by flashing clubland lights,
the doormen bow, the waiters laugh.

And laugh they do with tired eyes,
thinking of their late night bus,
the life they thought of passing by,
today dismissed with a sigh.

This London life, its double lines,
the rules that keep all in check,
the rules that often seem to warp
for the few that bend them best.

This life, this town of workers,
these hordes of slaves and toilers
from distant lands and furthest corners,
having left behind their fathers, mothers.

This town, this place of sorrow,
this city of Sodom without Gomorrah,
its church spires and museum domes,
its stone palaces, and forbidden walls.

Each passer-by with glazed eyes,
each step a step just too far,
each look a furtive glance,
each bump or touch just pure chance.

Every moment the Bow Bells ring,
"Where is God? Who is he?"
Is God some conjured myth,
set to keep us turning cheeks.

What thoughts churn on every face
passing by at such a pace.
Where are these folks going now,
have they arrived, or hurry still?

Who can judge, make prediction
of others' aims, their life's religion.
What goals are such actions for,
what door will open, to what land?

This London life, grinding on,
day to night, dusk to dawn,
while others sleep, others yawn
and pass into another dawn.

WINTER STORM (ARWEN)
for Stuart Gillies
[19.55, 27th Nov 2021, Iver Grove]

The winter storm has reached shore,
pounding on our battered doors,
howling at our shuttered glass,
creaking at our timbered floors,
seeping through every crack,
bringing cold and driving snow.

YOUTH & KNOWLEDGE
[23.01, 28th Nov 2021, Iver Grove]

Memories brought on by cold
can drown us in their depth,
leave us floundering and gasping
at why we were so inept
with our youth and knowledge
that now seems so wasted
on the young we watch paddling
in waters infested with sharks.

THE FIRST SNOW
[10.05, 2nd Dec 2021, Iver Grove]

The first snow arrived,
lay on the rooftops
like confetti at the church.

It blew in the wind,
the yellow sun blazing
on the frozen fields.

THE 2AM TICKING
[01.50, 5th Dec 2021, Iver Grove]

The two a.m ticking of the clock,
all is quiet, there is no talk,
only breeze racing through the trees,
rushing on to somewhere next.

What know we of this world,
never silent, earnestly at work,
spinning on through time and space,
while we hang on to what we've got.

The void of night, long and dark,
the clock ticks on, the wind howls,
cowers the meek to turn to sleep,
to hide away until the dawn.

PRAYING FOR PROSPERITY
[01.10, 10th Dec 2021, Iver Grove]

Prosperity eludes the wanting,
happiness is lost on the wild,
envy is the disease of the wealthy,
greed is the worst kind of crime.

Hope fails to rekindle kindness,
pride loses the man in himself,
love is the refuge from despair
when anger is abroad everywhere.

Lessons never learnt are forgotten,
minds that are broken are hurt,
healing is time's only blessing,
wealth a gift beyond words.

MAY THEY ROT IN HELL
[00.35, 30th Dec 2021 Marbesa, Spain]

Wealth, power and money is nothing -
without morals the individual is bankrupt,
nothing more than a pimp of depravity,
an exponent of corruption and abuse,
a defiler of dignity and integrity -
a pariah on society and individuals

destroyed by association and connection;
all they touch is tainted and despoiled
by the involvement and influence
they waste to make our lives hell.

LITTLE SECRETS
[00.31, 31st Dec 2021, Marbesa, Spain]

Time will come again to save
the moments I thought lost for good,
found again to be renewed,
reunited by somehow freshly viewed,
each moment really something new
that comes into existence.

With each loss space is made
to occupy the vacant slot,
empty plots of unmarked time,
endless in the emptied mind
seeking moments to be refined
and kept as little secrets.

THE MARBESA BIRDS
[14.00, 2nd Jan 2022, Marbesa, Spain]

The Marbesa birds are full of chat,
back and forth from branch to branch,
they hop with all the joy of Spring
though we are in the winter months.

What joy to hear their endless chirps,
to watch their everlasting play,
devoid of all our human traits,
we are slaves whilst they are free.

THE WOLF MOON
[22.01, 17th Jan 2022, Iver Grove]

It hung overhead in the freezing cold,
cobalt shadows in the winter gloom,
the dogs were silent in their makeshift beds,
nothing stirred, not a leaf fell -
the hoar glazed the sheets of slate,
covering the night in a misty haze.

BENEATH THE MILKY WAY
[20th Jan - 9th Feb 2022, Iver Grove]

What is important in life -
bananas, sunshine and sleep,
simple joys, essential oils,
a lover on your knee.
No endless journeys going nowhere,
no dark nights all alone,
no egos getting in the way
of truth and love.

Why then is it not so,
not plain sailing on a breeze?
Why is there always strife
and companions full of fear?
Is there something in the air,
the planets playing with our heads,
pulling on our darkest thoughts,
revealing all our faults?

Why can't we just be happy,
grateful for the life we have,
accept that this is what it is,
and this is our given lot.
Is that too easy to accept,
to have a humble life of joy,
to ease through days with a smile
and never be at odds?

No, something in our stubborn nature
makes us rail against the norm,
forces us to wail and cry
that the world is unfair.
Unfair of what, or with whom,
the Earth rotates around the sun,
the sun drifts where it might
through the cosmic storms.

Do we know what that means,
what it does to our thoughts?
Can we control the sky above,
or beneath the earth we trod?
Can we grasp the air we breathe,
or touch the sky up above?
Do our dreams exist at all,
are we real or not?

What forces then guide us on
to do the things we always do,
the things we repeat each day,
the blood coursing through our veins,
our ever beating fragile hearts,
our breathing done without thought,
all that's taught, or learned along
the ever winding way.

Day in day out we carry on
as if we have a special plan,
as if we are in control
of all we think we can -
Our schemes, so ably laid,
too often are of a mould,
a dozen times done before,
a hundred times or more.

Our genes dictate who we are,
what we will in time become,
our fate is what our fathers were
or what our mothers bore -
a timeless pattern to observe
the warp and weft of humankind,
we are the fabric of the past,
the cloth of time.

You may say it is not so,
each and all are unique,
I protest we are clones
with mutation sequence flaws.
The flaws that give us our quirks,
give us all our different looks,
leave us with the oddest views
that destiny ignores.

And so with our hidden secrets,
strewed across our wrinkled brows,
there are no tales to unfold,
they have all gone before.
We present nothing new,
our actions are just as tame
as those folks now long gone
who thought the same.

The danger lurks in belief
that this time round we are special,
somehow different from the past,
a breed somehow set apart.

But what folly in such talk,
blind we walk towards the cliff,
without a glance up ahead
we come to grief!

The sun will spin around the skies,
we will spin around the sun,
the Milky Way will always be
the place where we come from.
Two hundred million years or more,
our planet whizzes off and back,
our lives are but a single blink
of the cosmic eye.

What wisdom can we add to that,
to know we know not a thing,
our mindsets fixed upon ourselves,
not what has made all of us.
It is not some woolly thought up God,
conceived and watching us with love,
it is not some unseen hand
turning us back to dust.

If we know what life's about,
we would loudly shout it out,
but timid as we are at heart,
there are some convinced they know
that life is one endless wheel
where conscious thought is not real,
it is some long waking dream
we must escape from.

If so, then why all our fuss
to etch and scratch, make our mark,
record our time with our pens,
erect tall buildings with our names?
Why put our dates on our tombs?
Why etch in marble *lest we forget*?
Have all our rituals set in stone
while our planet spins?

Can we not see beyond the stars,
blinded by all that glimmer,
the black we think is a void,
that void containing what we are?
And what we are is not clear,
its something strange to ourselves,
that all the knowledge in the world
cannot explain.

And so we spin none the wiser,
hung in space going nowhere,
well, not in any cosmic terms
rooted here on planet Earth,
with our lovers on our knees,
our endless journeys somehow stayed,
no dark nights on our own
beneath the Milky Way.

ALL THE TRAINS ARE BOOKED
[23.52, 9th Feb 2022, Iver Grove]

All the trains are booked,
all the flights are full,
I'm going nowhere fast,
I'm stuck here for the now.
The country's on the move,
and I'm not in the loop -
folk are acting busy
and I'm a Betty Boop.
Winter is hard upon us,
I'm pressed to understand
why folk are whizzing off
with all their travel plans.
Its not our British nature
to go to and fro
when there is cold weather
and the threat of snow.

Perhaps I'm missing something
broadcast on the news,
perhaps I am muddled,
somehow most confused?
For all the trains are booked,
all the flights are full,
and I'm stuck here sitting
on my suitcase like a fool.

Oh well, I better unpack,
take off my winter coat,
hang my woolly hat
and scarf behind the door.
I won't be off to somewhere,
countryside or coast -
for all the trains are full,
and all the flights are booked.

HOMEWARD BOUND
[00.25, 22nd Feb 2022, Iver Grove]

The stag stood on the crest of the hill,
the loch below flat and still,
the afternoon sun on the mountain tops,
snow on the peaks, sleet on the slopes,
the air cleared by yesterday's storm,
the winter halted just for the morn.

Homeward I traveled on snaking roads,
southwards as rivers flooded and rushed,
broken mud banks, green meadows engulfed,
washed away fences, floated off trees,
felled by the fury of the gale force winds,
from far far out on the wild west seas.

TWENTY TWO, TWO, TWENTY TWO
[22.22, 2.2.22, Iver Grove]

Twenty two, two, twenty two,
the hour clicked on to twenty two,
the minute hand ticked to twenty two,
and all the twos aligned as they do,
but never again will the twos read,
forwards, backwards and upways too!

WAR
[01.10, 26th Feb 2022, Iver Grove]

What does war do for every man
but steal his freedom, rob his plans.
What does war do for women
but kill their children, make them cry.

War offers nothing but wild despair,
anguish, grief and endless mourning,
loss of faith that God exists,
debates on whether life's worth living.

War smashes all that's in its way,
does not distinguish right from wrong,
orders passed down are obeyed,
chaos defeats, leaves us decayed.

War destroys all our highest hopes,
makes us flee from all destruction,
makes us turn our back on those
who are not us, who now are foes.

This is war, that thing we dread,
that thing we cannot stop once started,
for we are led by idealists
whose pride prevents a fresh departure.

Thus war rages on with no end,
with no solution but tanks and guns,
this is the way men proceed,
while children pray for lasting peace.

INSTAGRAM
[00.00, 8th Mar 2022, Iver Grove]

I picked up my phone,
I felt incredible calm
as I looked at my babe
I knew she would come,
to pull me in closer,
hug me, and hold me,
and love me forever
if I could forgive her.

ZELENSKI
[20.18, 10th Mar 2022, Iver Grove]

I am not responsible for your problems,
all I want is guns and planes.
I don't care if you somehow starve,
go cold and cry into your borshe.
I believe I'm in the right
and you are all just talk.

I am not the one killing children,
bombing schools and our care homes.
I am not firing missiles,
shelling whole apartment blocks.
I am standing up for freedom
while you won't let me in your club.

Yes, I will take all your warheads,
line them up and face them north.
Yes, I will take all your aircraft
and load them up with nuclear bombs.
I am not the biggest problem,
I am the righteous of us all.

THE ORPHANED CHILDREN CRY
[22.20, 3rd Apr 2022, Iver Grove]

I will keep my counsel,
withhold my thoughts in public,
for I fear I am out of kilter
with a Western world bent
on destroying all our futures,
believing it is right,
and I am wrong.

The lambs will always baa,
for that is all they know,
they will follow the flock,
fall in line as they always do,
the dogs nipping at their heels,
the shepherd with his crook
hooking out the lame.

We are all lambs to slaughter,
knowing not our futures,
led off to war's abattoir
without the slightest whimper.
We are lost and helpless,
hostage to our leaders
and their talk of freedom.

If we were somehow free,
there would be no conflict,
surrender would be victory,
avoidance of all misery
would be the end of war;
the intelligentsia would cry,
the workers thrive.

The root of freedom is love,
love for one's native land.
Bound to a piece of Earth
by some magnetic force,
we give up our lives
for each blade of grass,
each gram of soil.

This is the folly of war,
the means by which we destroy,
obliterate all our progress,
return to the self same soil
as corpses turned to dust;

in the name of freedom,
we destroy.

Call an end to this cause,
lay down your arms,
pack away your bombs and missiles,
disband your soldiers, go home.
The weeping mothers wail,
the orphaned children cry
for those who're missing.

OUR DREAMS
[22.20, 3rd Apr 2022, Iver Grove]

Our dreams are as fragile as ice,
they melt on our aspirations
when we discover we are not in control
of anything at all.

THE ANATOMY OF MY WORLD
[9th Apr - 16th May 2022, Iver Grove]

When I go out into the world,
I fear not what I will meet,
nor who I will greet freely.
I think not of what is out there,
nor of what I will encounter
in the street, or pub.

For as a man of our times,
I enjoy the comfort of companionship,
the beauty of the human form -
for what better is there to look on
but the fair complexion of youth
or the twinkle in an eye.

Thus is conveyed the secret of life -
draws in our attention as such,
as we look to find the uncommon,
the rareness of human nature,
the unique individual of thought
who does not hide their knowledge.

Who does not enjoy the human
who reveals their inner nature,
who happily shares their companionship.
What more can a stranger want
than to receive a nod to their existence,
that we are alive, living now -

not in some ideal world imagined,
nor some dream like member's club
where I am not welcome, for I
seek the company of open friends,
individuals with no inhibitions,
with talk that transcends conditioning.

How else do we know one another
if we live with a false perception
of who we should be, or act like,
for acting is the human condition,
the means by which we lie -
tell our untruths to protect our egos.

Not so when we are well met
to confide with a total stranger;
we discover that we are not alone,
that we are only lost, looking to be found
for who we are as beings -
children wandering, looking for a home.

This home that we have lost,
that we left without knowing where
we were going, or when we would
return to where we started -
that child without preconceptions
of who we are, or will become.

So goes life, and how we revel,
discover the joys and pleasures;
how we love to indulge,
take hold of what is delivered,
served to us without payments
or expectation of some return.

Thus the greatest gifts are free
of consequence and commitment,
given to us without cost,
enhanced and loved with loss,
or pain, or remorse for enjoyment
of being alive and happy.

Oh how these times sustain us,
prevent the Devil from succeeding
in warping our hold on existence.

We discover what we do, not know -
we unravel the complexities of nature,
behold the wonders of the Earth.

Seeing these wonders for the first time,
we comprehend their meaning,
the hidden essence of their structure.

Such joy is always short lived
as we crave some new experience
to lift us from our worries.

For do we not crave distraction
to free us from our concerns?
Our concerns of war, of poverty,
of suffering when it is needless,
the cruelty of men on children,
the neglect of mothers for their sons.

There is no escaping the human condition,
that throwback trait we all harbour,
the cave-man, the tribal traditional
that makes as resentful of strangers,
that makes us suspicious of outsiders,
those who are no different from ourselves.

We make outsiders with our words,
with our imagination and indignation,
our indifference and our behaviour.
So we crave laughter, hide such thoughts,
embrace those we know with warmth,
trust those who are just like us.

We can fall into a sense of well-being,
put up with bad behaviour from some,
the enemy within, those who subvert us,
those who are envious of our ways,
want something from us, some gain
they can take away to profit on.

Who needs rancorous friends,
such shallowness will always out,
will always reveal itself to others,
be made plain and in full sight,
for us to condemn, or forgive,
depending on the severity of the slight.

Is this not the Christian way?
Our capacity to be hard done by
that somehow we willingly overlook
to make allowance, to offer pity
when it is not deserved, even then
we still find some saving grace.

This is the trap of the meek,
the flaw that permits exploitation,
the state of mind that repeats mistakes,
until all self esteem is eroded,
whittled down to loss of status,
diminished joy, and unhappy stasis.

All around us are the broken,
the lost, the seekers of redemption
who stretch for a reaching hand
that we will not refuse to take -
for today we can offer help,
tomorrow we may need the same.

How life turns back on itself;
we climb our hills, take our views,
then homeward, we reach the woods
and lose the path in the dark,
until at last we find we're lost
without a light to guide us home.

Many times and many places
I have found myself thus lost,
yet always there comes a time
when the darkness falls away -
shows the path out the woods
towards an open sunny place.

There the breeze freely blows,
there the sun warms our face
there we find some respite
from all our personal strife,
far from all the inner fights,
the anger and the doubts.

For homo sapiens that we are,
with our warlike take on life,
why do we create our saints?
Why do we present our art
as cultivated, thoughtful, loved
while we destroy all other life?

How can we lie, be so false,
promise those requesting help,
offer up our arms and bombs
to any nation fresh invaded,
when we know that such supplies
will lead us to our own destruction?

We are led by vane idealists
caught up in their need for fame,
drenched in their sense of history,
we somehow will get the blame,
for such leaders lead us down
a path that's in our name.

Is this how we treat our foes,
how we evolved so long ago -
wiping out our Erectus fathers,
erasing evidence of their triumphs,
by discarding their advancements,
leveling all their grand achievements?

I do not know, my life is short,
so short that there is little time
to find out why life is cruel,
so that all I achieve is to survive
until I'm robbed of that spark,
my brief flame before its snuffed.

How nature saves us from ourselves,
glares back at us on darkened pools,
knocks our senses with perfume,
roars at us with spray and fume,
until we know we are small,
and we as humans are such fools.

If I knew how to right all wrongs,
to lead us to the promised land,
then delusion would be my fate,
I'd lead you up the garden path,
line my pockets with endless gold,
write my memoirs before I'm old.

I'm not fit for public office,
who then is qualified to lead us?
I scan the horizon, do not see
a leader standing tall, erect
who I would follow with my heart
and want to vote for with my head.

Am I alone in my disenchantment,
this notion that I'm badly served,
that all we get is fibs and lies,
rogues who justify their acts
with half-spun truths, weak alibi's
they somehow think we will buy.

How delusion blinds the blind
to all but their own self interest,
life repeats itself in endless fashion
like nature reborn in the Spring -
with all its glory budding forth,
ivy poised to stunt and choke.

If we cannot weed good from bad,
then one bad apple taints us all,
such rotten fruit at the top
should be discarded before the rot
permeates to those below -
me and you and countless more.

Our only friend is the sun -
our saviour with each coming morn,
dark forces cannot hide from it,
it reveals all mankind's wrongs,
though we are trying to blot it out
with carbon fuels, atomic bombs.

We are the losers in this fight
to save the planet as it is,
while far off in the distant dark,
a billion light years from now,
destruction lurks beyond our know.
So worry not, ignore such woe.

I say, cherish this life we have,
make it sweet, not a sweat,
not a toil to make ends meet -
live not for your children born,
live not for your selfish wants,
live to laugh, cry, enjoy.

For there are those wrinkled brows
warning us of all life's ills,
their whispers echo in the streets,
rebound along the prison walls
that they try to bind us with -
do I give into their talk?

And health? This will fade from us,
drain away with the years,
pain our gut, bow our legs,
bend our backs until we stoop -
with wretched aches and countless ails,
life will be a long travail.

Will we give up? We have our minds,
to guide us through our later life,
our strength will be in our talk,
our gestures and our kindly acts,
these will soothe our body pain,
help to numb our nightly turns.

While in some far distant land,
an actor squares up to a bear,
a boxer paces round the ring,
the circus crowd blankly stare -
the thud of shells loudly blares
from the backs of elephants.

War is never too far away,
though we may never see the carnage;
death is never in our face,
yet death is going all around us -
the Irish know how to atone,
to wake the living gone.

Someday this will be our end,
yet still we carry on mundanely
to scrimp and save in penny jars,
squirrel pounds, save in tens
saving for some rainy day
that will not someday come to pass.

For pass we will, there is no doubt,
to burn or rot in the soil,
to leave behind our piggy banks,
our treasures, and perhaps a house
bequeathed to our kith and lot,
deserving, or deserving not.

Thus we'll speak beyond the grave,
to sow resentment, strife and anger;
for what is our life's labour worth
but labour unspent in our life -
and with our wills we divide,
calculate our total profit.

How so then, born naked, poor,
do we not depart just as clean?
How have we acquired wealth,
objects hoarded, retained in bulk
just because we've grown attached,
because we've spent a lot of cash?

Wealth is an abstract notion,
totted up on our balance sheets,
how it reads defines statistics,
does not reflect our true worth -
for each life has equal value
in the eyes of us all.

Who does not think this is so,
for if they do, strike them down,
there is no place in our world
for life to have no worth at all -
yet we see at every turn
that this indeed is what unfolds.

Can there be justice in refugees
being carted to some foreign land,
corralled into fenced off camps,
saying it is for their good.
Are we blind to human misery
and to the love of brotherhood?

I wrestle with such noble notions,
how to be the perfect man,
and time and time again I fail
to be the kind of man I can,
or perhaps become, now too late
to help all those in my past.

I struggle with my Christian faith,
not the God bit, heaven forbid,
I tussle with my moral code,
which laws to breach without cause -
the ten commandments are my guide,
that I have broken many times.

Not all, not many, not that often,
I am loathe to state my flaws;
yet I admit I have fallen,
made selfish choices, indulged in sin,
made profit from my neighbour's weakness,
my neighbour's wife, and forgone Sundays.

Yet, I keep only one God,
do not take his name in vane,
I have honoured both my parents,
and never never have I killed -
I have refrained from common stealing,
I do not lie, nor falsely name.

Perhaps then, I am bound for heaven,
or some variation on that theme,
who knows what's beyond that point
if there is such a place at all -
I do not seek to have such comfort,
I'm strong enough for when I'm called.

But och, my head is full of things,
nonsense I need not share aloud,
the sort of stuff that dulls all sense,
the stuff that makes the world turn -
the spin of such minor things
that topples a much bigger world.

What know I of others' thoughts,
of how they think day to day?
How do they cope with God?
What things are in their prayers?
I look about and only see
people working, not their thinking.

Is this the world we inhabit,
a veneer of human concentration,
hands moving in rhythmic action,
completing tasks in automation,
robots in a mindless system
existing in a mindless vacuum?

Perhaps not, not all the time,
the deeper self gets revealed,
spills out in gushed emotion,
opinions shared midst high elation -
then too soon external pressure
returns the robot to safety mode.

Heartless, you may dismiss me cruel,
senseless in a fragile universe,
that I am somehow out of whack
with mankind and mankind's acts
of goodness, kindness and remorse
that I somehow cannot grasp?

Alas, I have no swift defence,
I am bare of all my armour,
I have revealed without pretence
all the thoughts I can present
within the time I've been given
before my time is spent.

For what is a man without a beer,
his loins bared to his lover's quim,
his passions built on his ideas
as he accepts his lover's kiss,
as she offers all that's bliss
to take him off to Timbuktu!

Returning from such fetching journeys,
I realise that life is such -
that moment when in a gush
life is summed up in a rush,
all that's wanted, all there is,
that nothing else matters much.

Enlightenment, how gurus search
for that same thing with their OM's,
and yet its clear to every man,
the reason that we're meant to be -
to carry on, make life continuous,
the purpose of our entirety.

When I forget, my *reason d'etre*,
my mind gets foggy with silly things;
before I can help myself, I have
convinced myself of higher purpose -
I am here to combat wrongs.
I am above all human flaws.

How we delude ourselves,
time and time, and time again,
forget the lessons of our loins,
the clarity of such special joy -
until we once more search for love
to satisfy our primeval lusts.

This is the anatomy of my world,
a beating heart, a throbbing mind,
a passion fueled by senseless acts,
an anger dowsed by loving hands,
my reason stayed by sharing thus
all the stuff that haunts me.

There is no stopping mankind's folly
that scoops us up, slaps us down
in ways we have no voice against,
no way of making madness cease
as headlong on chaos comes,
sweeps us over madness's cliff.

I close my eyes, try to cope,
come to terms with selfish views
driven by a privileged few.
We see clearly they are wrong,
but life is structured in a way,
we cannot rely on our Gods.

Thus each day travels on,
leaves behind a bit of us.
Which part that is its hard to say,
we shed our woes, our memories,
until a birthday card or note
becomes the sum of our decay.

This is life, we can't escape it,
it is not what we were told
when we were young, in our bloom,
with all our hopes and expectations -
no one prepared us for a time
when all our bones would wither.

What then must an old man do
to grasp at something fresh and new?
How does a pensioner reposition,
find himself with new ideals?
How does he throw off the shackles
binding him to his views?

Escape is in all our minds,
but routine dulls, and destroys
most of the thoughts we possess,
pass through us without a stir -
no finger lifted, step-out made,
inertia is the natural state.

The wearied body sags, and sits,
forgoes the use of brain, and legs,
lounges in the summer heat,
wraps up in the winter bed,
moves not an inch without creaks,
groans and huffs, puffs and more.

This old age world is not for me,
though aches and pains may exist.
I live with all my life-worn scars,
all the honours of my wars with
work and foolish misadventures
that have transpired, let me be.

If I have led a different life
that took me down a different road,
I'm sure it would have turned out fine,
I'd still be me, who I am,
perhaps not whole, for who knows,
the roads we take are often potholed.

While money makes up for time,
time becomes far more rare.
Yet how do we value time,
so the exchange is somehow fair?
We give time, get our goods -
coin, or gold from endless crooks.

That is the feeling of those neglected,
left to rot in their dotage, the folks
that faithfully played the game,
obeyed the rules of their betters;
those swine intent on robbing them
to offer crumbs towards their end.

Ah you say, that is not me!
That is some unlucky, lesser sod.
No its not, its most of us,
caught up in this fool charade,
that what we do is for mankind
when in fact we fuel division.

Let's be frank, what are wars
but idiots bent on being kings.
While thinking that they are saints,
they destroy all that's built,
all that has been achieved,
they bring down around our ears.

Nowhere do they note this better
than in that ancient eastern land -
India where Brahma dwells,
where Vishnu tries to keep the peace
while Shiva waits to unleash hell
if all else fails to quell unrest.

The West will never understand
the endless cycle of this order.
We rush into our endless wars
without a thought for tomorrow.
We point our fingers and our guns,
we bully, cajole, don't ask why.

I am no Hamlet seeking revenge,
racked by indecision I am not.
Do I see the world as barren,
a place where there is no light?
No, I am happy in my skin, while
perhaps less happy in my head.

Alas, are we not all a little giddy,
stirred up by our raging hormones,
influenced by our friends' opinions
when sound advice should be silent,
their wild passions pour on out,
and only add to the confusion.

It is little wonder we wish to run,
perhaps to sleep, or to dream,
not to the extent we do not wake -
such thoughts are for the birds.
Whatever life throws at me,
I must endure the worst.

My worst is but a trifle,
to those fleeing for their lives.
What is a moment of discomfort,
compared to the maimed and dying?
How can I declare I am suffering
when there are millions on the run?

These are our times, our present days
as history replays old scores,
revenge carries with it no honour,
only heartache for all involved,
none get to sit on the sidelines,
war's whirlwind wastes, destroys.

Better then to create, and record
the sins of our leaders, their hordes,
their followers of misguided fashion,
the murmurers of certain propaganda;
for truth is in between the lies,
hidden in a cypher of hypocrisy.

In these times, knowledge is useless,
it has little purpose for those in charge,
knowledge is ignored, replaced with slogans,
evil language that thwarts diplomacy.
We are bombarded with hate and loathing -
God is lost in the bellicose fog.

Yet, still we must survive, get on
with our daily mundane chores,
find ways to feed our children,
devise a living from our resources,
keep our minds from exploding,
keep our heads down, obey the law.

What laws are these? Just laws?
Our loyalty to our country's laws?
Without the need to abide by others,
so we can justify great acts of violence
against those beyond our shores
that we have robbed oft times before?

This was Empire, long gone I thought,
then lo, a new era bubbles forth,
the ashes of the past are stirred,
new patriotic fervours soon awake,
young men, the bravado of their youth,
line-up to save our democracy.

What folly have we not remembered,
the blood-shed, all that's gone before,
the millions who lie in Flanders fields,
the countless in the Second War;
Korea, Vietnam, Iraq, Afghanistan -
when will it stop, death be gone!

As Labour Day comes on us again,
I ask why are brothers thus opposed;
the soldier in the field on duty,
the politicians ratcheting the rhetoric,
making their black tie dinner speeches,
believing they have saved us all?

It is not my world, not my dream,
not the fresh air of the hills,
it is the dullness of government thought,
not the waters of the empty dales,
where life eternal springs anew,
far from the contamination of the few.

For few they are, these Oxford men,
debase, immoral, an elite cabal.
Posing as our moral saviours,
they are hiding out in Babel's tower,
shut off from the endless chaos,
they unleash without remorse.

Their grand ideas, their global schemes
that somehow impoverish us all.
Those less literate read the headlines,
the intellectuals soak up every word,
and in between this wide divide
we all get lost.

Yet still, the roses bud into bloom,
the bluebells shelter in the shade,
the blossom falls to our feet,
the brambles ramble underfoot,
the moss bleaches in the sun,
the summer comes despite the gloom.

The cares we have are all internal,
emotions bubbling from our minds.
Injustice creates the greatest anger,
inherent wrongs will make us boil.
Cry we will at evil deeds,
lash out we shall at evil doers.

These precepts are thoughts eternal,
truths that rule our behaviour,
but only lone souls, not collectives
where influencers sway the crowd,
convince with their warped rhetoric,
the reasons to warp the laws.

How do we cope with such situations,
times where we have no control?
Do we riot? Burn down police stations?
Tear up shops? Loot and rob?
How do we show our disapproval
that is now not worth a jot?

Vote? For whom? For what?
The same old lot with different faces?
I have no answer for you here,
I fail to offer any help -
Revolution is not for old men,
and I am old, my youth spent.

This is the anatomy of my world,
the man who pushes on for seventy,
the white male, English speaking,
the type of human in decline -
I'll gladly crumble into dust,
my race has committed untold wrongs.

For whom does that bell toll?
For us and all that's gone before,
the crimes of which we'll never know.
I sense that they are countless,
the sins of the father stick,
and now those sins are woke.

Should we take on our father's sins?
Hell, yes, we are their flesh and bone,
we cannot whitewash out our blood,
pretend we are not the same,
we are clones, remade again
to repeat the self-same wrongs.

And so our children go to school,
unknowing of what they do not know,
their mothers go about their chores,
doing what they always do,
their father's set out their stalls,
life goes on, each day renewed.

Need we care what else transpires
beyond the patch we inhabit?
Can we not ignore these things
far from us and unimportant?
Our focus on our food and home,
leaves no time for far involvements.

Death stalks us all without exception.
An old man gives out to dementia,
thus today, I mourn my loss -
my father firmly left his body,
passed beyond this known dimension,
that place beyond all comprehension.

I will mourn, try to fathom, how
I could have been a better son?
Dredge the depths of my remorse,
dredge the sins I've inherited -
come to terms will all his flaws,
and all the good I've been left with.

Farewell, father, God bless you now,
pass on to a place of peace,
the torture of this life is over,
you can now rest with grace.
Sleep like you always dreamed,
dream on as we cry for thee.

It is with grief we come to terms,
set out on our pilgrim's trek,
walk the long Camino way,
face our trials each new day,
sleep in simple hostel beds,
rise to greet our fellow sufferers.

To contemplate and mourn,
may be all that is expected -
each mile traveled on the road,
another mile to be accepted -
that loss is a load to bear,
to be unburdened with great care.

What then does a pilgrim learn
when sanctuary is finally reached?
Have all the tears now been shed?
Has all the anger now been spent?
Has the mind been fully cleared
of all the troubles death presents?

Perhaps the lesson is less sharp,
for life is blinding at its most,
the aches and pains of being alive
can numb the troubles of the mind -
cramp can offer up some respite
from the torturous unseen kind.

I think somehow this is true,
fatigue of limb can dull all thought,
a pilgrim walking for ten hours,
a little wine to help his legs,
seeks to flop in a bunk,
sleep, to lay his mind to rest.

What happy days, what great joy
to kneel before St James's church,
to have trekked three hundred miles,
or less, or more, however far
to finally reach your pilgrim's end,
to know you've done your penance.

So then, my father gone, I must
come to terms with my loss,
find a way to make my penance,
shed my tears, dismiss my anger,
walk my own Camino way, ask
my questions, find my answers.

I might as well kick off my shoes,
put up my feet, remember when,
a beer in hand, a joint the other,
was the way I could forget,
that life was not a human rat race,
but something meant to be enjoyed.

It is worth reflecting, that youth,
that time of inexperience and blunder,
gave happy days of 'fuck it!',
an overthrow of controlling older folk
trying to mold my existence,
in a way I unceremoniously rejected.

And now here I am – old,
wondering where it all went wrong.
What may have been, only if?
If only I had listened more intently,
or taken all my given opportunities,
joined the rat race, and got on.

Alas that was, and is not me.
I see no racetrack before me,
no predefined white stripped road
leading me on to nirvana -
that happy place of happy people
who have fulfilled their destiny.

The illusion, the misty perfect life,
the ideal that centuries never change.
Marriage, house, children, retirement,
the middle road explained to Crusoe,
the safe unimaginative contentment
he rejected to leave him shipwrecked.

I have monitored my own shipwreck,
the constant need, the desire for rescue
that never comes as the middle road,
that place of safety I abandoned
to be replaced with endless storms,
followed by lulls, calm, and deep peace.

Is this what I recommend? How life
should be lived by you all? -
No, not at all!, it would be folly
to leave the middle of the road,
cross the white line to the verge,
then beyond into the unknown.

There lie dangers – poverty, madness,
crime, murder, and dangerous strangers,
car-wrecked folk, down-trodden wasters,
con-men, prostitutes and their agents;
corruption that knows no borders
on how to break your morals.

There lies the rub, our moral nature,
the depth of our spiritual education,
that upper part of our inner being,
that streak of decency, compassion,
the part that cares for right and wrong
as taught to us as children.

Without a moral compass, that pathway,
that middle road heading to heaven
has a white line that's wonky, broken,
that can veer off in a curve to the verge,
and over, disappearing into the morass
of loss, despair, 'til white is black.

I wouldn't wish that on anyone,
well, not anyone who has a good heart;
for many are ill-suited to wandering
and unable to find their own path.
Better then they take the middle road,
than test their moral fortitude.

At my age, it is too late to re-trek,
return the way that I have passed.
But I have re-found the middle path,
I am back on the white line road -
and on this ancient worn way, I have
re-encountered many friends of old.

Yet still, I am tempted to regress,
return to that wicked, lawless verge,
disappear into the sodden morass,
lose myself in all that mess,
expose myself to the perverse,
and believe I am being progressive.

What delusion wraps the selfish,
those individuals escaping from themselves,
the malcontents full of imperfections,
always attempting to find solutions,
solutions to their own inner flaws
that somehow can never be resolved.

And what of location, where we live?
How we live to get through our days?
The cooking that we do, the eating out,
when we are too tired to labour?
What are the daily chores we do,
the cleaning, and the rubbish recycled?

I am not proud of my humble abode,
two rooms with a kitchen attached,
a spare room for my impoverished friends
who are more nomadic than myself;
those friends who want more from life
who possess nothing but their names.

I can applaud such reckless living -
for they are alive, not dead inside;
they seek out that alternative pathway
that we know they will never find -
they travel with faith and great hope,
with no care to arrive.

A beer to their lips, a sip of wine,
this makes their world go round.
There is always talk of children,
that somehow they have not had -
and though they live for romance,
love never stays beyond the last dance.

What kind of living is this charade?
Are my friends fools, or lost?
No, I say, they are God's people,
kind in their ways, and in their hearts -
they have a love that is not returned
by lesser mortals intent on harm.

Let such friends inherit the Earth
as they surely do with their modesty,
their get-rich-schemes come to nought
as they do not believe they can be rich -
richness is a notion far removed
from those folk who live for profit.

In every age there are great potentates,
individuals who rise out of the muck,
ascend to such heights, that looking up
they make many others dizzy with envy -
they attract many imitating disciples
who replicate by trying to be like them.

Not for me, my friends are angels
compared to the avarice that abounds,
permeates every aspect of our culture,
makes decent honest people bent,
corrupts the young at an early age,
bends morals to the will of the state.

I am not adverse to bending the light,
Einstein proved that nothing was straight,
but how much bend can we make
before we break the stretching line -
infinity at both ends, yes ….
but not until broken beyond repair.

This can be a very lonely world.
My charity is not universal -
I can walk by beggars in the street,
look them in the eye, say hello,
but I do not extend a hand
to lift them from their poverty.

What is wrong with how I am made?
Why can I not help the most needy?
I will lend to a friend without repayment,
but to a stranger my purse is shut.
Is not the beggar sunken in despair
worth helping all the more?

Dickens is silent on this matter,
his foundlings, the boys of the rich,
underwent the greatest deprivation
in order to emerge as a super breed -
the blood of a distant relative, always
made the foundling crave for cream.

Not so for the stories still untold,
the slavery that inequality brings,
the attitude that the poor cannot cook,
they reason they must be given food,
excused as too lazy to feed themselves;
how absurd such statements look.

This is how revolutions begin, first
the hunger, then nowhere warm to sleep.
It is little wonder that mobs collect,
ransack stores, break into houses
when they are living on the edge
with not a thing to lose but their souls.

For this purpose has all learning been
a selfish journey to a pointless end?
A hedonistic sojourn to please myself,
my bouts of altruism but a thin disguise
for my failure to change this world
not made in the fashion I desire?

God, where am I in all this?
This void of human chaos and turmoil,
this Earth hell-bent on being destroyed
for some vague advantage I cannot see?
Some advantage I cannot condone
so our descendants can survive on Mars?

What folly permits such stupidity?
What reasoning dictates such policy?
We spend our Saturdays watching football,
our Sundays, Mondays, watching football,
until we are numb of all feeling -
until we are zombies with no freedom.

This is how we use our leisure,
vent our tribal affiliations through sport,
pick sides, curse the opposition,
take every little skirmish as a war.
For men believe their tribe is special,
worth the fight, worth dying for.

This is how nations come to clash,
take up arms, kill each other,
not because of right or wrong,
not because of greed or want,
but something more akin to loyalty
to their tribe, their clan, and lords.

What store they put in their faith
that they are the chosen ones -
that God is wholly on their side
as they maim, destroy, wipe out
any opposition to their tribe,
blind to all other ways of life.

This is democracy, devised by barons,
it is feudalism by another name,
the gatekeepers of Oxford, Cambridge,
educate the lackeys to do their bidding;
thus the sons and daughters of the poor
are corrupted to the barons' system.

This system of learning ingrains inequality,
for the barons cannot function without serfs,
and serfs we are to our jobs,
and serfs we are to our houses,
and serfs we are to taxation
until the day we die.

It is no wonder we search for an exit,
try to get off the white lined road,
attempt to find a better end-game
than the one we are currently on
as we zigzag and dodge convention
with our own internal monologue.

This is the anatomy of my universe,
retreating to my shed to make manly
things, not to slave, but to resist,
to contemplate life and to wrestle
with the complexities of my universe -
the world I have created in my head.

Existing solely in my inner temple,
my scrolls, the summation of my thoughts,
my tabernacle unseen by others,
the laws by which I live my life,
at odds at time with convention,
at other times, falling into line.

Then, when something wrong is right,
when enough people buy the lie,
when for some the only way to succeed
is to lie all the way to the top -
woe betide the liar when found out,
descent is swift, the fall immense.

And so master criminals run countries
from the greatest nations to the small,
liars abound at every government level,
as lying is how politics is done -
the vassals of the robber barons
trying themselves to be barons in turn.

As I drag my pen in contemplation,
I look up and gaze at the sun,
nothing matters, they'll soon be gone,
the politicians and their baron gods,
dictating all their daily dodges
while the sands of time run on.

What part play I in this rot,
all this shameful grab for wealth?
What time can I give to this desire
to live my life like a lord?
I'm little more than a beggar
writing this for no reward.

Happy thus to speak my mind,
on no man's time am I being paid.
I don't expect to be well read,
but I'd like my friends to understand
that all the things I do or say,
there's some thought to my rants.

For in old age, you are forgotten,
rarely seen at fine events,
rarely asked to come to dinner,
rarely visited by old friends;
for they too are kept in hiding
by illness, children, and long regrets.

What an age this is, Covid years
laying low the very best -
destroying joy in every way,
preventing us from shrugging off
a decade of festering waste of
xenophobia and financial chaos.

Will the good times soon return?
I cannot see how this can be,
the West has made its wicked bed
and now must lie with its partners;
I dream the bear will not wake
and set on us Armageddon.

Still we stumble on oblivious
to the events that may unfold.
No one can fully know the future,
but history shows what's gone before.
How the past once more returns
to haunt us, make us abhor war.

Not yet, the call for peace is called,
no whispers in our listening ears;
the silence is like the ocean's roar,
a constant static, nothing more,
no single voice to say aloud
what I feel my heart craves for.

Peace, to sleep, perhaps to dream,
to have my final years in quiet,
an old man's hope in a time
when others are for causing strife -
I'll say my prayers, keep right from
wrong, cherish time before its gone.

Thus is the anatomy of my universe,
in part of course, not the whole,
for who can set out in words
the wide expanse of their mind?
For when I go out into the world,
my mind is mine.

BLOOD CLOTS ON THE LUNGS
[20.50, 20th May 2022, Wexham Park]

Lying in a hospital bed,
oxygen tube up my nose,
my hand stayed by a finger clip,
my breathing shallow
as my blood clots thin.
I am no way near death,
but I am nearer than
I've ever been before.

NURSE KRISHNA
[22.26, 21st May 2022, Wexham Park]

Krishna pushed down on my tubes,
red, yellow, green and white,
checked my data every hour,
watched o'er me throughout the night,
turned the lights down on my sleep,
returned at dawn with my pills,
helped to save me from myself -
Oh Hari Krishna, nurse of mine.

OVERWHELMED BY LOVE
[23.15, 25th May 2022, Iver Grove]

Rarely have I been brought so low
in life, to discover my mortality;
but now that it has occurred,
I can rejoice at the care and kindness
given to me so generously by
those who know we are vulnerable
to illness and near death scenarios.

With love I have been overwhelmed
by those who surround me,
those folk who know me best,
those who care for me most,
those who I can rely on -
that small troupe of friends,
in number more than I knew.

To this loyal band, I thank you,
for showing me I am not alone.
You have restored my flagging faith
that life had gone to the dogs.
Not so! I am now reassured
that all is well with people
and that it is I who is flawed.

MY FINAL ABODE
[22.38, 4th June 2022, Ardbrecknish, Argyll]

Back in the land of my birth
with the mountains and lochs,
with the green and the blue,
with its wide expanse of freedom,
free from the London muck,
from the Southern money grubbing,
dragging me down to the Devil
while God lives in the hills.

If you are in the know,
then you will know my feeling,
my longing for clean air,
my desire for wide space,
my foregoing of the rat race
to find my own place -
where I can grow old
and rest without fear.

Where are the swifts and swallows,
the martins and the small buntings,
the wildlife that abounds, missing,
not found in old London,
where no park can replace
the diversity of nature
found on the wild hillsides
of the land that I love.

When will I break free,
realise that I have traded
a life of mid-wealth

for the price of my health.
While the wilderness calls me,
to be where I come from,
I'm a foolish old man
to ignore such advice.

And there rests my quandary,
the old ways and my ways
always tugging on me
to make up my mind -
making me restless
to give up on success,
to reject all I've built
in return for long life.

I live by my choices,
make my many decisions,
foolishly or selfishly,
peddle my code -
while the mountains and lochs,
wait for my homecoming
that I cannot guarantee
will be my final abode.

THE THINGS WE SEEK
[22.13, 12th June 2022, Arbrecknish, Argyll]

Those things we seek are eternal,
love, friendship and respect -
there cannot be a lesser goal,
nor wealth beyond such aspects;
for human nature so triple bound
demands we find this for ourselves.

NOTHING LEFT TO GIVE
[22.39, 12th June 2022, Ardbrecknish, Argyll]

When there is nothing left to give,
emptiness fills the void of being,
day to day in some shadowed life,
between the memories and the hours
that pass without paused respite.

From drudgery to the banal,
the minutes tick with the tide,
fast running the seconds slide
into the abyss of lost time
without a record of their passing.

Doomed to repeating *ad infinitum*,
the sum of errors made before -
there is no escape from the certainty,
that there seems to be no purpose,
none at all - to give any more.

AS THE GROWN-UPS PARTY
[23.33, 15th June 2022, Ardbrecknish, Argyll]

And so the days go by,
the actors deliver their lines,
the clouds drench the mountains,
the day never becomes night,
the laughter rings out loudly,
the swallows dart to their nests,
the loch shivers in the mist,
the children all sleep soundly,
as the grown-ups party.

THOSE WHO DEPART
[02.01, 18th June 2022, Ardbrecknish, Argyll]

As friends depart, new ones arrive,
this is life, how it works.
No-one is here to take our hand
to guide us to the promised land.
We are travelling on alone,
or think we are to the end -
as we are watched from afar
by those who have departed.

WHEN YOUTH WAS ON US
[20.19, 26th June 2022, Ardbrecknish, Argyll]

What happened to the Monday poker nights?
The chilly and the Texan beer?
The guys from Austin with their talk,
the gals from Anchorage, their walks,
the sun coming up on their love,
the days when youth was on us.

Those days rest in crop-farm grass,
gone into the distant world,
the rain descends like mountain mist,
jungle drenched the wildlife hides,
no sun to warm their sodden nests,
unlike when youth was on us.

YOUR DRAMA
[23.47, 6th July 2022, Iver Grove]

Your drama is not my drama,
but I wish it was -
then we would see eye to eye
that all that divides us
is actually what unites us,
and the drama would go away
to be replaced by the love
that we know we have.

THE WOMEN ALL LEFT
[20.05, 8th July 2020, Iver Grove]

The women all left, there is bliss,
silence in the house, quietness,
space to dream and float,
to rest and listen to the sounds
beyond the open window, the summer
heat stifling the distant muffle
of cars and cackling rooks.

MY ALTERNATIVE TO KILLING
[23.45, 10th July 2022, North Wraxall, Wilts]

I am not of this generation,
all that I create is worthless,
it has no value to my peers.
There is no doubt that some is good,
but does not sell, give return.

I know that I am an artist,
I make my art for myself,
to give purpose to my life,
otherwise I might want to kill
or blow my brains out.

TODAY WAS PERFECT ENOUGH
[00.08, 11th July 2022, North Wraxall, Wilts]

Summer can heal all ills -
the wild abandon of nature,
proof that eternity extends
beyond all human folly -
the heat of the midday sun,
the shade from the afternoon warmth,
the shadows of lingering evening,
the moon in the deep blue dusk -

tomorrow may bring new troubles,
but today was perfect enough.

IF I SAY TOO MUCH
[22.29, 11th July 2022, Iver Grove]

If I say too much to you,
I will recall my depravity, my sins,
expose too much of my mind,
cloud your vision of my nature,
turn you from a lover to a hater
of all that is me, who I am.

THE MAN WITH KNOWLEDGE
[23.29, 11th July 2022, Iver Grove]

Perhaps it is better to have nothing to say
than going on about the weather;
too much prattle, not enough thought,
too much nonsense, not enough wisdom;
the man with the gab can be interesting,
but the man with knowledge a treasure.

THE LITTLE PINK COTTAGE
[19.25, 13th July 2022, Withindale, Longmelford]

The silence is high in the trees,
sparrows hopping on the garden swing,
white umbrellas on the lawn,
cocktail in a dark stemmed glass -
the candelabra under an awning,
spread before the little pink house.

California culture in staid village England,
poetry blasting out from white speakers,
scooter parked on the driveway,
cat licking eagerly on its paws -
marijuana billowing in the evening air
as the hostess serves up her art.

FORTY DEGREES
[21.00, 17th July 2022, Iver Grove]

This heat, this record heat,
baking our skin, burning our grass.
Is it what they say it is?
Global warming? Perhaps it is so,
the proof that we are selfish,
that we are incapable of change.

We are stuck in our ways,
unwilling to compromise, give in
to the notion we are stupid,
incapable of reading the tea leaves -
that many will perish elsewhere,
and here, because of our conceit.

AS OUR PLANET SLOWLY BURNS
[19th July 2022, Bilbao, Spain]

Love the Earth, or save ourselves,
is each the same, or different worlds?
The collective whole is the goal, or
is individual survival more important?
I know not which is right,
the socialist in me for the former,
or the capitalist cad all for survival
at any cost to the world.

And thus our little planet suffers,
human selfishness, personal greed.
The poor lament their stricken state,
the rich lament that the poor exist.
So none know what is right,
though each has their own view,
helplessly we all plod along
as our planet slowly burns.

LIFE IS A CHORE
[14.28, 20th July 2022, Santander, Cantabria, Spain]

God on my left shoulder,
beer in my right hand -
surviving somehow.
Oh life is a chore!

THE MIND IS A TANGLE
[14.28, 21st July 2022, Oviedo, Asturias, Spain]

The mind is a tangle of thought waves,
rippling with torment, never calm,
wave after wave on a surf board,
the ride is rough, brutally hellish,
yet somehow it comes to an end;
the storm abates, the sun comes out,
a coffee or beer numbs the pain -
joy returns to make the day okay.

LEON
[20.57, 21st July 2022, Leon, Castille, Spain]

The light played on the Roman wall
as evening fell on old Leon,
the chatter rose into the night
as young and old strolled the streets.

Arm in arm the lovers drifted
with quivered lips and hungry eyes,
those beyond such tender love
watched wisely as they passed on by.

THE PILGRIM'S DORMITORY
[14.53, 26th July 2022, Santiago D'Compostela,
Galicia, Spain]

They sleep like children in their bunks,
the pilgrims tired and worn,
no sound from their lifeless forms
resting in their hostel dorm.

Bunked in fours, some in eight,
their boots lie scattered on the floor,
backpacks propped against the walls,
drying clothes, draped on the doors.

These modern pilgrims in their shorts,
sporty gear and logo'd caps,
on the march across the world,
trudging on come what comes.

Sleep they now in their beds,
is God somewhere in their prayers?
The window open to the night,
stars shining light on their dreams.

THE SUN
[17.28, 26th July 2022, Santiago, Galicia]

All that free energy,
burns as well as warms,
desert life is no life,
we crave it in winter,
curse it when it scorches -
that blazing orb of fire
we cannot blot out,
nor wish to hide.

OUR MODERN MAGAZINES
[20.29, 26th July 2022, Santiago, Galicia]

Our modern magazines are on the web,
pictures of 'me' and 'me's' friends,
Hello magazine without the cost,
free to look at, free to toss into
the bonfire of vanity tosh -
to be reminded many years hence
that what we post, outlives our death.

HOME TO UNFINISHED THINGS
[00.24, 2nd Aug 2022, Iver Grove]

Home to work on unfinished things,
home to my small rented abode,
home to recall everything wrong
with all the years that have passed.

Is there comfort in homely things,
or something sad, that this is all -
the summation of a life's work,
a few soft comforts despite the slog.

Is this the burden of age -
a looking back with some regrets,
wishing that time had dealt
a better hand than the one I played.

Home then to unfinished things,
home again, to get on with life,
home to discover I have traveled
and arrived without a glitch.

FOREBODING
[23.44, 3rd Aug 2022, Iver Grove]

It is to move on in life,
always there is a sense of loss,
foreboding that things will worsen,
go from bad to downright rotten.

THE SUN BEATS DOWN ON US
[22.25, 10th Aug 2022, Iver Grove]

The sun beats down on us,
shows no mercy,
boils our blood, dries our sweat,
until we are almost dead.

This is our daily life,
we run from the sun,
migrate north in survival,
run the perils of traffickers.

We cross seas in tempest,
to be detained in camps,
to be returned to our desert,
too thirsty to escape.

NO GRAND PLAN
[00.29, 12th Aug 2022, Iver Grove]

The heat soaked my bones.
Benin a distant mystery,
elephants always in my thoughts,
bad politics bringing misery,
the cold months to come,
business as usual someplace,
love just over the horizon,
never far away.

NO WAY TO BE
[00.23 18th Aug 2022, Iver Grove]

The battles rage on in the East,
now the heatwave has passed,
autumn is on its way -
that cold Russian winter wind
will bite us all, make us freeze,
for we have not found peace,
found no way to talk.

There is no resolution, just war,
only more artillery and bombings.
It is no way to live,
it is no way to be -
when will we ever learn
that war brings on death,
leaves us nothing at all.

TIME TO TURN OUT THE LIGHT
[23.18, 22nd Aug 2022, Iver Grove]

Have I any more to say to myself?
Any more images to drag from my past?
Any more emotion I have not vented?
Any more bullshit to get out?

Is there anything left to put down,
to drag from my tired soul?
Any glimmer of wondrous fact?
Any information worth some note?

No, I reckon I am burnt out,
ready for the scrapheap of life.
I've nothing more to say on anything.
It is time to turn out the light.

DREAM OF ESCAPE
[23.35, 24th Aug 2022, Iver Grove]

Oh to escape to some unknown place,
up in the mountains in southern lands,
somewhere olives drop from the trees,
where vines hang over the eaves,
where morning comes with a gentle breeze,
and sunset lingers forever.

AND SO SUMMER ENDS
[00.49, 1st Sept 2022, Iver Grove]

And so summer ends, autumn comes
as it always does without fail.
There is sadness and some regrets
for time lost while making hay.

The changes have been too few,
with plans not fully thought out,
going into autumn without a vision
of how the winter will pan out.

THE RAIN HAS FINALLY COME
[22.45, 1st Sept 2022, Iver Grove]

The rain has finally come
to end the drought, the burnt
soil, the scorched grass, ochre
coloured, the severed leaves
lying thick on the dry wasteland
of this summer's pastures -
the meadows parched, the fish
in the ponds left thrashing
on the dust cracked earth.

WHETHER TO COMMIT THE CRIME
[00.43, 3rd Sept 2022, Iver Grove]

I sat in the bar with my pint,
debating whether to commit the crime,
white collar worker paperwork scam
that could lead to doing time.

I wrestled with my dire state,
penniless and hopelessly facing debt.
I tried to pretend fraud was fine,
it harmed no-one but the state.

I pondered the enormity of my situation,
the desire to escape, get ahead,
I imagined my future, my other life
if I corrected some figures creatively.

I slowly drained my ultimate pint,
put on my coat, made for the door,
left the pub in a sober mood,
determined to change my life for good.

As I staggered homeward quite drunk,
a little voice told me to stop,
to consider all that I would lose
if I siphoned off what I proposed.

No, I was foolish, silly at most,
to even consider committing fraud,
so I went home, lay on my bed,
woke up innocent with no regrets.

THE THUNDER ROARS
[01.04, 5th Sept 2022, Iver Grove]

The thunder roars. Clear sounding,
echoing as the rain falls heavy
outside my open window,
the roller blind sucked out
as the lightning flashes.
There will be flooding
on the empty roads.

THE QUEEN IS DEAD
[16.12, 9th Sept 2022, Rottendean, Sussex]

The Queen is dead, now we have the King.
Life will change, Empire finally gone.

We can now give up all glory,
adjust to our post imperial past,
stop throwing punches about
like a boxer past his prime.

We have done our allotted rounds,
lets quit before we are on the ropes.
The Queen was the link to Commonwealth,
the nations we dictated to before.
Its over. Let's not prolong the pain.
Elizabeth is dead. King Charles reigns.

THE CHINESE DELEGATION
[01.00, 17th Sep 2020, Iver Grove]

They have banned the Chinese delegation
from attending the funeral of the Queen;
fifteen hundred million people
snubbed by our haughty politicians.
How blind they are to mourning,
how petty in their motivations
to act like petty potentates
while guarded by tin soldiers.

THIS IS HOW IT IS
[01.07, 28th Sept 2022, Iver Grove]

Empty. This is how it is.
How days pass, mornings come,
nothing seems to stick.
Women come and flee,
friends stay for a bit,
cousins die, memories fade.

MY SILENT FILM FLICKERS ON
[01.01, 6th Oct 2022, Iver Grove]

The road ends, the day goes,
my silent film flickers on -
pictures of lost summer fun,
raindrops wiped away like tears,
apes swinging on a rope,
cricket but a distant dream,
time passing like my ship
on its voyage to Zanzibar.

I'M RUNNING OUT OF WORDS
[10.20, 8th Oct 2022, Iver Grove]

I'm running out of words, my energy is spent -
nothing new to speak of, nothing new to trumpet.
I'm a worker tired by labour, my routine is numbing,
I see no quick escape but that of slumber.

I AM DONE
[00.05, 12th Oct 2022, Iver Grove]

I am done, can do no more,
I have reached the cliff edge
of my stock and trade.
This is the end, my final poem
to complete my work.
I cannot predict how long
I will live beyond these words.

The poet in me is dying -
I can no longer rage against the light,
I am seeking peace,
my anger is spent,
I am discarding my pen.
I wish you a sweet adieu,
farewell friends, farewell,
with tears I say goodbye.

THERE ARE DIFFICULTIES IN LIFE
[15.45, 6th Jan 2023, Calahonda, Spain]

There are difficulties in life,
health, wealth, weather, shelter,
but none taxes the human mind
more than our own kind – people.

Wisdom – that ability to learn,
confirmed by famine, plague, and war
proof we are perennially in competition
with everyone we ignore.

Some argue against such assertions,
some will go on causing more strife,
for it is in our nature to fight,
play out our fears on others, right?

This is the spiral of difficulty,
the obstacles to much better lives -

the monks in their caves meditating,
the loners hiding in the wild.

NEIGHBOURS
[6th Jan - 6th Apr 2023, Calahonda, Berlin, Iver]

John is middle aged and full of sorrow
for all his tomorrow's never come,
alone he sits on his back-door stairs
contemplating what he has borrowed
without saving a penny for his heirs -
the children he never had,
the lovers who had always left,
the tears he has never shed
now held back by his fear of death.

Ann got up, looked in the mirror,
where had time fled to leave her so,
bereft of all that once was good,
left her with her aging looks,
she crossed herself, crossed the room,
poured a gin, picked up a book,
immersed herself in Norma Jean
and tales of woe in Hollywood.

How time passes like a bus
full of people going home,
every stop a painful lull,
every jerk and bump a trial,
the weary hanging on for life,
the impatient cursing every time
the bell's pushed to stop advancement.

George creates his own misdeeds,
needs no push to curry mischief,
from dawn to dusk he's at work
applying his arts to his advantage -
he wastes no hours on self inspection,
digs no dirt on his actions,
he whistles off his own deceptions,
notes none of the consequences -
without an ounce of weighed reflection.

Mrs. Winthrop doesn't feel so sure
the world is spinning very smoothly,
she's been spooked by the theory
that houses will be built on the moon,
then Mars, then a hundred other planets
so far from home there's no way back,

that for her is totally shameful
as she doesn't like to travel far -
for she has to feed her cat.

Doctor Bob is the local quack,
he dispenses of kinds of advice,
no sooner than he's cracked a back,
he is off on a roving rant -
for he can fix every ail,
he can cure every pain,
he is trained to bandage sprains,
massage all aches with his training,
gleaned from years of observation
of actors on his television.

How life spins like a Dervish
to leave us all in a tizz,
common sense goes out the window
when presented with a *wunderkind*.
Modern wizards fool us all
with their sparkling fizzing arts,
who can resist the lure of magic
when bedazzled by such bewitching craft -
in a flash we are blinded
as the carpet-bagger steals our cash.

Nothing can stay our onward movement
though gravity may slow us down,
Uncle Tom still staggers forward
towards the pub just down the road,
blindly tapping his thin white stick,
he knows the worn flagstone way,
the smell of curry on the left,
the sound of trains just ahead,
a right turn at the broken pavement
that leads past the kiddy park.

Out of sight, Sarah cries
her heart is broken, yet again,
this time it is a traveling salesman
who blurted out he had a wife
back at home in Swansea town -
a place she'd never ever been,
now no hope to ever visit,
her life now shattered without hope
of ever having her own bloke.

The tears will wash to the sea,
where Tiger Jack plies his trade,

a giant with hands shovel-like,
big enough to crib a babe -
his gentle nature washed with laughter,
his mighty shoulders full of power
trained to guide oil-well pipes,
put to turning drill head bolts
on a hot-burning derrick floor.

Such worlds there are out at sea,
far beyond our peering eyes -
the choppers flying to and fro
with workers on the come and go,
until no-one really ever knows
where the oil eventually flows.

Mister Jones turns up the heating,
blue with cold from economising -
he can't afford to waste his pension
on keeping warm with some months more
before Spring arrives with the tulips.
He wants heat into his bones,
but daffs just give him false hope,
cherry blossom a sad foreboding,
he knows from gazing at the sky,
that Spring is still a long way off
unless the sparrows come chirping back
from their distant winter homes.

Gareth's far more optimistic,
he sees no writing on the wall,
his head is far above the muck
that many others wade on through -
for every day is filled with joy,
every hour is his to enjoy,
every moment a maiden voyage
to some great destination.

So the world onward rolls,
pitching at its molten core,
switching its magnetic pole
without us knowing its doing so.

Glenda runs for the sporting club,
likes to do cross-country trials -
she is a cheetah up a hill,
but is a hippo in the mud,
yet somehow always comes in first,
for she is tall, strong and blonde,
she is the club's pin-up girl

to all the middle distance men
who kiss her every time she wins.

Jerry is a couch-potato,
eating crisps and guzzling coke,
his fingers fly across his keyboard
as he notches up another score,
earns fresh tokens to carry on
playing games well into the dawn.
He is all of fifty stone,
the largest bloke in the block,
but no-one knows he exists
except his mum who does his chores.

What state of mind propels inaction
to sit and stare at the walls,
Jackie knows no other life
for she has given into sloth.
'It's not my fault' she expounds
to excuse her procrastination -
her fear of getting off her arse,
the effort required to wash her face,
then slap on a bit of rouge
to go find herself another job.

None can say where we go wrong,
somehow, somewhere along the road,
the slopes turn into massive hills
with no sign of downhill ahead -
we can lose all will to carry on,
the hike no longer just a jog.

Mr. Brown knows no resistance
to his happy hippy life,
gone, of course, his student days
of booze, drugs and sexy women.
Instead he's opted for retirement,
endless cruises around the Med,
what better life than in the sun
aboard a floating swish hotel
providing all his daily needs
offering widows all his love.

What better chance is there of joy
but to take what's offered up -
a smile from a pleasant face,
a whiff of air, car-fume free,
a blackbird chirping in a hedge,
a lonely cloud passing overhead,

a spot of rain to still the heat,
the ocean breaking on the beach -
such joys so short, so brief,
we barely think we have such need.

Georgina gets through every day
with a little bit of spice,
mainly wine, sometimes beer,
when she's pissed, slugs of rum,
for Georgina cannot cope with life,
living every moment's real,
something has to give – not her,
her mind needs to be a blur,
in order to make sense of things
that occur to her every hour.

Helen tries to sell her art
though it is something quite far-out,
yet she believes she is commercial
despite her friends and their doubts
that what she puts in her visions
does not quiet match their taste -
They are all bell-weather bods
who float on fashion, shallow taste,
they wouldn't know tit from bum
if pressed right up against their face.

Alas such pleasures elude some folks,
busy with their stamp collections,
Tony with his pre-war horde,
Cyril with his Victorian lore -
can there be any other interest
for these dedicated blokes,
who find joy in a lick of ink
stamped across an envelope -
with a date and place of issue,
neatly sealed in sheets of tissue.

And so it is with those who wait
for life to catch its breath on them,
until they find there's no time left
with which to make their escape -
for they are happy in their pursuits
engrossed in their binding loves
and who can say we are wrong
to find their niche in this world -
for they have found their equilibrium
while many others go wobbling on.

THEN IT STARTED AGAIN
[21.31, Thurs 11th Apr 2023, Iver Grove]

Then it started again, the constant noise
shattering my peace with grief,
covering my shame with wicked thoughts,
cowering me with my own doubts,
coercing me to think badly of myself,
regretting my existence as a man,
instead of rejoicing in who I am.

THE BABBLE THEY THROW OUR WAY
[22.29, Wed 12th Apr 2023, Iver Grove]

Why do all artists ask the same questions,
leave us no answers in our prisons,
high walls that shut out the sunlight,
bars that cast shadows on our faces.
We are left to ferment our fears,
torture ourselves with our nightmares;
never finding an exit from our nightmares,
we stagnate in our own bleak hell.

What use then are our dreams of heaven,
as princes and princesses trapped in our towers,
there is no rescue sent from Camelot,
or caravan bringing gifts from afar.
We linger on our beds of torment,
trying to shut out the evils of the day,
we languish in the hope of rescue
that will not come despite our prayers.

What then for all those revered artists,
shining torches skywards in the dark,
what questions do we hurl back at them
to silence the babble they throw our way.

BEYOND OUR GRASP
[02.52, Sat 15th April 2023, Bathford, Somerset]

Who can say what others think,
the fire burns, leaves us warm,
while others cold, linger on
despite the cold upon them.

We lucky ones curl up together,
never lonely, nor underprivileged,
what we know is not worth knowing
for we do not know the suffering.

Suffering is a common ailment,
contagious in our neglectful midst,
the laughter always so short-lived,
no-one asks why it gives out.

We know that life is brief,
that tragedy is on us all,
the sweetest smile hides the truth
that we are all broken souls.

How do we fix all our ails,
start to see our human flaws,
we want to hug every wrong,
put right the things we cannot solve.

And on we go in this mess,
hoping we can do our best,
try to help those distressed,
even though we are the cause.

Perhaps it is a noble art
to solve the problems of the world,
while we know that it cannot be
that all our ails can be relieved.

Perhaps all we have is hope,
nothing more, we struggle on,
come to terms with this world
before it spirals beyond our grasp.

WHY DO WE SUFFER FOOLS
[23.47, Mon 17th Apr 2023, Iver Grove]

Why do we let ourselves suffer fools,
those folks who vex us, make us old,
those who seek to be forgiven
despite their remorse being nothing more
than a cheap facade, a mask,
to cover all their selfish flaws.
Damn them all! They are lost,
and time only makes them worse.

WINDING DOWN
[00.13, Fri 28th Apr 2023, Iver Grove]

Winding down with little to do -
tomorrow's tomorrow
no worries about little things
everything is nothing

roses are red after the rain
the world will continue without me
until the sea disappears
and there are no clouds left.

MRS. ELLIOT
[17.28, Mon 1st May 2023, Iver Grove]

The fish swim in different directions
but she is left holding the dog,
she cannot counter all the aspersions
but knows they're all utterly false.
So she sips her wine every morning
hoping for change to eventually come,
while the clock ticks on increasingly loud,
time passes on without any pause.

THE WIDOW
[00.25, Thurs 4th May 2023, Iver Grove]

So I wait for her to call me up,
no doubt a time when she is lonely,
but will I wait an hour or day,
or never hear her voice again,
for who can tell what she thinks
living in her ivory tower -

That trap that offers no escape
into a world she knows she wants,
yet she somehow can't imagine
to live the dream she sleeps upon.

This far flung place she inhabits,
free of strife and daily chores,
where she awakes each new day
to find she has no work to do -
except to think the reason why
she lives but her love has died.

Unhappy then, the days drag on
without a purpose, without a cause,
the guilt of being thus unchained,
and lost and pained by remorse.

THE TIDE OF TIME
[05.44, Thurs 11th May 2023, Iver Grove]

The tide of time is against us,
we are paying for our ancestors' crimes -

nothing now can stop this progression,
marching on, the toll bell chimes.

This is how Rome fell in past times,
how all empires eventually decline,
to leave behind a legacy of cruelty,
that is the essence of their design.

We cannot wipe out our history,
we are the sum of empire's wrongs -
we live in empire's fading shadow,
and the echo of its tolling gong.

A SEA OF TROUBLES
[21.40, Sat 13th May 2023, Iver Grove]

Asleep, in dream, in cinema-scope,
I watched the pictures, enjoyed, enraptured,
I relished the narrative with immense joy ...
then the picture cut! Went to black.

Still asleep, the picture stayed blank,
it would not switch on, my dream gone,
no images to take me through the night,
no imagined world filled with light.

Why then did the film switch off,
disturb my sleep, I was not awake,
but left to question my darkest fears
of why my dream was sadly gone.

Habitually, I do not remember my dreams,
I wake to discover all is lost.
How strange then to recall from sleep,
my dream going off, not switching on.

Is this how we one day pass
from sleep into the other realm,
where the dream we had disappears
and we are alone in the dark.

I AM BLIND
[00.20, Thurs 2nd June 2023, Iver Grove]

Dear Lord, let me fully understand
the ways of this land, this world -
I cannot see why things are so,
why many wrongs are this way
when life is simple in my eyes?

Others complicate my clear view
of what is right, what is not.
Is it me, or am I blind,
to all our human flaws -
Lord, help to keep me strong.

ODE TO GERMAN SALAMI
[22.17, Wed 7th June 2023, Iver Grove]

What use is this ditty, this ode,
I have nothing to say. I am tired,
spent by office labour, mental anguish,
unfit to compose a long tirade.
Lost without a cause, I tarry
with my pen in utter uselessness,
I stutter across this white page
in the desire of some usefulness.
Alas, I am no expert on salami,
and I admit I am no sage.

I KNOW WHAT IT'S LIKE TO BE LONELY
[0.45, Thurs 8th June 2023, Iver Grove]

I know what its like to be lonely,
there's nobody just for me ...
so I sit and I drink my vino,
ponder how this came to be.

LOVE IS WISE, WAR IS DUMB
[23.33, Thurs 8th June 2023, Iver Grove]

All we try to do is love,
find the time to show ourselves,
no hiding out in ourselves
with the world watching on.
We cannot pretend to hate,
loathe the folk that we know,
they are us, and we are them,
we can't pretend we are alone.
No one can say I am myself
when we are all part of one,
in between we soldier on,
for love is wise, war is dumb.

A COCK AND BULL STORY
[00.32, Tues 13th June 2023, Iver Grove]

The heat eats at our strength,
governments collapse beneath its weight,

the sunflowers turn their heads away,
the storm comes, drops its rain.

Sunday lunches served with radish,
young folks pretending to be adequate,
churchyards filled with war graves,
letters waiting for absent guests.

Empty lanes edged with tall grass,
fox faces painted on pub walls,
poppy heads drooping on to lawns,
cottages for sale in charity shops.

The silence of the ticking clock,
the hum of voices in the dark,
no breeze to stir the drawn blinds,
no flies or bees, not a buzz.

No rumble from a rising jet,
no creaks from aged timber joists,
the cobbled yard quietly mossed,
the air hung with hot intent.

Tomorrow but a stone throw off,
the night a sleepless humid toss,
the bull will stare at the moon,
the cock will crow all too soon.

UKRAINE
[00.32, Tues 13th June 2023, Iver Grove]

The war goes on, so do the lies,
this is the nature of this war -
the defenders falsifying their claims
they can drive the invaders out;
while all the time the real bad guys,
supplying tanks and bombs and guns,
spin their web of mass destruction
on the ones that they support -
the body count in hundred thousands,
machines and armour turned to rust,
all for what but some ideal,
laid upon all of us -
who can you trust with the truth,
not the ones who thrive on war.

JOHN'S SON (BORIS)
[23.11, Thurs 15th June 2023, Iver Grove]

The little boy has finally cried,
all his toys are out the pram,
his little soldier lads are chipped,
his Churchill hat is all skew-wiff,
his tears are for his spoiled self,
his ship has long gone adrift.

All alone he wails and bawls,
his teddy bear has lost its legs,
no-one now will hear his cries,
the boy has howled all his lies,
all alone, he'll snivel, mope,
learn nothing from his temper strop.

For he is such a damaged child,
he cares nothing for the adult world,
by trying to trick, to take control,
he causes chaos, fills with woe
all those he bullies with his bawls,
'til Nanny comes and slaps his bum.

FRANCESCA
[00.41, Sat 1st July 2023, Iver Grove]

The kayak took her down the stream
to meet a swan wanting love,
she stopped to greet the queenly bird
then onward went into the sun,
to sit and sip on Alsace wine,
propped up upon swallow pillows,
she fed a robin from her hand,
spoke to me in dulcet syllables,
woo'd me with her English charm,
lulled me with her country wisdom.

BEYOND THAT DARK PLACE
[23.24, Sun2nd July 2023, Iver Grove]

Is the universe expanding ...
or is our galaxy shrinking down?
Are we descending, swallowed whole,
being sucked down a cosmic hole?

Black are the thoughts thrown about,
as we turn in on ourselves,

Planck and Einstein at the fore,
above, the sky churns some more.

The light bends, warps our view,
throws time off into space -
beyond sight lies the cusp,
dark matter distant, far from us.

Shall we ever know for certain,
what lies beyond that dark place?
No, we will never, ever know,
why things are just ordered so.

HER LOVE FOR ME
[22.14, Mon 3rd July 2023, Iver Grove]

She fell into my arms, she swooned
like a child lost, then found,
she clung to me with all her strength,
kissed my hands, then my neck,
and soon her lips fell on mine
and I responded back in kind,
for I had no defense to give,
she had numbed my mind.

GREAT MALVERN
[21.48, Tues 4th July 2023, Great Malvern, Worcs]

The Turner sky turned grey
as evening settled on the hills,
the sleepy streets, silent, still,
the windowed shops poetry filled,
stacks of books towering up
to fill each inch of wandering eye;
an English flag half-unfurled,
the twinkling lights far below,
once part of Wales long ago.

SEXY PIC
[23.22, Thurs 6th July 2023, Iver Grove]

She sent me a snap of her beautiful legs
with a tag that said 'sexy pic'.
I replied that she was tempting me,
flaunting her body to entice me on.

She replied that she was only joking,
that I was probably used to racier things.

Slighted, I texted back prudently
that she was flashing her wares.

Then she admitted, it had all been a test
to see if I wanted her just for her body.
Of course, I did! I wanted that too,
along with the mind teasing me to.

I'LL LOVE YOU IN THE MORNING (song)
For Frankie
[10.30, Tues 11th July 2023, Iver Grove]

I'll love you in the morning
I'll love you through the day
I'll love you in the evening
then I'll say my prayers.

I'll love you in the mountains
I'll love you in the glens
I'll love you when the sun sets
when we're lying in the ferns.

I'll love you when its raining
I'll love you when it's cold
I'll love you for your youth
I'll love you when you're old.

I'll love you with my last breath
as I've done since we first met
I'll love you now and ever
and love with no regrets.

SWEET AS CANDY
[19.48, Wed 12th July 2023, Iver Grove]

She was as sweet as candy
and smelt like a rose,
she made love like an heiress,
but was still daddy's child …

She was haughty like a diva,
yet caring like a nurse,
she had the walk of a model,
but the talk of a chorus girl.

MODERN LIFE
[20.52, Thurs 13th July 2023, Iver Grove]

We waver to find our place,
struggle to understand our position,
falter when questioned … when
we have no answer to give.
We don't think through our options,
have no time to contemplate,
we are forced to make decisions
without any kind of pause.

Worse still, we are hustled,
made to do things we hate,
ordered to hurry up and act
while we wish to wait.
This is modern living,
there's no time to prevaricate,
we career on into rashness,
regret the mistakes we make.

MY LITTLE APPLE
01.20, Sat 15th July 2023, Iver Grove]

I saw my little Apple today,
she had fallen from the tree,
life had caught up with her
and I observed her fear -
I shuffled in my bistro chair,
smiled and nodded on,
I loved her just the same
though her summer bloom is gone.

Life is cruel on beauty,
it eats the thing on show,
but her inner essence shone
like I had known of yore.
In awe I watched her nibble
on her haddock stew,
knowing that our time
was all we had anew.

We parted with an embrace
that imparted all our love,
we had shared a bed in Berlin
and knew we were apart …
yet something in our nature,
we knew that we were souls,

cemented aye forever,
and forever bound 'til old.

LET'S TALK AT BREAKFAST
[23.40, Sat 15th July 2023, Iver Grove]

We're going nowhere fast,
nothing's meant to last,
so let's make love now ...
and talk at breakfast.

DEMENTIA
[00.24, Sun 16th July 2023, Iver Grove]

His mind wanders in riddles,
unravels as the evening draws,
there is no call for order
as random thoughts fall on -
the spouting of gibberish,
like brushing rubbish with a comb,
a sweeping in the darkness
of endless, pointless talk.

So tired, he lumbers onwards
to get a handle on himself,
there's hope of mild success
in combating ailing health -
but such struggles remain a challenge
to maintain his failing life ...
we cannot say he's winning
but he keeps up the fight.

IT WAS FOUR A.M
[04.25, Tues 18th July 2023, Iver Grove]

Woke up thinking about you,
wanted to call but it was 4 a.m,
put on the light, lay there naked,
wondered when I would see you next.

Did I think I would be happy
without having you by my side?
Wrapping the bedclothes around me,
I turned out the light.

LOVE IN THE DARK
[23.30, Wed 19th July 2023, Iver Grove]

Into the dark, blind, feeling something
familiar to touch, to find without fear,
edging slowly, limbs tense and wary,
each moment uneasy, a slow easing on
into the pitch black, listening intently,
the heave of her breathing, beads on my brow,
into the unknown without any idea
where I am going, or how it will end.

ALONE IN THE DARK
[05.58, Sat 22nd July 2023, Iver Grove]

Dawn is up, the birds are in the trees,
the city wakes to a mild weekend.
She makes herself a cup of tea,
looks down on the uncut grass,
the grey sky stretching up above
reminding her of Africa -
gutters filled with last year's leaves
that fell when her lover departed.

THE TREES WILL COME BACK AGAIN
[06.15, Sat 22nd July 2023, Iver Grove]

When we are gone, the trees will come again,
repossess the land we have stolen,
they will cover over all of our failings,
hide for good all our crimes.

For we have forced trees to the fringes,
ignored their place in our world,
they have suffered by our actions,
We have hacked, and built and burnt.
The trees will come again sometime soon,
for soon - we will all be ash.

NESSIE SPOTTER TEAM (song)
[13.18, Sat 22nd July 2023, Iver Grove]

They hang out by the lochside
looking kind of sheepish,
they are kind of clannish -
the Nessie Spotter Team.

Loch Ness is a haunt
that tourists love to visit,

to hear about the Beastie
from the Nessie Spotter Team.

If you go down to the shoreline
with midge spray to rub on,
take your binoculars to spy on
the Nessie Spotter Team.

HER LIFE WITHOUT ME
[00.44, Tues 25th July 2023, Iver Grove]

Naked and bare, I wanted her there,
naked and wanting beside me -
but what could I say to make her stay
more than a night, before giving flight,
back to her life without me.

THE UNDONE TASKS
[04.29, Wed 26th July 2023, Iver Grove]

Another dawn emerges from the dark,
the violet shimmer of another day.
I am breathing, wide awake,
not quite ready to engage,
to tackle all the undone tasks
waiting to be wrestled and subdued.

A SUMMER WITHOUT RAIN
[23.32, Wed 26th July 2023, Iver Grove]

A summer without rain is a summer lost
to eternal heat, and infernal fires,
moors burning, forests blazing,
houses raised and livelihoods lost -
No-one wants such natural disasters,
but this is the lay of our present world.
Temperatures rising, ice-caps melting,
El Nino raging, and nowhere to shelter.

Such is our planet buffeted, fanned,
swept with a heat we cannot abide.
If it is the result of our human folly,
then we only have ourselves to chide,
while some believe we are not to blame,
they change not, weigh not the cost ...
perhaps one day all will acknowledge,
summer without rain, is our world lost.

A KISS AT THE END OF THE LINE
[00.54, Sat 29th July 2023, Iver Grove]

No-one really knows what is going on
after midnight when the lights go out,
messages exchanged, travel like lightning,
fingers type as fast as the mind,
innocent texts become little love notes,
desire climbs into a climax of memes,
the moment expended, leaves love in limbo,
until the next chance to fire a salvo;
to compose a sweet little *bon mote*,
signal that love is foremost the message
with a kiss at the end of the line.

HIPPIES
[21.38, Thurs 3rd Aug 2023, Iver Grove]

We were cool, nothing touched us,
we were knights in tie-dye armour,
we were high in the clouds,
we Freaks, we trucked, traveled on,
we never let them bring us down,
as spaceships headed for the moon,
we flowered, seeded, saw peace bloom.

THE WAR WILL BE OVER SOON
[21.48, Thurs 3rd Aug 2023, Iver Grove]

If ever there is a time to stop
it is now ...
The war will be over soon,
the vanquished are all but done,
the victors, soon will come
to occupy the vacated land.
The people will return
go back to ruined homes,
to the pitted landscape ...
they will rebuild their houses
midst the ghosts of the dead
who will parade in the fields
where relatives keep their memories
by laying flowers on their graves.
If ever there is a time to stop,
it is now ...

SHE CALLS ME UP
[23.41, Thurs 3rd Aug 2023, Iver Grove]

She calls me up, sends her love,
talks about the things gone wrong,
tries to sell herself to me
but knows it's just a tease -
sends me hearts and double xx's,
wakes me up with her texting,
rings when I least expect her,
sends me pics and little bits
of info I already know -
or stuff she's told me all before,
and still I listen to her so,
until she's finally bored with me,
decides to hang up, let me go.

ONCE MORE I CROSS TO FRANCE
[22.57, Thurs 10th Aug 2023, Dover-Dunkirk Ferry]

Once more I cross to France
on the midnight sailing -
the kids prattle in their different tongues,
language foreign but filled with laughter,
small children restless, vacate their chairs,
babies cry disturbed by engine rumble
whilst older folks cuddle, try to sleep.
Others on the move for different reasons,
who is free, and who is fleeing?
A thousand stories, a thousand theories.
I have one that I'm repeating,
like I have done so many times before.

JIM HAWKINS and MISTER HYDE
[23.17, Sat 12th August 2023, Valence, France]

What do I have in common with RLS,
his first name, of course, and then
we were both born in Scotland.
Is it enough that we are both writers,
no, for Robbie gave us Treasure Island,
Doctor Jekyll and Mister Hyde,
and a slew of memorable stories
that fired my young questioning mind.

What then will I leave behind?
Some dodgy verse, some suspect plays,
a gaggle of topsy-turvy films,
a smattering of indulgent novels,

some diary entries devoid of merit.
This perhaps will be my end -
a failure to inspire the young,
to lead adults to understand themselves.

This is the haphazard life I live,
given lofty heroes to follow,
given the hope that I could be equal
to the challenge those before set down.
I could argue that I am spent,
a notion without utter conviction,
for this would be mere excuse
for why I'm not a foremost mind.

So I stumble on, scribble ditties,
hope the muse will set me free
to create some *opus magnus*,
or at least write something of weight,
for despite all my love for RLS,
it cannot make me as great as him.
Jim Hawkins, God rest his soul!
And Mister Hyde! Immortal evermore!

THE VAR
[17th-20th Aug 2023, Le Thoronet, Provence]

The river runs slowly by,
the bamboo twitches in the sun,
quietly all about is calm,
the evening now is just begun.

This is the way of Provence life,
a stillness in the summer heat,
existence but the will to breathe,
to be at ease with what it brings.

The cliffs tower into the shade,
the breeze wafts the last of day,
night comes on without much haste
as if its counting centuries.

There's no rush to get things done,
all in time will be self-made,
nature goes about its chores,
with no pause or long delay.

So it is, its rivers flow
between the Alps and the sea,

the valleys giving life to all,
the soil on which the vineyards sprawl.

This is the way of Provence life,
the stillness of the summer heat,
the lull that hides all things well,
alludes to a mere idleness.

Not so, this land, this factory,
this place of great inventiveness,
this hub of talent, artists, dancers,
musicians found in every quarter.

Its sailors home from the sea,
captains home to plant their seeds,
cabin girls tired of labour, cooks
sharing truffles with their neighbours.

This is the Var, in Provence,
not yet on the tourist maps ...
wild, and far from the crowds,
where life is simply paradise.

THE OFFENSIVE (Robotyne)
[23.30, Fri 1st Sept 2023, Iver Grove]

Eighty thousand men are dead,
and still we hear the same old song -
"We'll be with you to the end!"
"Fight on, lads, we'll break through!"
While in the fields, mined and shelled,
those lads lose their arms and legs,
lie crying through the bomb-lit night
caked in dust by morning light,
and dead before they are found.

What purpose to this futile fight
in the fields they once ploughed,
who can praise such reckless folly.
"Victory, boys, advance to glory!"
Cluster bombs and jet-fired missiles,
tank rounds landing midst the chaos,
comrades, now just mere soldiers
sent to die on higher orders -
and still the line no further forward.

COMMON SENSE PUT OFF 'TIL TOMORROW
[21.24, Wed 6th Sept 2023, Iver Grove]

No-one listens to common sense
until the senseless has overtaken
all reasoned chance of success
in endeavors so easily resolved.

Reaction is the normal trait
as hidden anger bubbles up,
overtakes all rational action
to situations hardly worth a jot.

This is human nature
to solutions simply proffered forth,
rejection is a point of honour,
acceptance the hardest pill to swallow.

Conflicts simmer into war
because of pride and false bravado -
the senseless overtakes today,
with common sense put off 'til tomorrow.

FACEBOOK
[00.29, Thurs 1th Sept 2023, Iver Grove]

So many pictures telling a story,
where do I start to tell my own?
Perhaps I haven't got the right look,
or a body to make others weep -
how can I make a lasting impression,
compete for the Likes everyone wants,
what is the answer to my deficiencies?
Perhaps a photographer, just to keep up?

Didn't it used to be just the neighbours
we had to impress with our stuff?
Now its a world of friends, acquaintances,
many I'll never meet in the flesh.
What hope is there of being loved
with so many in love with themselves.

ANOTHER RAINY SUNDAY
[14.03, Sun 17th Sept 2023, Iver Grove]

Its another rainy Sunday,
but at least its not Monday,
I can watch the ran fall
rather than sitting in my office

typing endless emails
that do nothing for my health -
there is more to life than business,
like dancing naked in the wet.

DOING SOMETHING DIFFERENT
[23.37, Sun 17th Sept 2023, Iver Grove]

Its not easy every morning to wake up
and think of something new to do today,
its far simpler to perform the same routines
to get into the groove of daily living.

But what if you do not have a routine,
live in the moment, and on whims,
feel your way through each second,
make decisions as circumstances dictate?

How can the mind be so reset
that it does not blindly work on default,
for is routine not the ideal condition
that allows us all to interact?

Perhaps it is dangerous to be free thinking,
to go against the flow of routine thought,
but I for one will continue to look for ways
of doing something different every morn.

GOLD DIGGERS
[03.29, Thurs 21st Sept 2023, Iver Grove]

Oh how unhappy some people are,
they have the whole world, but its not enough,
they always want more than they have,
and by hook or by crook they connive,
employ solicitors, then onward drive
to an end that they have imagined
that will get them what they want.

NARCISSIST
for Michael
[21.04, Fri 29th Sept 2023, Iver Grove]

Its not what you do, its who you are -
Who are you? That false person
that one who vexes all, who
spreads false rumours and spite,
that individual sent to try us,

to make us all curse our lives,
instead of cursing you!

What peace is found far from you,
beyond the range of your words,
beyond the influence of your bile
hidden behind a factious smile -
you stalk our daily thoughts,
impose your malignant persona
on our purer minds.

How were you born, you monster child,
how were you fashioned into you?
What molding hands made you thus,
selfish and beyond all redemption -
how does your troubled mother sleep,
how must your dead father weep
for the sins I mention.

The time has come for your reckoning,
the tallying of all you have done,
not for all your vile actions,
not for all your deeds performed,
but rather for your twisted nature,
for the web of deceit you have spun,
to be the evil person you have become.

THE RUSSIAN TEACHER
[13.53, Sun 1st Oct 2023, Iver Grove]

Her hair was as black as the universe,
her eyes like shining stars,
her skin like alabaster
left outdoors in the sun.

Her voice like that of a whisper
of breeze passing through a lock,
her choice of dress for the evening
black like that of a nun.

Her neck was finely wrinkled,
draped with a silk red scarf,
her breasts adorned with an necklace
that came from somewhere afar.

Her nails were clean, unpainted,
her hands devoid of hard work,
but her boots were bling encrusted
with heels that lifted her up.

She walked with poise and purpose,
unsure of what was ahead,
and into the depths of London,
she looked back with a little laugh.

HAMAS
[23.52, Thurs 12th Oct 2013, Iver Grove]

What brings men to commit atrocities,
a conditioning, an internal hatred,
the need for vengeance against their foes,
that defies all rational logic to us,
the witnesses of their atrocities.

What makes men so cold blooded,
to do such acts, the maiming,
the torture of their hostages,
the barbarism that strikes fear
into every God loving soul.

Perhaps not what, but who created
these desperate men devoid of love,
men pushed beyond all morality,
angered beyond desperation,
to be heard, to make their point.

IS THIS IT?
[00.17, Sat 14th Oct 2023, Iver Grove]

Is this the end? Some backwater.
Alone, staring at the ceiling.
Where has it gone wrong?
Could there have been a way,
a different life from this,
these four walls, my prison?
All that has gone before me,
my ancestors, the heroes of my youth,
did they lie here wondering?
Is this all there is?
Why am I here at all?
Will I ever know I existed?
Is this the end? Is this it?

WHERE IS THAT YOUNG MAN
[19.12, Sat 14th Oct 2023, Iver Grove]

Where is that young man
who once knew of heaven
who sang with the seals

and flew with the falcons
gone now to hell -
in his old man's prison.

Where is that fine hero
who once rescued maidens
who proclaimed all his love
gave his heart in an instance
now rigid and cold -
the old man has taken him.

OTHER WORLDS
[01.07, Tues 17th Oct 2023, Iver Grove]

Beyond the borders of reality,
lie other worlds, far beyond me
into these landscapes I will trek
in search of truth, and love, to find
all the vacant spaces in my heart
to fill with joy and bounty -

For I am an empty drifting vessel
out upon an open sea -
if I cannot find love now
then I am bound for eternity -
that place where the devil dwells
and there's no God to save me.

MAJOR O
[circa 05.30, Tues 24th Oct 2023, Iver Grove]

Sweet between the sheets
with her well endowed physic,
she was a force of soldier nature
with her medical behaviour,
she was out to save me,
and I was out to tame her.

A night of wild enchantment,
a morn of pure enrapture,
I explored all her battles,
she overran my defenses,
I salved all her wounds,
surrendered without questions.

I saluted her bravado
stood to her attention,
at ease with my advances,
she took full advantage,

an officer and gentlewoman,
with an open loving nature.

THE STORM WILL COME
[13.40, Sat 4th Nov 2023, Iver Grove]

The storm will come, but planes will fly,
the trees will dance like madmen;
the flood will wash away the muck,
erode the tracks of ancient ways,
deport the waste of the Fall,
bring on the call of winter.

MY BONNY LASS
for Lynda
[01.47, Fri 10th Nov 2023, Iver Grove]

Alas, my bonny lass,
things don't last, always pass,
so we must grasp with a gasp
the life that we've been gifted.

TANGIER WITH SUZIE
[23.32, Thurs 28th Dec 2023, Grand Hotel Via De
France, Tangier]

Far lies the near distant shore,
the full moon drifting on the clouds,
lifeless palms in dimming light
towering o'er the terraced grove -
where you and I outward gaze
upon the town spread out below.

BETTER TO BE IN MARBESA
[14.45, Sun 31st Dec 2023, Marbesa, Andalucia]

Once more in Marbesa,
catching the final sun of the year,
a long year, much labour and toil
for I am getting on in years.

This is how it is,
no one can rest on their laurels,
for soon the leaves of success wither,
tighten round the wearer's head.

Not so for the restless,
those seeking room views like Matisse,

those disenchanted with the status quo
from which they feel somehow excluded.

Perhaps it is their childhood,
those things they cannot unfathom,
the faults of their fathers, mothers,
that they repeat as their enduring songs.

So there we have it,
knowledge is a thing kept from us,
there is no point to endless dwelling
on the things that disrupt love.

Better to be in Marbesa,
catching the final rays of sun,
for tomorrow may not come again,
and the laurels never worn at all.

BITCOIN CRAZY
[00.10, Tues 9th Jan 2024, Iver Grove]

How the rich get richer still
swallowing the orange pill,
filling all their trusts with coins,
pushing up their index funds
as if they're at a jumble sale
before all the coins are gone.

How fear of missing out creates
panic in the market place,
profit foremost in their minds,
they hock their stocks, then exchange
every penny for a stake
in the greatest deal of the age.

Winners always come with losers
who buy in just before the crash,
yet no-one knows when that is,
for speculation comes with luck -
a savvy early bird feeds well,
late comers at just the worms.

Get rich schemes rarely come
but when they do, the gloves are off,
the fight is on to beat the odds
stacked against the little guy,
who holds his coins with diamond hands
and vows to all he'll never sell.

DISAPPOINTMENT
[10.30, Sat 13th Jan 2024, Iver Grove]

Disappointment taints us all.
"Just me. Why me at all?"
The axe swings on the fallen tree
to cut it further, until gone -
wood chips are all that remains,
washed off in the heavy rains.

Expectation thus so destroyed,
sets hope upon a renewed voyage
to load our ships with fresh goods
sent to markets far from us -
in the belief we'll overcome
the ills to which we've succumbed.

No other notions can succeed
other than those we believe,
we may expect better terms
than those life throws our way -
for disappointment is soon forgot
when opportunity comes to stay.

WORRY AT 4AM
[06.47, Tues 23rd Jan 2024, Iver Grove]

Worry came at 4 am,
then passed like a summer storm.
The dark clouds now far gone,
the rain easing, all but off -
the calm as the sun emerged
sometime after dawn.

WHITE BARBARIANS
[21.52, Tues 23rd Jan 2024, Iver Grove]

What is it with these circling crows
always ready to gorge on war,
to sink their beaks, sup on blood,
to tear apart, to feast, grow fat
with the cry "It's them or us!"
"It's self-defence! It is a must!"

What Hippocratic oaths are these?
To main and kill, these profiteers
blind to their sick, evil ways,
none pausing long enough

at the trough to stay and watch
the genocide their greed creates.

How sad it is, we watch dismayed,
our voices muted, our cries silenced,
shouted down by vested interest,
as horror plays on our minds,
the guilt builds for every child
and mother killed by our kind.

What kind are we? White barbarians,
towards an end we blunder on,
slaughtering all that oppose
our ways, our every selfish want.
May God strike our people down
for we are not the chosen ones!

JANUARY GALE
[02.25, Wed 24th Jan 2024, Iver Grove]

Blow your hardest, wind!
Knock the slates from my roof,
rip the branches from my trees,
sweep my bins down the street,
do your best to tumble my walls,
rattle on my old shed door -
You scare me not a single jot,
with your gushing puff and roar!

WHEN PEACE COMES
[Sun 28th Jan - Sun 11th Feb 2024, Iver Grove]

Now is not the time to waver,
to deviate, go off track,
to hang a hat, hook a coat,
wrap a scarf around a peg,
ignore the goings going on,
blindly turn our heads away
refuse to notice.

War may wither our resolve
to engage with cold reality,
yet the angry cries are heard -
the crying of a foreign child,
the wailing of a grieving spouse,
the marching of the chanting crowd
demanding peace.

Genocide, what crime is this?
So now, we know not it's form?
Shame upon all who believe
self-defense absolves all slaughter -
he who lies shouts the loudest,
protests his innocence without proof
to escape all justice.

Thus the war wind cruelly blows,
leaves all hope in disrepair,
saps the will to raise dissent
or take up arms against aggression.
Wrapped in cozy warm abides,
we get on with our idle lives
while others suffer.

Rain no longer falls in Africa,
ice flows melt in far Antarctica,
barbed wire seals besieged America,
missiles mire western Asia,
bomb craters pock-mark Europe -
the world at war with itself
and its people helpless.

Life throws much at us unprovoked,
we wipe it off, then move on,
we seek to find happy days,
leave behind the horror shows -
things that eat at our souls,
gnaw away at our integrity
to leave us cold.

We crave for peace's warm embrace,
shed our clothes to let it in,
run to the stretching sands,
dive headlong into the waves,
wash ourselves of all our woes,
emerge baptised, filled with joy
for being alive.

Not so now, these war hours,
these ticking restless seconds gone,
for gone they are, not to return,
but more come on just the same.
Peace is a long way off,
we heap our burdens on our backs
until we snap.

What beast of burden does not bray
as the load breaks its back,
to expire with a final groan
or utterance "I've had enough!"
Something always has to give,
to rip or rent apart in two
our mental state.

This is the war of our folly,
to assist our self-destruction,
to blindly steer off the road
that leads to the peaceful hills,
where rest awaits, joy abounds,
where all our troubles, packed away,
we learn to smile.

Such happy times! Gone!
Like coal smoke on the wind,
grey glimpses of what once was,
a hint of something now unseen,
a feeling that something's there,
while all the time what we perceive
its just fresh air.

How can we grasp what is lost,
regain that longed-for peaceful vibe,
that feeling that life is good,
that every moment is our last -
where the present is our only life,
that those we're with is who we love
without remorse.

Then there! Just beyond our gloom,
a candle burns just for us,
lit to guide us through the dark,
we find ourselves fumbling through -
hope is just an arm's length off,
faith returns as we emerge
into the light.

But Mother Mary never comes to us,
she's never there to smooth our waters.
Should we ask God to send her?
Is that just a futile prayer?
Can there ever be salvation,
can all sins be washed away
in a cease-fire.

Can we place our hope in science,
find remorse in some equation,
will the wheels of life spin on
while we are still rotating -
with minds in a senseless fud,
with brains occupied with crud
and speculation.

Let the music play, dull our senses,
fill us with false emotion,
let the drugs take effect,
protect us from all affectation -
surely we must have escape,
find a way to run away
from all approbation.

Oh how we all fall from Heaven,
angels giving into the Devil,
we turn to find we are broken,
not because we are forsaken -
abandoned by the curse of time,
we run out of hours to fix
our endless crimes.

We would rather go blind, then,
leave all our woes unfixed.
But how? What guarantee is there
that time will not rob us of this?
Oh Mother Mary, why not come now,
pay a visit to your needing sons
before they're gone.

For gone we all surely must
depart before the sands have run -
well before our given hour,
we must arrange to be contrite.
There is no advantage to greed,
to stuffing riches in the bank
for our needs.

Too soon such folly comes to light
at the ritual for our departure, when
near-ones ask why such wealth
when life was lived in such squalor?
Poverty of mind, bareness of living,
hoarding of emotion, love and giving,
a total nothing.

Is that me? Ask yourself again,
ask yourself every chance you can.
What will be the lasting effect
of everything you have done to now?
Does it matter, perhaps not, no,
but to yourself? That, my friend,
you only know.

How that little voice nags away,
works upon our inner guilt,
gnawing at our chance for peace
until we are finally swayed;
I will conform, go with the flow,
agree to everything I disagree with
and find acceptance.

Capitulation, now the war has come,
makes all resistance a futile act,
our guns may fall silent,
our bullets spent, our fight gone -
yet we remain alive and breathing,
alive to fight another day
in the future.

There is an upside to this fud,
the bottom of the curve is found,
from here on in its only up,
no more downward trend to come -
time to reinvest in hope,
time to rebuild all our trust
and our luck.

Freed from all that weighs us down,
bereft of all our former woes,
we gift our time to newer things
we should have done long ago -
the bucket list of daring deeds,
our dreams of being like the breeze,
and free to breath.

Aw, how that thought unchains the mind
from all the shackles binding us,
our former woes dropped away
as we go through that open door -
that leads us to that better life
where sunshine fills our every day,
our every hour.

Is there need for Church and State
when we have such self-assuredness?
Surely now we have both things
we need no intervention -
God is us, who we are,
to govern ourselves on better terms,
in finer fashion.

This is freedom! The perfect goal!
To break free of our inner jails,
to run from our tiny cells,
to climb the walls surrounding us -
to look beyond the prison yard
where we have exercised our thoughts
watched by guards.

Somewhere there waits a boat or us
to push into the blue beyond,
a craft to take us to a place,
a paradise we can touch -
a place where every day brings joys,
where we can roam all alone
in perfect peace.

And when our horses are released,
we will ride them 'til they tire,
we will lead them then to drink
but not force them to imbibe -
for now that we roam free,
we must not then enslave
all other kind.

Thus, in control of all we do,
we see that others still are trapped,
lost in the fog of war,
drowning in the depths of debt.
Are we then to cold to help?
Will we protect what we've got
and let them rot?

Oh, sad beings that we can be,
selfish beyond our own beliefs,
caring with our thoughts and words,
hands in pockets, we shrug things off -
let all ills we fixed by others,
ignore the pain and all the suffering
being inflicted.

Inaction thus blots out the sun,
clouds the sky, brings on war,
those peaceful days we have found,
return us to being on frozen ground -
all gains we've made, quickly lost,
all joy we've had turned to frowns
and despair.

We weep for those lost happy times.
There is none to blame but ourselves
if we blind ourselves to genocide,
condone the oppressors crimes -
we too are then in the dock,
we too are the guilty ones
who didn't stop.

Stop what? How? I didn't know!
Of course you did. So did I.
We nightly wailed and sighed,
as each new story made us cry -
but it still did not let up,
the killing mounted, more on more,
uncounted dead.

Therefore I ask, when will peace come?
When will we say "We've had enough!"
When will we push and shove,
instead of uttering useless words.
If peace ever comes again,
it will be because the war is lost
and we are found.

EACH DAY ARRIVES
[00.55, Wed 14th Feb 2024, Iver Grove]

So each day arrives afresh
on each night of no regrets,
tomorrow comes with all renewed
without review of past missteps.

WORRY
[10.23, Mon 19th Feb 2024, Iver Grove]

I worry about things I cannot change.
I worry more about things I can.
But my worries go when I react
and erase them with my acts.

BERLIN
[00.57, Sat 24th Feb 2024, Berlin]

The snow is gone, the crowds too,
the bear stands lonely in the cold,
the city moves as it does,
Berliners going about their chores -
a steady beat, a measured breath,
a confidence despite the times,
a quickened pace, but hardly much
more than what's gone before -
if there is angst beneath the smiles,
in lowered eyes, it briefly shows.

CHECKPOINT CHARLIE
[15.43, Mon 26th Feb 2024, Checkpoint Charlie, Berlin]

What is Checkpoint Charlie now?
Cafe mocha, chocolate cheesecake,
the Wall down, the tanks gone,
the Allies back in their box.

The war rages in the East,
now we see they have returned,
their tanks in Ukrainian bogs,
their missiles fired at Russian soil,
intent on building another Wall
along the 'Neiper riverfront.

BEFORE I WAS A GENTLEMAN
[23.50, Mon 26th Feb 2024, Iver Grove]

I've given up being a rogue,
my ship has sailed, I'm o'er the hill,
my bills are paid, my time served,
I'm now a perfect gentleman.

That rogue has gone with the wind,
my mind free of all his tricks,
for I am rich, done with crime,
I'm now a fine old gentleman.

What roguish traits I once possessed,
the broken hearts, the wives that wept,
I've now made friends with their men -
I'm now a fellow gentleman.

No more a scoundrel, nor a rogue,
no debts are due, my slate is wiped,

I pray each night on my knees
and rise a humble gentleman.

Perhaps one day the mask will slip,
the rogue revealed for all to see
that part of me, of who I am,
although I'm now a gentleman.

THE MARCH RAINS HAVE COME
[06.18, Sat 2nd Mar 2024, Iver Grove]

The March rains have come
in like a lion, the weather goes mad.
March the month of Mars,
the month of the Ram,
when the storm gives in
before going out like a lamb.

WHEN THINGS COME TO NOUGHT
[22.13, Sun 3rd Mar 2024, Iver Grove]

When things come to nought,
I am at a loss to know why
much time and effort
has been wasted.

The answer is always the same -
human folly, insufficient knowledge,
skills that are not honed
that produce failure.

THE WANDERER NEVER SLEEPS
[20.28, Mon 4th mar 2024, Iver Grove]

The wanderer never sleeps
as her dreams are all
in her waking hours,
searching for something
while it is within her
and not the miles.

KNACKERED
[21.07, Mon 11th Mar 2024, Iver Grove]

The day is done! I'm stabled by nine,
sighing like an old horse seeking rest,
the chores of the day quite tedious,
plowing my way, endless furrows
with many more furloughs to go.

This is the way to the knackers yard,
to be recycled as marrow and bone,
stiffness in every taut sinew -
will I be harnessed tomorrow,
or will I sleep, done for ever more.

WHY DO YOU LOOK SO YOUNG
[07.50, Sun 17th Mar 2024, Iver Grove]

How do you manage to look so young?
I look in the mirror and wonder too,
I drink beer, eat what I want,
work ten to six, stay up late,
stare at my phone 'til eyes are sore,
sit in a chair all day long,
touch my toes when stiffness comes,
can't say I'm different from anyone.
Perhaps its the lighting, or something,
I only see the old man I've become.

I DREAM OF LEMON TREES
[22.35, Sun 17th Mar 2024, Iver Grove]

I dream of lemon trees,
I hear the ocean breaking-in -
far from here the breeze sways
the tall grass on the cliffs -
I am there, free to fall
into the blue there below.

I look up, see endless grey,
wish I was not here today
beneath the bland London sky.

OH BRIAN BORU (Song)
[01.35, Tues 19th Mar 2024, Iver Grove]

Oh, Brian Boru, if you only knew
what Ireland thinks of you now,
the O'Neill's in the north hanging on
to the land not with the south.

A thousand years, slain in Clontarf,
caught with your trousers down,
if only you'd lived to rule as king
for Ireland is still not united.

What would you say to all Irishmen
unable to finally unite?

March to Armagh? Take over Howth?
Lay siege out on Dublin Sound?

Ireland doesn't know, I doubt you do to,
what's to be done with the Isle,
you tried your best, and its said
you united Ireland for a day.

Oh Brian Boru, High King for a day,
you sent the Vikings away.
If you were here now, with any doubt
All Ireland would sing your praise.

NOW IS THE TIME
[23.10, Wed 20th Mar 2024, Iver Grove]

Now is the time to rest, do nothing,
let the world spin in a whirl,
no need to keep up with the madness,
the rushing about without end.

Those days are now numbered,
finished and gone without any doubt,
the desire to peek over the horizon
traded-in to watch the sun go down.

SEVENTY
[00.39, Wed 27th Mar 2024, Iver Grove]

Seventy plus a day, now two,
Eton's deserted night-time streets,
the Thames flooded to the boards,
no-one out, no-one abroad.

Angry men in the theatre,
Guinness black and so inviting,
kebab shop lights taunting,
the rain still pouring down.

Seventy now, plus a day,
I am now officially old -
don't feel life is any slower
despite time ticking on.

My friends saw me through the day,
Proseco, cake, evening cheer.
There is nothing better in the world
than having friends who're there.

RAGE AGAINST THE WAY WE'RE BORN
[23.07, Wed 27th Mar 2024, Iver Grove]

Sometimes what you do
makes no difference to the world.
You breathe, you go about your chores,
it changes nothing, but your moods -
You're left to feel that what you've done
is nothing but the will of others.

Don't you want to shout "Enough!"
and get off this wheel of trouble?
I want to, every single day,
I want to stop being a slave.

Is it easy? No way, for sure,
yet we somehow struggle on,
to fight the fight every day,
to rage against the way we're born.

ANTIBES
[10.59, Mon 1st Apr 2024, Antibes, France]

The Roman wall held back the waves
smashing on the oolite rocks,
the promenaders looked in awe,
wiped the sea-spray from their coats,
scurried off to favourite haunts.

The gulls pitched in the storm,
the lashing rain swept all before
with increasing violent force.

SOMETIMES I FEEL MY LIFE IS WASTED
[20.50, Wed 3rd Apr 2024, Iver Grove]

Sometimes I feel my life is wasted,
I have not made the world a better place.
What more should I have done
to stop the anger I see everywhere?
I despair but cannot openly weep
for the suffering and the cries of woe.

How is it possible to save more souls
from the reverses that constantly unfold?
Must I stand up on a soapbox,
denounce every evil done by men?
Should I join an organisation
that liberates all those trodden down?

Yes, is the answer, but I am weak,
too weak to give up what I have.
I have given into avarice, temptation,
I line my pockets as the world burns.
What charity can I thus offer
when I am selfish beyond all hope?

I waste my life in pointless sloth
without helping those I should.
I am not alone in my inaction,
my silence is echoed far abroad.
God help me if I do not change,
the Devil waits to burn us all.

DUNES OF DOUBT
[23.08, Sat 6th Apr 2024, Iver grove]

We know not what we do, we try
to see beyond the bent horizon,
seek to find Zanadu, trek unfound
plains unwalked in our imagination,
limit our dreams, settle for Majorca,
the seaside piers close to our homes,
unfit for us or those we love.

We march into history, tell
stories that will not be reheard,
cry into the wind, sip our tea,
drink into oblivion all our achievements,
leave behind nothing but dunes
of doubt for future generations -
to ponder what we were about.

HOT SUMMER NIGHTS
[20.43, Mon 8th Apr 2024, Iver Grove]

Those hot summer nights, window open,
naked on the bed, numb, content
to let the darkness fall, the rain
wash the heat away, the storm
come and my lover turn to say
she loved me more than I'd ever
know, or will ever know again.

THEIR LOVE IS MISSED
[22.10, Tues 9th Apr 2024, Iver Grove]

Do you feel that no-one loves you,
or somehow they've forgotten you exist,

that you are lonely, need attention
as the world spins on in a whiz -
while you are left picking up the pieces
of a life that is no longer what it was,
as living on your own, you are a name,
a footnote in other peoples' lists -
a birthday card or a Christmas message
being the extent of their kindest wish,
their kisses somehow just a symbol
of how much their love is missed.

THE WORLD IS FULL OF IDIOTS
[20.52, Fri 12th Apr 2024, Iver Grove]

The world is full of idiots,
fools who make us weep,
they think we are laughing
at their jokes, all their means
of keeping us from seeing
the tricks they play on us,
they think we are fools
who've fallen for their schemes.

Where are all the wise men
to sweep away these fools?
Men with skills and morals,
ideas, command of speech
to counter propaganda,
to dismiss all these clowns
with their crazy woke commotions
and the bile they preach.

These idiots should be arrested,
locked into public stocks
so we can throw tomatoes
and bananas at their mugs!
The world needs to see
these fools for what they are -
con-men, peddlers, wide-boys
of who we've had enough.

THE SICK REDWOOD OF IVER GROVE
[00.54, Thurs 18th Apr 2024, 2024]

They stand tall against the sky,
towering over all the land,
except for one, thin and bent,
born a dwarf, in neglect
left to stoop, forlorn, bereft

of what the others all possess -
stature, form, full erect,
magnificent in their proud intent,
while our poor, single, sick redwood
struggles on, survives at best.

THE DEMONS COME
[02.55, Tues 23rd Apr 2024, Iver Grove]

The demons come, eat all the food
life has given, leave nothing
to feed the mind, give nourishment
to barren hope, on how to proceed
to overcome the doubt, that all
will be well by dawn.

SAILING WITH THE WIND
[20.19, Fri 26th Apr 2024, Uxbridge, London]

O Lynda, distant Lynda,
sailing with the wind,
will it blow in my direction
as you go with the flow -
it's a long way to harbour
and the storms are wild,
the oceans are connected
but the seas are wide.

YESTERDAY
[22.43, Tues 30th Apr 2024]

A day in bed, after a shandy lunch,
escape to watch two classic films -
black and white, made me laugh,
until evening fell, brought on the dark.

The need to eat made me rise
to cook enough to last three days,
before hunkering down with a tome
on how the world's broke for good.

Nothing it seems is as it looks,
everything is somehow misunderstood,
all is not as good as it should,
when certainly it could be.

On that thought, I closed the book,
took to brood on darker things,

I pondered on the world's plight
as April's rain chilled the night.

I'M A COUNTRY BOY
[11.11, Mon 6th May 2024, Iver Grove]

I have no country villa
though I'm a country boy,
I grew up in the city
on the edge of it all;
fields a stone's throw,
the hills within sight,
the city was my youth
but my love was countryside.

Those grey granite streets
bound by cherry trees,
I climbed the nearest hills,
played in the fields;
a country boy inside,
not a hard city lad -
when I finally go,
it will be from no city land.

NO-ONE KNOWS ANYTHING
[21.16, Mon 27th May 2024, Iver Grove]

No-one knows anything!
They pretend they have a plan,
a method for living life,
a way of getting by
that is better than our own.

Lost like the rest of us,
they guide us ever on,
dictate their better knowledge,
espouse their perfect plans
then leave us in the dark.

It is obvious they are lost,
stumbling on the path,
grasping hold of that they can,
learning nothing as they fail,
to find out who they are.

THE DEBT MEN WILL COME CALLING
[14.16, Sat 1st June 2024, Iver Grove]

Know not what I do,
know not what I say,
the debt men will come calling
on you without delay.
For you are my debtor,
the credit call has come,
the due time has arrived
and you deny it all.

Oh silly little fellow,
you know not how it works,
they'll take all your goods,
your chattels and your dog.
You cannot hide from bailiffs,
they will knock and call,
until you are in court
and I've had all you've got.

THE GREEK GIRL
[23.11, Sun 2nd Jun 2024, Iver Grove]

The Greek girl beckoned,
I fell from the Acropolis,
I lay on the beach naked
as she beguiled me
to swim in the azul water
where she waited open-armed
to welcome me to immortality.

I EMBARK UPON ADVENTURES
[02.29, Sat 8th Jun 2024, Iver Grove]

I embark upon adventures,
then wake from the dream,
the reality of each journey,
questions my ideals -
makes for inner conflict,
sets me on a course
that puts me in danger
instead of staying home.

JURY OF TWELVE
12.22, Tues 25th Jun 2024, Iver Grove]

Another film canned, how many more
before age closes in, shuts the door

on being able to continue some more
with the work that I'm known for?

ANOTHER BRICK REMOVED
[00.01, Sat 29th June 2024, Iver Grove]

Nothing is certain … another day gone,
nothing but steps taken,
breath spent, miles driven,
another brick removed
from the crumbling wall.

THE GENERAL ELECTION 2024
[07.12, Fri 5th Jul 2024, Iver Grove]

Last night I made my cross,
there was no passion, little choice,
it was a vote for change,
not a vote for leadership.
just tired of things being the same.

Now as the morning rain falls,
I wake to a new desire,
a need for fresh clarity
from those now in charge
without any hope of change.

THE OLD GREEN TREE
[15.26, Wed 10th Jul 2024, Bath]

Flat our worn, done in
by afternoon sex and Proseco -
dozing over a pint of lager.
Eyeing up the open pub door,
sun in and out, like this summer,
tourists drifting like the brooding clouds.

No-one certain on what to do,
prepared to open their umbrellas,
dive into the pub for food.
I linger with my pint,
half awake, half alive too.

WE ARE FOUND
[21.19, Thurs 11th July 2024, Iver Grove]

We are found, but barely so,
much has been swept downstream,
sunk to the bottom of the lake,

lying there, being covered in silt,
until it'll be lost forever.

That is our destiny – lost,
all that is gathered – scattered,
covered over and not remembered,
useless bric-a-brac, our treasure
washed away, no trace remaining.

Nothing can change our history,
our memories gurgle from us,
drain clean, leave us found,
found as who we are -
but lost as who we were.

LISTEN TO THAT RAIN
[21.38, Mon 15th Jul 2024, Iver Grove]

Listen to that rain!
It was forecast to last all summer,
the wettest in a hundred years.
That sound! The beating on the panes,
the running into drains,
the splattered drops from leaves,
the hiss of bouncing downpour,
creating the desire to be indoors,
safe, and warm, and listening
to the drumming on the slates.

BACK FROM ATHENS
[21.10, Thurs 25th July 2024, Iver Grove]

I could do nothing, trapped
by the heat, the relentless shortness
of oxygen, the air heavy with sweat
as the conditioner chugged, failed
to draw the drench from the room.

Back to rain, cool wet England,
langering in a fitful summer
of wet, disheartening coldness,
each day a season of it own
with no refuge from it's storms.

DESPINA
[21.35, Thurs 25th July 2024, Iver Grove]

That face, delicate, refined,
her green eyes shining bright,

her movement easy and smooth,
her very step a simple glide -
her Thracian skin, soft and white,
her hair the colour of the night,
her sighs those of the wild,
her hopes the dreams of a child.

THE IVER TAVERN WENCHES
[00.24, Wed 31st July 2024, Iver Grove]

You lot need to piss off!
Get a life, stop being served by us!
You are malcontents and drunkards
abusing us with your craik,
using us as your butts
while we are working hard
to take home less than
ten pounds an hour.

What kind of customers are you?
Sloth like creatures, hanging on
our bar well past closing time.
We should throw you out,
ban you from gracing our tavern,
expel you for all time from
our presence before we hate
your guts.

You pretend you are in 'Cheers'
with your banter and your remarks
centered on making us lowly,
unworthy of joining your ranks,
you rich-heeled customers
talking about your foreign jaunts -
Your banned now, you horrible lot!
No more baiting us with your taunts.

LOVE KNOCKS ON THE DOOR
[20.57, Thurs 1st Aug 2024, Iver Grove]

Love knocks on the door.
Am I in? Or am I non receptive
to once again being coupled
to a woman I barely know?
This is the plunge, the wild beyond,
the land that lies far off-screen,
the landscape of desire, emotion,
in exchange for abandoning calm.

Will my life of rational days,
evenings with friends in the pub
be gone forever if love explodes
and obliterates all present order?

Love can be beyond all dreams,
but can also wreck the feckless,
for the rocks of longing are sharp
when life is ebbing and you are old.

LUNCH WITH DESIREE
[08.07, Sun 11th Aug 2024, Iver Grove]

Morning comes, I drink my tea,
look forward to a day of ease -
lunch at one, Windsor way
with a girl from Africa.

Will the sun shine today?
Will it rain on my parade?
Will love be in the air
as I dine with pretty Desiree?

FIFTY YEARS AGO TODAY
[08.46, Sun 11th Aug 2024, Iver Grove]

Fifty years ago today,
Maggi and me set off
over the sea, young and free,
ahead of us a wild adventure
that left her behind
while I went on to India.

What did we know then
that we know not now?
How time steals our adventure,
replaces it with repetition,
unless we escape routine
and sail headwind into life.

Time drags us into habit,
a war that molds us,
a battle of attrition
that wears us down -
makes us conform to type
so that we become defeated.

Yet, we do not surrender,
we engage in skirmishes,

though the battle is lost
we do not accept defeat,
we take our annual vacations
as proof we are warriors.

Not so fifty years ago,
the battle lay before us,
the world to be conquered -
fearlessly we went forth
across that choppy sea
to defy all convention.

GONE LIKE A THUNDER CLAP
[21.12, Sun 11th Aug 2024, Iver Grove]

The day went like a train downhill,
like a skier speeding beyond their will,
like a comet racing across the sky
in a blaze of light and a dying flash.

So went my hours with my lover,
kept at arms length while in public,
hand in hand, then arm in arm,
we went in time beyond all eyes.

There in the quiet beneath the trees,
we kissed each other with eager lips,
we devoured the minutes left to us
before we parted with panting touch.

When will I see my lover again?
The sun edged over the flat horizon -
those seconds in my lover's arms,
gone in a moment like a thunder clap.

IF I WAS A PAINTER
[20.30, Mon 12th Aug 2024, Iver Grove]

If I was a painter, I would die
for the sky I spied as it floated by,
the whiffs and wisps up there high,
the clots of clouds like big cream pies,
cake to make ancients cry,
for times when clouds pleased the eye
of lovers lying in the rye.

IF YOU'VE NOTHING TO SAY
[10.59, Wed 14th Aug 2024, Iver Grove]

If you've nothing to say, say nothing.
If you've something to do, get working.
If you've nothing to do, do something.
If you've someone to love, start loving.

I AM ABLAZE
[10.35, Mon 19th Aug 2024, Iver Grove]

My testicles are ablaze with desire's fire,
I know not how to dowse the flames -
my lover is off on some distant chore,
I toss and turn awaiting her return!
Can there be more cruelty than this,
when lovers are bereft of coital bliss.

HOW I TALK
[22.25, Mon 19th Aug 2024, Iver Grove]

Oh how I talk about the world,
all the wrongs I need to right,
the flaws that make me run away,
the endless reasons why I stay
to kiss someone I do not know,
wish to love, heart and soul.

LIFE IS LIKE A MUSHROOM
[11.06, Mon 2nd Sept 2024, Spala, Poland]

Life is like a mushroom
growing all the time,
the underside is brown,
the upside is white -
the downside is divorce,
the white a loving wife -
two sides of the fungus
eaten throughout life.

DESIRE
[07.57, Tues 3rd Sept 2024, Slubice, Poland]

My vitals are bull-like in appearance,
my mind that of a stag ready to mount you,
my hands cupped and tingling
to cling to your mounds.

VILLA VERA IN WETTER (Germany)

[19.36, Wed 4th Sept 2024, Channel Ferry]

It was wet in Wetter,
we washed all our woes,
the Villa Vera welcomed us
and our tired weary bones -
warm beds for tired travelers
traversing Europe's roads.

THE UNKNOWN ROAD

[23.43, 17th Sept 2024, Iver Grove]

What was that trip I made?
Begun in Dover, then to Poland
and back to John O'Groats,
seven thousand kilometers of road,
images flashing past at speed,
adventure in the comfort of a car
that rolled along with ease.

Where did it start? And how?
And why in twenty days
the trip unfolded as it did,
Belgium, Germany, on and on,
to rural Poland, the back beyond
where friends awaited our arrival
with food, and drink and warmth.

How can I fully set out here
the experience now in the past,
though I am just now returned
from those miles of open road -
my encounters with my fellow man,
the women who shared time with me
as the miles wore down my tyres?

What purpose is this without hope
that what you see is good for you?
Yet, while the eyes dwell on sights,
the mind is racing, running wild,
making stories where none exist,
making judgment on many things
that have no relation with reality.

Where do such thoughts lead us,
onward to the next town or country,
along roads filled with vehicles
racing to some unknown timetable,

while our own clock ticks in kilometers,
propels us like a steel pinball
to arrive at the dregs of the day.

This is the life of a traveling man
who cannot settle, stay at home,
find comfort in a soft settee,
or be happy with a mug of tea,
such luxury is beyond the pale,
a life forsaken for adventure,
traded for the unknown road.

NOT IN MY NAME
[21.10, Wed 25th Sept 2024, Iver Grove]

Not in my name, you politicians,
with your guns, bombs and missiles,
playing your games without consent,
crying wolf as the world burns -

crocodile tears at the General Assembly,
lecturing each other on global integrity
while all the while advancing invincibly
over nations that don't have influence.

Shame on you! You selfish individuals,
your power makes you into liars -
this is how you peddle doctrine,
justify your smug replies -

twist the facts, fabricate innocence,
ignore dissent, applaud compliance,
sit on your hands in defiance of
God's laws with unjust arrogance.

This is our present world, despair,
led by those completely lost,
lost to what justice is,
lost to know right from wrong -

lost to ideas that count the dead
as money spent for their ends -
to satisfy their warped perceptions,
to shape the world as they intend.

Not in my name, you politicians,
not at any time, nor year,
not in any shape or form
will you kill and maim for me.

Curse you all, you evil kind,
plaguing us with your disease,
with your guns, bombs and missiles
without cease, nor talk of peace.

AFRICAN WHISPERS
[21.03, Wed 2nd Oct 2024, Iver Grove]

She whispers in her native tongue
as we lie naked, ensnared in love,
I eat her wild worldly words
as she quivers with each touch,
her lips letting out the sun,
to burn me with her every breath,
her fires flare with every gasp
as she dreams of Cape Town's surf.

NETANYAHU
[00.56, Fri 4th Oct 2024, Iver Grove]

What goes on inside his head?
Every move a bible story?
He is David, he is Saul,
he is Joshua at the walls.

Isaac's tribe taking Caanan,
Syria's but a heathen nation,
Persia but a constant threat,
Egypt beneath his contempt.

Can he not recall Masada,
know that war brings disaster,
that God's wrath can be swift
to bring his people to destruction.

THE NEW MAN IN TOWN (song)
[00.50, Wed 9thOct 2024, Iver Grove]

There's a new man in town,
the girls are excited,
the wives, oh the wives,
the maidens looking for husbands -
the spinsters with dreams,
the teenagers in blossom,
the barmaids with smiles,
the shop girls with longing.

There's a new man in town,
and love comes a calling.

WINTER HAS COME AGAIN
[20.55, Tues 15th Oct 2024, Iver Grove]

Yes, it has come again,
that feeling of winter, the cold
eating into all that lives -
the damp moldering in corners
of drowned out shade.

My bones creak, my muscles ache,
craving for sun to come again
to clear away those rotten leaves,
those chestnuts frothed white
that crack underfoot in the mud!

Yes, winter has come again -
I wrap myself against its bite.

DESIRE RANG ME UP
[20.43, Thurs 17th Oct 2024, Iver Grove]

Desire rang me up and said
'Would you like to share my bed?'
What should I bring I replied -
'Bring all the gifts you possess.'

I wondered what she meant by that
'Your smile, your wit and your laugh,
those things are in short supply.'
Who was I to question why.

When love is put in such terms
I wipe my face, and underparts,
buy some flowers on the way,
obey Desire, and all she says.

Perhaps I am a simple man,
prone to being in women's arms,
but oh, the softness of her bed
and Desire's sweet long caress.

What fellow would not forego such joy,
love and comfort on her pillows,
companionship upon her cushions,
my head upon her puffed out bosom.

I cannot sat more on this -
Desire has locked me in a kiss,

as she unwraps all my gifts
I give myself to untold bliss.

BREADCRUMBS
[10.53, Mon 21st Oct 2024, Iver Grove]

When did I last have breadcrumbs
scattered on my sheets like sand,
sourdough toast, peanut and jam,
morning coffee mug in hand,
a gorgeous specimen leaning in,
sipping juice between her laughs.

This is missionary work at best,
exploring folds of unknown land,
surveying all that I command,
from pillows mounded at my back!

With a gulp my coffee's gone,
my beauty gives a little gasp,
she stretches out in long expanse,
I sally forth in sound advance
down her hills, across her fields,
towards her treeless fancy farm.

THAT GREAT POEM NEVER WRITTEN
[20.49, Tues 22nd Oct 2024, Iver Grove]

Oh for that great poem never written,
something now for all us Britons,
not some drivel about lost hope,
nor some rubbish about booze or dope -
something to lift us to the skies,
something to carry us from ourselves,
something to bring us back to Earth
when we are faced with life or death.

Such is the hue for higher art,
something to grip at our hearts,
something to make us cry or laugh,
something that takes us from the dark -
words to brave us for the fight,
to lift our heads into the light,
so we can have our world restored,
our wounds healed by words alone.

THE BITCOIN BOYS
[20.21, Tues 29th Oct 2024, Iver Grove]

Bitcoin is soaring like a phoenix from the fire,
the excitement is growing for those in the know,
the rich are investing hand over fist,
while the poor are filling their baskets with food.

Those in the know are planning their futures,
while those who're not are counting their pennies,
saving to get to the end of the month -
while the bitcoin boys are filling their trunks,
counting their gains and not saying a word.

WOKENESS
[22.56, Fri 1st Nov 2024, Iver Grove]

Should I say more than that
which I have expressed before?
Must I now lambaste the arrogance
of those risen up from the gutter
who dare tell us how to live?

I cannot stomach it, digest it,
for it is bile that fills my mind,
turns all my perfect thoughts against
everything I took for granted,
only now to find that such treasured
beliefs are mere moral trifles ended
by the march of time, to leave me
isolated in my aging temple, this body
that once carried me safely hither
to places that are now just dreams.

This is how perfection declines,
leaves all matter to rot, decay
until the very fabric of being
becomes poisoned, ill with doubt,
fogged by a cold valley mist
covering my village of certainty,
my safe haven from false ideals.

I am lost to my community, my
acquaintances all now laid to rest,
my old friends likewise gone, departed
to a place where we will not meet again.

Oh, I should dream of heaven -
but it is no comfort, no escape

from this present life, drawn out
with constant change, until nothing
looks the same except the stars.

Yet stars too are now obscured
by whizzing orbs of steel, mirrors
reflecting back images of ourselves.
No longer are there Gods to quell us,
make us tremble with fear, remind
us that we are imperfect, false,
flawed servants of the universe that
we know nothing of what lies beyond
our arrogance, our vain self importance
hiding us from truth, the reality
of our existence, of why we're here.

We listen to the shameful rhetoric
of those who lead us blindly onwards
with their will to silence us, their
rules to make us obey, comply with
muted acceptance their contrived agenda.

No! I will not have it! I will
fight to have my freedom, to speak
my doubts, spit out my poison
into the faces of those who wish
that I was dead, and gone from here
before my time! But I will not go!
I remain to land my blows at wokeness,
and all woke attempts to silence truth.

VEGAS
[16.09, 10th Nov 2024, Palms Casino, Las Vegas]

They chained the doors during lock-down
in a town that never slept,
those days now gone, the gamblers sit
roll all day, forego the sun
beating down on their luck.

Busier than it was before,
the money rolls like no-one knows,
the chatter lifts to the roofs
filled with bars and fancy clubs
high above the Vegas lots.

KILLINGTON LAKE
[09.21, Sat 16th Nov 2024, Killington Lake, Cumbria]

I've been here often to look at the lake,
the mist on the water, smooth like a mirror -
the sun coming up over the hills,
the wind blades turning almost at will -
fueling old thoughts that have painfully passed
during the miles homewards to Glasgow.

CLEANLINESS IS ONE WITH GODLINESS
[21.48, Sat 16th Nov 2024, Hillpark, Glasgow]

How do others live as they do
when all is provided for them,
a dwelling watertight and dry,
yet inside is like a sty.

How can decent folk thus live
with dishes piled to the sky,
bins overflowing with their waste
left to rot while they make haste.

Can they not make more time
to mend their manners and taste,
roll the blinds with each day starting,
make their beds before departing.

Such simple tasks are not taxing,
no big deeds in the asking,
tidying up is not an oddness,
cleanliness is one with Godliness.#

SLANDER
For Paul Wiffen
[23.05, Mon 18th Nov 2024, Hillpark, Glasgow]

Envy sows the seed of mistrust,
leads to gossip unwisely spread,
fertile soils turn sterile, barren,
where once there was no stony ground.

This is how bad words flourish
beyond mere rumour into fact,
striping truth, creating fiction
based upon precious lies.

Slander has a thousand friends
prepared to swear that all is true,

yet none can prove or validate
the poison spread by wagging tongues.

BURN HIS OLD MAN'S POETRY
[00.10, Sat 30th Nov 2024, Iver Grove]

A young man would burn his old
man's poetry, or bury it deep underground
where the worms could eat for all eternity
on the words created that dwell upon
his infirmities and litany of moans and whines!

The old man should erase his young
fella's poetry, tear it up, toss it aside,
let it float down the river that takes
all in good time, to settle as silt there,
to rots in the slime of his rhyme.

NO SONG IS LOUDER
[00.25, Sat 30th Nov 2024, Iver Grove]

No song is louder than a lament,
the crying of the soul seeking solace,
the seeping of pain up from the spleen,
the wrenching of woe from a deep sleep;
'til nothing can stop the girding of grief,
the wailing, weeping, grinding of teeth,
the lulling of anger, acceptance of lost,
the aching thoughts of better times gone.

BEAUTY
[01.05, Sat 30th Nov 2024, Iver Grove]

Oh beauty! Where can I find it?
In the sound of the winter wind?
In the rumble of a train going by?

The search for beauty never ends,
my nature makes me seek it out,
to search for it in brown-leaf woodland,
look for it in the clouds drifting on.

I crave to find beauty where ever I can,
in the things I can take in my palms,
the sense I interpolate with my ears,
the ocean breaking on jagged rocks,
or an elephant silently walking past.

Such beauty as in a spotted ladybird,
or the stillness found by a Scottish loch,
a polar bear bounding on ice,
a child looking up with infinite trust,
the smoothness of soft human skin,
or an accent with a lilting burr.

The search for beauty never ends,
'til I be blind, deaf and numb,
such beauty then would be the dark,
to find beauty in my inner thoughts.

I pray these days will never come
while the world spins forever on,
I'll seek to live for beauty's sake,
look for beauty everywhere,
rejoice on finding perfect things,
enjoy the joy that beauty brings.

I WANT TO APOLOGISE
[14.11, Sat 30th Nov 2024, Iver Grove]

Before I die I want to apologise
to all my enemies.
I meant it at the time,
but when I'm on my death bed,
I will not have the strength
to say sorry.

So I apologise now to all
you bastards,
all you who know who you are,
who made my life more miserable
than it should have been
before my death arrives.

THE SOUTHERN ENGLISH
[15.44, 30th Nov 2024, Iver Grove]

The southern English cannot be trusted,
they don't lie, they just stay silent,
they never answer the question emphatically,
they obfuscate in a measured fashion,
to make you believe they are courteous
in all their dealings involving finance,
while under the smiles a crooked mind
intends to fleece you down the line.

FIRST WORDS
[21.58, Sat 30th Nov 2024, Iver Grove]

The and of A, to I in on,
for that be my, with it is as,
by we all was, from you his me,
but their not are, or they no he.

At like have this, but who time out,
our one so where, her life what love,
an week she had, now there while up,
into day when down, your man may more.

NOTES ON THE POEMS IN THIS VOLUME

HIGH WYCOMBE (Sept 2015)

I moved to High Wycombe and lived there until December 2020. It was a beautiful flat at the Loudwater end of the town and I was happy there. Of course I was coming and going a lot after losing the bungalow in Denham which I had lived in for eight years. (I had been financially tied up in a tax inquiry). Three years had passed since the making of feature film *Heckle* and moving to Wycombe got me back on my film feet with the making of *Oh My God*. Wycombe itself was not an easy place to make friends but a good place for families to school their kids. [30/11/2024]

I AM SILENT (Nov 2015)

This poem was my response to the refugee crisis in the Mediterranean. Small boats were setting out from Turkey to cross to Greece. Hundreds were drowning. It was yet another humanitarian crises caused by the geo-political meddling of the West, this time in Syria. The British were in step with the Americans to remove Assad as president. They had learned nothing from the mess they jointly made in Iraq, Afghanistan and Libya. Yet, as a British citizen, they were doing it my name. To protest was to be shouted down. I felt it was better to remain silent rather than adding another approving voice. [22/11/2024]

GOZO (Dec 2015)

I spend that Xmas – New Year period in Gozo, Malta with my good friend Suzie Kendall. I had been to Malta before but the two week break there was refreshing. I came back with renewed vigour and determination to rebuild my finances. [30/11/2024]

BREXIT (June 2016)

A calamity for anyone who spent a lot of time in Europe. Any dreams of settling somewhere else in the European Union went out the window. The saga dragged on for another three and a half years until we were finally cut off on the 31st January 2020. See *No Longer A European*. [30/11/2024]

RAGE AGAINST THE LIGHT (Jan-Mar 2017)

Not all ws well in early 2017 as the wrangling over Brexit continued (and dragged on to the end of 2019). I wrote this poem in response to prime minister Teresa May's inability to articulate her thoughts to the nation. Cameron had abandoned us all to face the Brexit vote disaster. The war in Syria was still raging but we didn't hear any common sense from any politician. I believed May to be a decent human being, yet somehow her tight-arsed ecclesiastic childhood made it impossible for her to express herself with anything other than with the same monotone voice. She sat on the fence. In the end it did for her. Bad boy Johnston ran rings round her and she in the end got tufted out of office by that short-arsed oaf.

The 'wrongs of the world can not be healed by sociopaths'. There was so much to be unhappy about – climate change, austerity, my own struggle in coping with growing older. The one thing to look forward to was my planned trip to Southern Africa to film elephants. [22/11/2024]

WHERE ARE MY FRIENDS NOW (Nov-Dec 2017)

I had to abandon this poem. It was too painful to recall all the friends that I had lost, or had lost touch with. I am sure I am not alone in this sense of loss, the what-might-have been if friends had lived longer, or those that have been lost-touch-with were still in our lives. As I progressed with the poem I became overwhelmed by the sheer number of friends I have had in my life. Acquaintances we all have, but friends are special, people that we have confided in, helped, been helped by, miss. So, that is what struck me as I was writing the poem. It sent me off on an unhappy journey that I just had to stop. [22/11/2024]

NO ESCAPE FROM SHIPWRECK (Jan-Apr 2019)

When I'd finished writing this poem I posted it on Facebook. Maija Briede the painter told me that it went on forever and was far too long. I was rather pleased by that response. The whole point of the poem is the never ending thought processes that go on inside our heads.

The simile of a man stranded on a desert island wishing to be rescued but also having moments of contentment that makes him fearful of being rescue, well, that's all of us – we want to escape but we are fearful of that that escape might bring. Having spent a lot of time in my early adulthood on beaches in far away places, the shipwreck sailor is as much me as Robinson Crusoe. My own inner turmoils might be figurative rather than physical, but they are based on my real physical experiences and mental anguishes. Naturally, these experiences are amplified to the extent of being hyperbolic. However, all good tales are at best exaggerated in order to keep the listener intent on the story. [22/11/2024]

THE DRUNKEN JOURNEY HOME (Dec 2020- June 2021)

I had been in Spain for a week and I guess my mind was full of the images of that week. Anyway, I started the poem after writing *What Is There To Show*. If I recall, though I cannot be certain, the weather was colder than usual. I began with the idea of a Tam O'Shanter kind of tale, the drunk making his way home to his lonely wife with his drinking companions and getting way-laid by his own imagination. It sort of turned out like that though it took a while to complete. [30/11/2024]

THE WASTELAND MY HOME (Mar-Apr 2021)

This poem is about Pollokshaws were I grew up. It gets mentioned in The Wanderer many times, but on this occasion, its about how many of the landmarks of this old medieval village that have been demolished or gone to ruin. During my lifetime, the village's buildings have been flattened twice to be replaced with houses that look like they too will need to be knocked down in fifty years time.

This is the planning department of Glasgow – Pollokshaws is not dear to them, as it is to the Queer Folk of the 'Shaws, with its long history of industry, famous son's and well educated children.

BENEATH THE MILKY WAY (Jan-Feb 2022)
What do we know of the Universe? I come back to this time and time again. Still I have no answer. Nor does anyone else. Star-ships can fly off to the end of the Universe (if there is an end) but we will still not learn how the Universe came into being. God? Perhaps this notion sums up our complete ignorance of why we exist. So in summary, this poem is my understanding that we know nothing and 'that we spin none the wiser' in our orbit around the sun. [22/11/2024]

THE ANATOMY OF MY WORLD (Apr-May 2022)
My view of the world instead of the universe. During the writing of this poem my father died in Glasgow. I could not go to his funeral. I was recovering from a second bout of COVID and I was freshly released from hospital in Buckinghamshire. In my absence, my daughter Rachael read some the lines from this poem at his funeral. I read these lines now and remember so much about him. I know there is no heaven but I like to think he is there in a happier place. I've always appreciated how much my parents struggled to give me what they could to make my life better. How do we pay that back? We can't, we can only do the same for those who come after us. As for the bulk of the poem, its about me, or someone like me, struggling to get through life on a day to day basis, remaining optimistic despite all the tribulations that the world throws in our faces. [22/11/2024]

NEIGHBOURS (Jan-Apr 2023)
I initially called this poem The Apartments, but on reflection that was too tight a definition, and I changed it to *Neighbours*. I started writing these verses in Spain while on holiday. It began as just a few loose observations on fictitious oddball characters that were neighbours and it just flowed from there. They are colourful characters only in the sense that they are flawed individuals living in their own little worlds.
You could say they have an *Under Milkwood* oddness to them. I could have carried on and populated *Neighbours* with more weirdos, but I had the film *Helen Razor* to make. [22/11/2024]

WHEN PEACE COMES (Jan-Feb 2024)
I always seem to come back rested from Spain after New Year. I get time to think there, get rid of my jumbled up thoughts that inhabit me through each year in the film business.
And boy, how we need peace with the Ukraine war and the Gaza genocide, yet no-one seems to be able to stop any of it. There appears to be no will on any side to end the conflict. It is soul destroying to watch the ineffectiveness of modern day diplomacy. It is a constant blame game with none willing to apologise or say there sorry and offer a truce.

And none moreso than Zelensky, an intransigent man out of his depth who would rather bring on WWIII than come to a settlement with the Russians. What more can I say. I want peace, and it should be at any price if it saves lives. Basically that is what the poem is about. [22/11/2024]

COMPOSITION NOTES
By changing the size of the pages of the notebook I write in, changes the form of the poetry as the page confines the writing. I've been well aware of this for fifty years from my novel writing days. With novels, the pages had to be A4 line pages, but my poetry had to be written on blank A4. That however was quite some time ago. Now I am not so rigid, and I currently write on A5 sized pages. But I do still like to get to end of a notebook i.e. fill it before moving on to a new notebook. Composition has many rules, but the page it is written on is often the limiter of the scope and length of the poem due to lines and pages to be turned. [18/04/2024]

When I write my poetry, I usually write into a diary sized book of blank pages. Sometimes I am on film business and I will write into the notebook that I keep for jobbing down my business affairs. This might only happen three or four times a year, the rest goes into the diary sized book. These books can take up to five years to fill. The one I am currently using is about half way through. I have written on 162 pages over the last two years. This should give the reader an idea of how long it takes to fill one of these A5 diaries. [30/11/2024]

PUBLISHING NOTE
The main reason I have decided to publish my poetry in three volumes is because of the restrictions placed on the publication size. In this handy 5"x8" format that these pages are printed on, the maximum number of pages that the spine can hold is 830. I can no longer fit my complete works on to this number of pages despite using 7pt font size. In this three volume edition, I am able to increase the font size to 8pt and undo some of the layout condensing that the previous format has restricted me to. It also allows the printing on to cream paper which is easier on the eye. Hence the overall expansion of the three volumes to more than a thousand pages with no deletions in order to save space. Finally, it also allows future poems to be added to this volume without republishing the earlier works in Volume's 1 and 2. [30/11/2024]

ROBBIE MOFFAT

Born in Glasgow, Scotland in 1954. Educated at Sir John Maxwell Primary, Shawlands Academy and Newcastle University. Best known for his film work with Palm Tree as a writer, director and producer, Robbie formed Palm Tree in 1980 to publish his poetry work. Since then, the publishing arm of the company has printed all of his poetry and many of his novels and screenplays. Some of these more recent titles are listed below and can be ordered online.

Complete Poetic Works
What Prize Did I Win Vol 1 Screenplays
Punks (novel)
The Loving Series (4 novels)
Christine and Her Teachest (novel)
Lost In The Landscape (novella)
The Lost Summer (novella)
Glasgow Boy (bio)